THE
DEAD PIRATES OF
CAWSAND

STEVE HIGGS

VINCI
BOOKS

For my father, the saltiest of seadogs.

Vinci Books

vinci-books.com

Published by Vinci Books Ltd in 2025

1

Copyright © Steve Higgs 2018

A CIP catalogue record for this book is available from the British Library.
Paperback ISBN: 9781036708559

The EU GPSR authorised representative is Logos Europe, 9 rue Nicolas Poussion, 17000 La Rochelle, France contact@logoseurope.eu

By Steve Higgs

Blue Moon Investigations

Paranormal Nonsense

The Phantom of Barker Mill

Amanda Harper Paranormal Detective

The Klowns of Kent

Dead Pirates of Cawsand

In the Doodoo with Voodoo

The Witches of East Malling

Crop Circles, Cows and Crazy Aliens

Whispers in the Rigging

Paws of the Yeti

Under a Blue Moon

Night Work

Lord Hale's Monster

Herne Bay Howlers

Undead Incorporated

The Ghoul of Christmas Past

The Sandman

Jailhouse Golem

Sparks in the Darkness

Shadow in the Mine

Ghost Writer

Monsters Everywhere

Death by Misadventure

As Philip stepped out of the pub, the cold air reminded him that it was late October, and he was on the seafront where there was nowhere to hide from it. It was a relatively still night but there was mist about already. He had expected it. Having lived by the sea his whole life, he took pride in knowing what the weather was going to do without the need to see a forecast. He pulled his coat tight about his body and zipped it all the way up to protect his neck.

'Don't let the pirates get you,' said a voice from behind him.

He turned to share the joke with the landlord who had come over to shut the door. It was closing time and Philip was the last one to leave. He usually was and prided himself on being a great customer.

'I think I'll be alright, Dave,' he replied with a laugh. 'It's a load of superstitious claptrap anyway.'

The landlord frowned as he replied. 'Try telling that to those tourists last week. Or that nice Indian family that took over the old chip shop.'

1

'I hardly think they were set about by dead pirates, Dave.' He shuffled off in the direction of his house. 'See you tomorrow, Dave,' he called over his shoulder.

'See you tomorrow, Phil,' the answer drifted back through the mist.

Phil shuffled along the old, cobbled street back towards his house. He had lived in Cawsand all his life. He would die there too, he knew that and was happy about it. He had picked out his lot already, high up on the cemetery that overlooked the harbour.

The mist swirled around him as he turned away from the sea and headed inland. There were only two pubs in Cawsand, and he had to pass the other one both coming and going from his house to The Star. The other pub, the Sea Pilgrim, was owned and run by his sister-in-law which made it far harder for him to sneakily meet with Maggie Tanner. His wife knew he was having an affair, that he had always been having affairs. Clearly though, she was no longer bothered about it, probably even saw it as a relief that she was no longer expected to put in a performance herself. Her sex drive, what little there had ever been of it, had dwindled to nothing years ago. He was a stallion though. At almost seventy, he still wanted some action every night.

Not tonight though. Maggie had a headache she said, so their usual secret meeting had been cancelled. However, he had other things on his mind as he shuffled home: he was going to be rich. Maybe rich enough to leave his wife and move in with Maggie. A recent chance discovery had guaranteed his future, now he waited on a decision to be made. He would not wait much longer though. He had already issued his ultimatum, and they had no choice but to pay up.

A shadow moved ahead of him in the fog.

He stopped, peering into the murk. Had he seen something? The recent reports of ghostly pirates were making him nervous, that was all it was. Tourists and newcomers and superstitious rubbish.

He started moving again, then heard a noise behind him. He spun around or at least turned as fast as his decrepit, drunken body would turn. There was nothing there. At least, that was what he told himself, ignoring the fact that he could only see a few feet before the mist ate what little light there was.

He chuckled to himself for his foolishness. Shook his head and turned back to face the way home. Paying no attention to his feet he tripped over a cat as it came out of the alleyway next to him. It shrieked at him and shot across the street, the fright making his heart rate spike. He leaned against the wall of a house for support. His chest hurt suddenly, it felt tight, and he was struggling to breathe. Regret for a lifetime of drinking more than he knew he ought to dominated his thoughts. He sagged against the wall, thinking it was stupid place to die, then just as the pain in his chest was reaching an unbearable level, he let out a long, loud belch that seemed to start deep in his gut.

It went on for several seconds. When it finished, he wiped his mouth and stood up straight. Not a heart attack at all. His chest pain was gone all bar a lingering niggle. He chuckled to himself again, pushed off the wall and began tottering along the road once more. His house was just a few more yards away, just around the corner. Fishing in his pocket for keys, he saw another shadow in the mist ahead. This time he ignored it entirely. Nothing but the moonlight playing tricks on his alcohol addled sight.

'Philip,' called out a voice in a creepy, singsong, off-key

manner. It was behind him. He whipped around, but there was nothing to be seen in the impenetrable mist.

He looked about, worry gripping his pulse again and making it beat hard enough for him to hear it banging in his head.

'Philip,' the voice again. It called out from ahead of him this time. He spun around. Something moved in the mist and a figure emerged from the gloom, then another joined it. Both were dressed as pirates, complete with knee-high boots and hats. Each bore a cutlass in their right hand that looked wickedly sharp and eerily both were softly glowing as if lit from within. The scariest detail though was that they were both very definitely dead. They were virtually skeletal, their skin missing from their skulls and arms and wherever their ripped and rotten clothing had exposed what should have been flesh beneath.

Water was dripping from their clothing as if they had just emerged from the sea. 'Run,' the one on his left instructed. That the skeleton had no tongue and should not be able to make words didn't occur to Philip as he turned and fled.

With no idea where he was going, his only thought was to get away. Away from the horror in the mist.

The boat.

He remembered his boat. Ever reliable despite its age, Betsy would be his refuge. All he had to do was get there. Once he was cast off, they would not be able to get to him out at sea.

His pulse was hammering in his head from the effort of running, even though it was barely a stumbling jog. His chest ached from the exertion, but it was not far and all downhill. He checked behind when he reached the jetty, the pirates were still behind him, walking slowly, visible mostly due to the soft glow they were emanating.

Betsy was in sight though, right where he had left her earlier today. He tumbled onto the deck and scrambled to find a knife to cut the lines. There was one just inside the cabin, he kept it there for gutting fish when he caught them. So focused on reaching for it in the dark, he barely felt the cutlass cutting his throat. It was the warm liquid soaking his shirt that made him stop and look. Only when he looked at his hands to find them covered in dark sticky liquid did he question why his throat was stinging. He fell onto his backside. A shadow came over him and he looked up. The night sky was obscured by two dark figures. His vision was blurring but they looked different from the two pirates that had been chasing him a moment ago. The pirates were the same size, these two were not. He wanted to say something, but his lungs were beginning to fill with his blood. Taking a breath was no longer an option.

As he sank to the floor, his pulse hammering in his ears, he wondered why they had singled him out. He tried to speak but a sudden blow to his chest silenced his question before it made it to his lips. He looked down at his body as an old, rusty-looking cutlass was pulled slowly back out of his ribcage. It made a comedic slurping noise as it came clear.

He wanted to chuckle, but a hand gripped his chin, forcing him to look up into the face above him. The face was mumbling something, whispering perhaps. He could barely hear it over the pounding in his ears. There was something about him having ignored a warning. Then his vision began to fade, and it no longer mattered.

Rattler Cider

The first swig of the pale liquid washed over my taste buds in a soothing kaleidoscope of flavour. At the bar, I had found myself presented with an array of options I was unfamiliar with. On a whim, I selected the Rattler pear cider, mostly because I liked the look of the pump with its snake motif. Plus, I was in the West Country and therefore drinking cider felt obligatory.

I downed half the glass in the first go while standing at the bar. I was thirsty from the journey, hungry and a little sore. The drive had taken longer than I had expected. It was only two hundred- and seventy-miles door to door, but the route took me down the A303, which even on a Sunday afternoon got snarled up as it went past Stonehenge and drivers gawked out of their windows at the odd collection of rocks. It was a single-track road for much of the journey after that, my speed dictated by tractors and farm vehicles and then, as I got deeper into Cornwall, by the narrow confines of the roads themselves, which were often too tight for two cars to pass.

The five hours I had planned for the journey quickly became six and although the dogs slept most of the way there, it was necessary to stop several times so that they might stretch their legs and exercise their bladders.

It was dark by the time I arrived. There was nowhere to park near to my lodgings, the tiny seaside village streets far too narrow for cars. There was a road that led through the village and in front the pub but a large sign on the way into the village made it very clear that visitors were to park in the car park and walk to their destination unless emergency or disability prevented them from doing so. Turning the engine off, my first imperative was to get both the dogs and myself out of the car. I was not certain where the pub was exactly, other than it was on the seafront, so I left my luggage behind and set off to find it.

Pulling at their leads, the two miniature black and tan dachshunds dragged me downhill towards the sea. The streets of Cawsand were lit by streetlamps as one might expect, but the narrow streets reduced the distance the light could penetrate, creating far more inky, dark shadows than one might expect. Even darker alleyways disappeared into an impenetrable gloom mere feet from their start point.

What I remembered of Cawsand was a picture-post-card-perfect little fishing village where rows of tiny, but brightly painted terraced houses wound around the steep cliff the village occupied. Undoubtedly evolving due to a natural harbour, the streets themselves were winding and unpredictable, side streets would suddenly appear to my left or right revealing yet more houses tucked away. I looked forward to exploring tomorrow during daylight.

I found the pub easily enough by the simple expedient of heading downhill until I ran out of road and reached the water. Buzzing around my feet, the dogs were very happy to be somewhere new, the myriad unexplored smells causing them to dash here and there, constrained only by their leads. Where the road from the car park terminated at the seafront, there was a small pebble beach that could be accessed by stairs or by a ramp and the pub with its rooms was just to my left. It occupied an enviable position directly in front of the beach itself. I had probably sat outside it as a boy enjoying a bottle of cola with my twin sister though I had only a vague memory of doing so. There were no patrons of the pub sitting on benches outside it now though. It was a cool October evening so anyone visiting the pub would want to stay inside.

The dogs didn't resist as I pulled gently on their leads to steer them inside.

'Good evening,' I called out as I got to the bar. It was untended, even though there was a chap sitting at the far end of it, a half-empty pint glass in front of him and a paper in his hands. He looked up briefly, nodded in my direction but returned to reading his paper. He was the only person in sight. It was still early on a Sunday for the evening crowd, but the Dirty Habit back in Finchampstead would be full of customers at this time of day.

I heard footsteps approach from somewhere behind the bar. They were coming closer, clomping along wooden floorboards out of sight.

'Hello,' A lady said as she came through a gap in the wall behind the bar. She was close to sixty, or maybe slightly over, had a windswept face that spoke of living by the sea and she was quite short at what I estimated was a shade over five feet. Her hair was neatly styled in a shoulder-length bob and shot through with grey that she showed no interest in colouring.

'Hi,' I smiled at her. 'Tempest Michaels. I rather hope you have a room booked under my name.'

'Indeed, I do. I have been expecting you. I'm Gretchen, the landlady. I must say you were lucky to get a room. You called just moments after the last chap announced he was leaving earlier than planned. There has been quite a bit of interest recently with all that has been going on.' She didn't elaborate on what she was referring to. 'So, you are staying for five nights, leaving on Friday?'

'That is my plan,' I confirmed.

'And you booked the en-suite master bedroom bed and breakfast. You are going to enjoy the breakfast. My John makes it fresh to order every morning. He's such a talent,' she boasted. I assumed that John was her husband though she didn't say he was. The mention of breakfast made my stomach rumble lightly.

'How will you be paying, Tempest?' Gretchen asked.

'Credit card?' I replied, producing one from my wallet. 'Perhaps I can open a tab for drinks and food. Is the bar open?'

'Oh, yes. Would you like something now?'

'Indeed, I would,' I said, eyeing up the contents of the bar. 'I need to collect my luggage and the things for the dogs, but I would like a drink first I think.'

'Dogs?' Gretchen asked, her face a picture of confusion. She leaned forward and looked over the bar, whereupon she spied the two dachshunds sitting patiently by my feet. They saw her face appear and simultaneously started wagging their tails. 'Goodness, they are well behaved, aren't they?' she commented. 'I would never have known they were there.'

That exchange had led to Gretchen handing me a key to my room with instructions on how to find it, then showing me the range of drinks I could pick from. Ten minutes later I was placing the now empty glass of Rattler pear cider on the table in front of me and thinking that I should get my things from the car before I allowed myself the next one.

The room was easy to find and was a delightful space to spend a few days in. The bed itself was a giant four-poster constructed from solid oak. The uprights were beautifully turned in a spiral design and it had curtains hanging from each side so that the occupant could completely enclose oneself at night. In the days before central heating, I would imagine this feature was highly desirable. Less so now.

I left the dogs to sniff around the room and went to retrieve the luggage from the car. Finding my way to the car was easy enough, I just pointed myself back uphill, so despite the confusing, twisting streets and alleyways, I found the carpark again without becoming disorientated. Then, to avoid a second trip, I fiddled about until I could grab, hook or balance everything I had packed. Burdened by the weight of all the baggage, I struggled back downhill to the pub.

Looking about as I tottered along, I had to observe that it was jolly dark in the bits that the streetlights didn't penetrate. The moon was high in the sky though and quite close to full which created sufficient light to see by. I was curious to see how dark it would be on an overcast night and questioned whether the streetlights were on all night or perhaps went off at some point in the small hours. Did fisherman get up before dawn here? Centuries ago, they would have managed without streetlights, no doubt they could now as well.

There were lights on in most houses. In some, the curtains weren't drawn, so walking by the windows, I could see inside and had to make sure I didn't allow my eyes to linger too long on any particular dwelling lest I be spotted staring in. 'Would you like a hand?' asked a voice from nowhere which made me jump; I had not noticed anyone else about.

I turned slowly, a bit off balance by the weight of the items hanging from my arms to see an openly gay chap in his early twenties. He was wearing a full face of make-up, a pair of pink cowboy boots and ripped, bleached jeans that were so tight I wondered if he needed assistance just to get them on. He was just coming out of a house I had passed. 'Are you heading to the Sea Pilgrim?' he asked.

'I am actually. I'm staying there for a few days.' He was already walking towards me, raising his hands to relieve me of whichever items of luggage I could disentangle. I had received an injury to my ribs just over a week ago when I had a sort of job-related incident involving some men dressed as clowns. Several of my ribs had been broken beneath where my right arm naturally rests. They were healing but were still sore, so I was glad to reduce the load hanging from my right arm.

'Tempest,' I said, offering the man my hand as I put my suitcase down.

'John.' His handshake was rather weak – effeminate even, if I can use the term without being sexist.

'Were you on your way to the pub?' I was making conversation as silence would feel uncomfortable while the man was helping me.

'Yes. I'm the chef there. My mum runs it.' John was her son, not her husband.

'Oh. Well, I look forward to sampling your cuisine this week. Can I expect a lot of fresh seafood dishes?' The thought of a freshly landed piece of plaice or a John Dory fillet made my mouth water. My stomach reminded me again that I had eaten all too little today.

'Oh, yes. My aunt provides me with a fresh catch every day. She's the parish councillor and supervises the fishing activities. In fact, she's responsible for all the boating activities out of the Cawsand harbour.'

'So, you have a quite a family legacy here,' I commented to make conversation.

He laughed. 'I guess we do. My sister Roberta is the local bobby, so we are all quite well known. Lived here all my life, apart from a brief, but wondrous career in the West End.'

'Acting?'

'No. I was a make-up artist. I thought I was going to be there forever, but my boyfriend cheated on me and he was the theatre producer, so I lost my job as well as my place to stay. I tried to make it on my own, but in the end, I just came home. It's lovely here though and my family are all local.'

At the door, I thanked him for his help, took back the bags he had carried and went inside. As I went up the stairs he was heading into the depths of the pub, probably to the kitchen.

I had to dump my bags to get the key from my back pocket. It was a chunky brass item that came attached to a square of metal that was almost the size of my wallet. I figured this made it harder to lose. I could hear the dogs snuffling at the gap under the door as I fiddled to open it and of course, they were climbing all over me as soon as I got it open.

Shuffling forward to prevent them from escaping between my legs, I managed to get inside and close the door. I checked my watch: 1803hrs. I tussled briefly with leaving the luggage until the morning, but I was a stickler for routine and for being organised, so I picked the dogs up and placed them on the bed where I knew they would stay out of the way, then I tackled the task of unpacking.

Fifteen minutes later my clothes were hung up, toiletries were in the bathroom and the dogs' items were organised. It was finally pub o'clock.

Once we were back out in the corridor, the two dogs strained desperately against their leads. I could hear conversation coming from the bar downstairs. Lots of conversation. Now, it may be because my ears are attuned to hear such things now that I investigate the paranormal for a living but whatever the case, I heard the words, ghost, spectre, and pirate at least once while I stood at the edge of the room, looking around to work out where I was going to sit.

A Strange Tale

The bar was packed. There had to be fifty people in it now, which meant that most of the seats were taken, and it was standing room only at the bar itself. Perhaps this was normal. As I made my way through the crowded room, watching to make sure the dogs didn't tangle anyone or get trodden on, I picked up snippets of the conversation. The chaps I was passing were all aged between late twenties and mid-forties with just one or two exceptions and there were only a couple of women present. Scanning their clothing and appearances I noted that those present were almost certainly not tourists as they weren't dressed to be out somewhere nice. They looked like they had been working. Their hair was windswept, their faces were red from the cold wind outside and they had on layered outdoor, rugged clothing.

I spotted an unoccupied table in the corner and made a beeline for it. It was a table for four, making me wonder if I might end up sharing, but to secure it, I hooked the dogs around a table leg, left my phone on the table and went to the bar to order food and a drink.

Waiting my turn, I heard the word *ghost* again and then someone said treasure. I stared at the line of spirits behind the bar and listened.

'... dived out past the headland today. I got a ping on the sonar, but it was just some old barrels that someone had dumped over the side at some point. I'm moving the grid inland tomorrow.' The speaker was to my right, but I couldn't see him, and I didn't want to turn and stare overtly at him.

Then another man spoke, 'I had no luck either. Did you hear that a ghost hunter has arrived in town?' My ears pricked up at that. I would hardly refer to myself as a ghost hunter but what was really startling was that anyone knew about me at all.

'Yeah, some multi-millionaire girl from up north,' replied the first. 'After the death on Saturday night, she packed her gear and came to Cornwall.'

'Never,' replied his friend. So, they weren't talking about me after all. However, there had been a murder, and someone thought there was a ghost involved. I had taken a break away from home to avoid all the ghostly daftness for a week. How had I managed to find it here already?

'Yeah, I hear she's quite the big shot. Brought a whole crew with her, flashy gear, expensive looking all-terrain vehicles. Jimmy saw them rolling onto the fields above the east headland by Kingsand earlier today. I reckon he must have meant old Graniff's land. He doesn't do anything with it anymore.'

'What did you hear about the murder then?' I was listening as acutely and as surreptitiously as I could manage without making my eavesdropping obvious. In so doing, I had failed to notice the landlady asking me what I wanted to drink until she asked again and touched my arm to get my attention.

Snapping back to reality, I said, 'Sorry, I was miles away. I'll take another Rattler cider please and the plaice for dinner.'

'Where are you sitting, love?' she asked.

'Just over in the corner.' I pointed. She placed the pint on the towel in front of me and disappeared into the gap behind the bar again. I sipped my drink but stayed where I was.

'…on his boat in the morning with his throat cut and stiff as a board.' I had missed a chunk of what they had been discussing.

'Who was he then?' one asked of the others.

'Well, I heard…'

The old chap I had seen sitting at the end of the bar when I first arrived interrupted. 'It was the landlady's brother-in-law, Philip Masonberg,' he said, having dropped his paper low enough to see over the top. 'The pirates got him. Don't go out there at night alone, chaps.' He met each of us with a meaningful gaze, looking at us over the top of his glasses. Then he flicked his newspaper once and hid his face behind it again.

A second of quiet passed, then the two chaps resumed their conversation.

'Have you seen anything? Of the ghosts, I mean,' one asked of the other. I turned a little now so that I could take a better look at the two men. They were young, or at least younger than me but probably still in their thirties. They were wearing the rugged outdoor gear that most others in the bar had on. Several of the other patrons had starting stripping layers off, I noted. It would be cool at sea if that was where they had all been, but in the confines of the bar, the number of people in here was raising the temperature. There were no distinguishing marks on the clothing of the two men to label them as working for a particular firm, nor was there anything remarkable about the features of either man. Both were of medium build and height with brown hair. They had most likely been out on the water for most of the day and were now enjoying a cold drink during their evening off.

Curiosity got the better of me. 'Excuse me, chaps. I could not help but overhear your discussion of ghosts. Can you tell me what it is that I have clearly missed?' I had moved away from the bar slightly so that I was in their field of vision when I started talking. I found it preferable to tapping one of them on the shoulder. They both stared at me, not in a threatening manner, but more with a look of surprise that I was so poorly informed. 'I arrived less than an hour ago,' I answered their unvoiced question.

It seemed to fill in a blank for them. The taller of the two, the one furthest away but facing directly towards me spoke first. 'You don't know about the pirates?'

'No. No, I don't,' I replied, hoping I would now get some answers.

'Well, don't go outside by yourself after dark, mate. Like the chap with the paper said.'

'Because of the pirates?' I confirmed.

'Because there are pirates out there and they are already dead and have come back to life to protect their treasure and they will probably kill you,' he said while flaring his eyes to show me how serious he was.

I took a sip of my drink, waiting to see if he had anything more to say on the subject. 'And you say that someone was killed by them recently?' I asked when he didn't speak.

'Old fella was found this morning. Run through with a sword,' he said while miming the sword action and pulling a face.

'A cutlass,' his friend cut in.

'Yeah, a cutlass,' he agreed. 'And there have been reports of ghostly dead pirates wandering the streets and scaring people for weeks now.'

'Ever since they found the gold,' his friend piped up again.

'Yeah, that's right.'

'What gold?' I asked.

'Crikey, mate. You don't know much, do you? It has been all over the news.' Now that he mentioned it, I did remember a short article on the national news a week or so ago about some gold being found. An old sunken treasure or something. I had probably been cooking dinner at the time and not really paying attention as I could not remember any more detail than that.

I pressed them for more information, which they willingly gave. A handful of gold coins had been found on Cawsand beach sixteen days ago by a chap out walking his dog. He was then spotted getting excited by the local copper who was out for a run at the time. Before anyone knew what was happening, the story was out and a fight over the ownership of the gold coins had begun.

A historian, probably with a dedicated career in marine tragedies was summoned from a nearby museum to examine the coins. It took him two days to confidently claim that they were lost when a ship called the Merchant Royal went down somewhere off the Cornish coast. The wreck had never been found, but now it looked like a storm, or something, had thrown the coins onto the shore and a gold rush of treasure hunters had beset the village hoping to make their fortunes.

The ghosts had appeared the next night – skeletal figures in pirate dress.

'They want their gold back. That's what I heard,' the man concluded in a hushed tone, leaning in to get closer to me like he was delivering a stark warning to stay away and be very afraid. I locked eyes with him for a moment. 'And they are going to hunt down anyone who goes after it,' he finished.

'But you are out trying to find more of it,' I pointed out.

He sniffed and straightened up. 'Yeah, well. Gold is gold.' He took a sip of his pint and checked his watch looking bored now.

It was all a bit odd. I thanked them both for their time and went back to my table to wait for my food. The dogs had gone to sleep on the old floorboards beneath the table. They looked up as I sat down but having seen that I was not carrying food to share, they saw no need to do more than that.

Dead pirates walking around the village looking for their gold, threatening people and stabbing one chap with a cutlass. That there had been a murder I believed. That it had been perpetrated by a centuries-dead pirate skeleton I could not accept. Sitting quietly and sipping my drink, I could already feel myself getting drawn into the mystery. With a sigh of resignation, I accepted that I was going to ask questions and investigate it for myself.

Fifteen minutes later, I was approached by a chap bearing my dinner on a plate. I had seen the same man working his way around the bar collecting empty glasses and serving dinner to other customers. The dominating feature was his muscular frame. He was a bodybuilder, if not professionally then he was most definitely dedicated to lifting some serious iron. His biceps bulged massively under his cheap, white shirt and his back formed a deep triangle that tapered into his lean waist.

'You waiting for fish?' he asked slowly.

'The plaice?' I attempted to confirm.

He stared down at the dish, the movement slow and deliberate, then looked back up at me, his expression unchanged. 'Fish,' he said again, placing the plate in front of me. It was indeed my plaice, a large piece, in fact, and exactly as I had expected the dish to look.

He seemed satisfied that the dish was delivered and wandered away feeling no need to furnish me with cutlery or condiments, or even a napkin for that matter. He seemed a little low on the ability scale, so I figured it might be simpler for me to sort such things out for myself. I got up and went back to the bar.

I waited to get the landlady's attention, glancing back at my fish hungrily and wishing I was already tucking into it. She spotted me, then tutted and rolled her eyes. She reached to a shelf behind her, producing the items I needed without me needing to ask for them. She indicated that she would bring them to me at my table.

'I see you met Thirty-three,' she said as she was laying out my knife and fork.

I raised my eyebrows in question.

'Our server,' she said as if that made anything clearer. 'The chap that speaks as if he's being played at the wrong speed. We call him thirty-three because when he speaks, he reminds you of a forty-five RPM record being played at thirty-three RPMs.' I was too young to have owned a record player, but I understood the reference. 'He's completely harmless and works for food and lodgings, but my lord he's as thick as they come.'

I shot my head around to stare at her, surprised she would be so negative about someone she employed.

'He's worked here for a few months. He just turned up one day. Walked in the bar looking for some work and has been here ever since, and it takes half the time to get the beer barrels in from the delivery van now because he carries them in three at a time.'

Thirty-three. It was a fitting name having listened to him speak, even if it was a little insulting and insensitive.

'What is his actual name? What do people call him to his face?'

'Oh. I don't know. He did tell me his name when he first arrived, but I forget what it is now. Everyone just calls him Thirty-Three.' She bustled off back to the bar, leaving me to enjoy my delicious fish, which was indeed delicious.

The dogs came out from under the table to stare intently at me. I was used to it, so I cooed at them between bites, assuring them I would find them a worthwhile treat later. As I scraped the plate to get the last few morsels, they began climbing my chair. I glanced across to the bar, checking that I was not being observed and put the plate down for them to lick clean. Then I finished my second pint and went to the bar for a third. The two chaps I had spoken with earlier were gone, replaced by two different men. These were much younger, perhaps twenty or twenty-one. They were talking about the ghosts and the spectral ship. Once again, I interrupted them to ask what they knew.

'We're The Spook Sleuths!' one announced proudly in a tone that suggested I should have heard of them. He was, to my mind, a little inbred looking. His ears and nose were more pronounced than they ought to have been, he had a schoolgirl complexion with flushed red cheeks, and his thin brown hair was already receding badly. He looked like he would grow up to be a Tory politician.

'What does that involve?' I asked, taking an interest.

'Not much,' answered the second chap.

'Geoffrey,' his partner complained.

'What, Tarquin? We have been on three of these little ghost hunts now and never seen a thing,' snapped Geoffrey.

'Why do you keep coming then?' snapped Tarquin.

'Might meet some girls,' said Geoffrey. Geoffrey was about as butt ugly as his friend but taller and thinner. At least his features were in proportion and his hairline seemed intent on staying put for the time being.

'What will you do while you are here then?' I asked. 'Are you out to catch a ghost or just see if you can spot one?' I had wanted to press them for more information about the ghosts, but I was fast arriving at the conclusion that they knew nothing worth learning.

'We plan to photograph the ghost ship when it next appears.' Tarquin was fiddling in his pocket while he spoke, producing a phone which he then swiped to reveal a picture. 'This was taken on the headland above the village a few days ago.'

The photograph was of poor quality. It showed the sea at night with the night sky dipping down to touch the water at the edge of the Earth. Centre focus was a white blob which looked mostly like a ship but could have been anything.

'This is really poor quality,' he explained. 'It was taken by someone on a phone camera. We have much better photographic equipment, so for the next few nights, we will be camping out on the headland to see if we can capture a better image. If we do, we shall sell it for thousands and get famous.'

'If we don't, then we go home broke again,' added Geoffrey in what was clearly dig at his friend.

The two took to bickering, so I left them to it. I wondered how many of the people in the bar were here because of the supposed treasure or the supposed ghosts. Were they treasure hunters, or ghost hunters or a mix of both? I decided my fatigue was more pressing than my curiosity though, took a rum and coke from the bar instead of another pint and after collecting the dogs from the table, I headed up to bed to read. Maybe tomorrow I would poke around and ask a few questions or maybe I wouldn't. Maybe I would just walk my dogs and visit places where I could get a cream tea.

Yeah right.

Heading up the creaking, rickety wooden stairs, I already knew I wasn't going to let this go until I had solved it.

Exploring Cawsand

I woke in the dark. I was an early riser, I had been since I joined the army many, many years ago and got used to the benefits it brought. Both Bull and Dozer were on the bed with me. They had snored loudly most of the night, but despite their deep sleep they were both eyeing me suspiciously now in case I was going to dictate that it was also time for them to get up.

I ruffled their fur, then left the bed heading for the bathroom. I was going out for a run. I didn't run much; I tended to visit the gym and lift weights or go to a martial arts class to get my heart rate up and burn calories. However, there was no gym here and I wanted to take in the view over the village that the cliff paths would offer me. The sun would not peek over the horizon for a while yet, which gave me time to find the way out of the village to the cliffs above.

I quietly let myself out into the dim light of pre-dawn, shivering against the cold as I stretched in place and berating myself for not stretching upstairs where it was warm. I was wearing nothing but a thin t-shirt and shorts to

24

keep the late October air at bay. I would warm up soon enough once I was running, so my only real concession to the time of year was a pair of gloves. I hated when my hands were too cold to undo buttons or use a key.

Sitting on a steep cliff as Cawsand did, the run was going to be a challenge both going up and coming down. I was right about the reward though. A twenty-five-minute indirect route to climb out of the village and up to the cliff path above, gave me a view I would remember. The dawn sun was clipping the top of the waves in the harbour and highlighting the colourfully painted terraced houses in a diffused manner as if the sun were being filtered through a darkened lens. Out to sea, there were several boats heading back towards Cawsand. Even from this distance, I could tell they were fishing vessels returning with an early morning catch. Out of breath, I stood and watched until I began to get cold from the light breeze hitting the perspiration on my exposed skin. I turned and started back down, picking out points that I recognised. There on the seafront was the small exposure of pebble beach, which placed the pub roughly halfway along the line of roofs I was looking at. I picked out my car in the car park. Its bright red sleek lines made it easy to spot. Along the shore, there were many wooden buildings, fishermen's huts most likely; a place where they could store their gear. A newer looking building, designed to match the others, had a bright white sign that dominated the side. It faced inland, advertising Scott's water sports. I soon lost sight of the shore though as I came down to the village outskirts and the houses there.

Coming back into the village, I spotted my first person of the day. There was another runner out, but unlike me, the lady running up the hill towards me was fully sheathed in layers of clothing, all stretchy fabrics and thin materials designed to move with the body and remove sweat. She looked like a runner, toned legs beneath an athletic figure with her brunette hair yanked back into a ponytail. It was swishing from side to side behind her head as she came towards me, gawping slightly at the fool out in clothing barely more substantial than pants and vest. I nodded and smiled as we passed in the street but left her to run as I picked up speed for the last mile.

Going hard for the last minute or so, I arrived out of breath at the pub door. A little shy of fifty minutes had elapsed which I considered quite sufficient for one day's fitness. The wound to my ribs was still sore but was not stopping me from training nor affecting my ability to breathe. The dogs leapt off the bed as I went into the room, showing me that they were keen to get out, their little bladders most likely full now. I stripped off my damp t-shirt, selected a fresh one from the drawer I had placed them in, paired it with a hoody to keep me warm and took them out for a walk. I would rather have taken a shower but didn't wish to run the risk that one of the dogs might pee on the floor. The old wooden floorboards might let it run straight through to whatever room was below.

Walking my little dogs along the path that bordered the seawall, I saw boats both setting off from the harbour and others arriving back. The dogs were fascinated by the new smells, though I kept them tethered to their leads in case they spotted a seagull and chased after it.

Suitably empty of fluids, the dogs seemed content to be led back to the pub where their breakfast awaited, and I remembered that I needed to text various people to let them know that I had gone away. I made the decision to leave and then left within the space of a few hours, pausing only to set Jane up to work from my house since my office had been burned to the ground on Friday night. Calling people to let them know where I was, wasn't a task I relished, so I put it off just a little longer, telling myself I would deal with phone calls, emails, and text messages after breakfast.

Breakfast itself was a sumptuous affair, and it might be the case that there's nowhere else to go for breakfast in Cawsand, but the room was packed. The people filling it were the same chaps that had been in the bar the previous night. I recognised many of the faces, although there were plenty of new ones. There were also very few seats left available, leaving me no choice but to share a table with someone else. I realised this could give rise to a conversation where I could ask questions about the ghosts and the treasure though. I selected a seat next to a chap that was just being served his breakfast and sat down.

He was hungrily tucking into a convincing plate of bacon, eggs, sausage, mushrooms, beans... the list goes on. It was quite the full English. The bacon looked to be a quarter inch thick. John the chef appeared almost the second I sat down as if he had been waiting for me.

'Good morning, Tempest. Did you sleep well?' he asked.

'Very well, thank you,' I replied with a smile.

'Were you not lonely in that big, sumptuous bed?' It was an oddly personal question. I let it pass.

Keeping a frown from my face, I said, 'Not a bit old boy. Why do you ask?'

'Oh, no reason.' He got on with pointing out the buffet of cold options available behind me. I asked him to make me a copy of the plate the gentleman opposite me had. When he left, I turned my attention to the buffet he had indicated. I needed tea, so helped myself to a cup of that first, then spotted some granola. The fried breakfast was a treat to myself – a special meal because I'm on holiday was what I had told myself as I guiltily ordered it. The granola was a healthy choice and would thus balance it out. I knew it didn't work like that at all, but I was hungry, and the granola looked great. However, before tucking in, I introduced myself to my breakfast companion.

'Daniel Russo,' he said in return, offering his hand to shake. He had on a dark grey fleece top with a zip that came down from the neck to the chest. On the left breast was embroidered the words, *Gold Rush*. I asked him about it.

'It's a boat,' he explained. 'I work as Mate for a chap who made his fortune finding treasure. It's a three-hundred and thirty-four-foot Halberg-Rassy kitted out for diving expeditions in deep water. He had it specially made to his specification.' I didn't know a lot about yachts, but I knew that ordering a bespoke yacht meant the man was seriously rich. 'We were in Ireland five days ago, diving on the wreck of a second world war supply ship when he heard about the caper here. We left immediately. Arrived here Saturday.'

'Do you think you will find it before the others do?' I asked, taking a mouthful of the granola.

'That depends if there is anything there to find,' he replied but I barely heard the words. I was too busy staring at my bowl. The granola was incredible!

'I'm sorry. I missed what you said then.' I had to ask the man to repeat himself because I had just found the best granola on the planet. Tucking into it, I felt even more guilty about the full English I had just ordered. I didn't need it if the granola was this good. I committed right then to stick with the granola for the rest of my stay and pair it with fresh fruit and yoghurts. I had eaten badly last week and could not out-train a bad diet. If I wanted to keep my waistline, I needed to employ some discipline.

'I said it's not uncommon for there to be no ship to find.

Ships wrecked hundreds of years ago can be amazing finds, but more usually they are elusive and when someone does find their location the supposed treasure inside is either missing or was a small fraction of what was reported. Still, I get paid either way, so it doesn't matter too much to me what happens.'

'What do you know about the ghosts?' I asked.

'Not much,' he said between mouthfuls of bacon. 'I heard that someone spotted an ancient looking pirate ship sailing past the headland in the moonlight about a fortnight ago. Then it disappeared, but ghosts of the pirates were spotted in the village the same night. Now there are ghost hunters watching for it because every time the spectral ship is seen, the pirates come ashore looking for their gold. Sounds like a load of crap to me.'

It sounded unlikely to me as well, but I was prepared to believe that something was going on. Daniel's knife and fork rattled onto his plate as he finished his meal. He checked his watch, quickly drained the last of his tea and excused himself. He needed to get to the boat. I bade him a good day and watched him leave just as my fried breakfast was arriving.

The fried plateful looked appetising, but all I wanted was another bowl of the healthy granola from heaven. I ate what I was served anyway and can report that it was filling and tasty. I vowed though that I would find something healthy for my lunch. My watch assured me it was 0830hrs. As I left breakfast, I took out my phone; it was time to tell people where I had gone.

The first person I called was Amanda. We had not spoken for a couple of days which was unusual for us. We had only known each other for a few weeks, having met at a murder scene when I began to investigate the vampire murder spree in Maidstone. She had been a uniformed police officer at the time but since then had quit that job and taken a position at my investigation firm. She still had a couple of shifts left before she was officially finished with the police on November 8th but was already working on cases for the firm and had solved one just a few days ago. Unfortunately, she had betrayed my trust last week when she chose to not divulge that I was being tailed by the police who were using me as bait to lure in a group calling themselves the Klowns. The Klowns had subsequently tried to kill me and several of my friends and I was unhappy with her. However, I had cooled a little in the last couple of days and just wanted to move on.

'Good morning, Amanda,' I said when she answered the phone.

'Good morning, Tempest,' she replied, her voice sounding like angels singing as always. 'I was just about to call you. I was heading to work but realised that I don't know where we will do that now. What can I do for you?'

'I needed to let you know that I'm going to be away for a few days. I decided I needed some time off.' I let that sink in for a few seconds.

'What about the business?' she asked.

'I have no live cases, Jane can handle calls and emails, and I will be back at the end of the week. If you wish to tackle anything that comes up, please feel free to do so. Jane can handle the paperwork and billing.'

'Really? Just like that?' she asked. 'Where will Jane be working? The office got burned down.'

'I bought new IT gear and office supplies and set her up in my house,' I explained. 'The customers will not be able to tell the difference until they wish to arrange a meeting. I asked Jane to put everyone off until the end of the week.'

'Okay,' she said after a while. 'I guess that all makes sense. Tempest?'

'Yes.'

'Tempest, look. I wanted to talk about what happened with the Klowns...'

I cut her off. 'Amanda, I really don't want to talk about it. Not now at least. Let's pick it up when I get back, okay?'

'Okay, Tempest. Have a good week,' she said while stifling a yawn. We said goodbye and disconnected.

I sent a text to Big Ben so that he knew I was away and wouldn't pop around to my house. I did the same for Jagjit and then with a sigh, I called my mum.

I was one of those lucky kids that had grown up with parents that stayed together and didn't fight about it. My father was the kind of man that was kind to animals and small children, who put others before himself and was satisfied with the life that he had at a very base level. He was a great father to have been around growing up and now that I was a man, he was still a great father and someone I tried to emulate. My mother was... well, my mother was lovely, but she was also quite hard work. Mum knew with absolute unshakeable certainty that she was right about everything. From astrophysics to fine art, my mother was the ruling opinion in any room. This, while annoying, was not that much of a problem. The issue, in simple terms, was that she also knew best about how I should be living my life. The same concerns about who I should be married to, how many children I should have produced for her by now and what I should do for a living did not, however, apply to my twin sister who was considered to be more or less perfect.

Anyway, I dialled the number for the phone in their house, knowing that my mother would be the one that answered. So, imagine my shock when my father's deep voice came on the line.

Caught off guard, I recovered and said, 'Hello, Dad. You haven't answered the phone in a decade. Where's mum?'

'Hey, kid. Your mum is in the bathroom. What you up to? We figured we would see you for dinner yesterday.'

'Yeah, about that. I'm in Cawsand,' I replied, getting the news out quickly like ripping off a band aid.

'Cawsand? Cawsand in Cornwall?' he asked, sounding confused.

'That's the one.'

'Okay. Why are you in Cawsand?'

'I felt like I needed a few days off work. I haven't had so much as a long weekend since I opened the business back in the Spring. I booked a room at a B&B, packed the dogs into the car and took a drive.'

'Will you be back for dinner next weekend? Mum has some jobs in the garden I could use a hand with.'

This was typical dad behaviour; he had processed the news and moved on. 'I intend to leave on Friday morning,' I replied. 'So, I'll see you for Sunday lunch.'

'Right,' dad said. 'See you then. Have fun in Cornwall.' That was all dad had to say on the matter. I exchanged goodbyes with him, wished him a peaceful week with my mother and we disconnected.

Task complete, I put my phone away and considered what I wanted to do with my day. I had come to Cornwall to relax, so what could I do that was relaxing? Solve a ghost related murder case?

Oh, okay then. If I must.

I collected the dogs from the room and headed out to

32

poke around in Cawsand. Strangely, I was looking forward to it.

With the dogs on their leads, I left the pub, stood in front of it flipping a mental coin then turned left instead of right purely on a whim. The street undulated as it wound around the coastline. Sometimes there were houses on the seaward side of the street and sometimes the path was hanging right above the water. I was doing nothing other than exploring the village itself, getting a feel for its rhythm and observing the activity of the people that lived here.

I spotted a yellow note, about the size of an A4 sheet tacked to the front door of a house and crossed the street to investigate. At the top of the sheet, which was, in fact, a laminated A4 sheet of paper was the word WARNING in a large font. That was what had caught my eye. The warning note was from the local parish councillor, advising the occupant of the house that their property was in disrepair and not in keeping with the tone of the village. It further warned of fines and corrective action if the property were not brought up to an acceptable standard within one calendar month of the date shown. The date shown was a week ago.

What did corrective action mean?

The note was signed at the bottom next to a printed name: T Masonberg. I stepped back to look at the property. There was some flaking paint around the windows and the windows themselves could do with a clean. Inside the windows were net curtains which had seen better days and needed to be cleaned or replaced. The guttering was loose, and the downpipe had shifted so that it was no longer properly lined up with the exit from the guttering. When raining, the water would spill out and run down the front of the house and there were a few weeds growing in the cracks where the brickwork of the front façade met the street. However, these were all quite minor points. I had a little bit that I needed to do to my house and would feel rather put out if someone left a bright yellow notice on my door demanding action.

I filed the information away and moved on. I walked another few feet, then a thought occurred to me. I pulled my phone from my pocket, swiped the screen and called Jane at the office. Jane was a man that I had employed as my assistant who then turned out to have some cross-dressing interests. Each day upon waking, he let his mood decide whether he would dress as a boy or a girl. There was never any ambiguity or need to wonder which one he had gone for as when he dressed as a girl, he looked utterly convincing. Until he opened his mouth that is. I was fine with it. He was gay, he liked to wear girl's clothes. There was probably weirder stuff going on within a few yards of my house.

'Good morning, boss,' he answered. 'It's Jane,' he filled in helpfully, having learned that people could not tell which gender he had gone with over the phone.

'Good morning, Jane. Are you settled in okay?' I asked.

'Yup. Got everything I need.'

'Jolly good. I need you to do some research for me.' I explained where I was and what was going on, then asked her to look up any newspaper reports, witness statements, the names of those that had claimed to have seen the ghosts and anything else she could find that seemed pertinent. Jane was a whizz at researching odd bits of information. I left it in her hands, knowing she would update me by email with what she had found later and would keep going at it until I told her to stop. I decided that I myself would investigate the ship that had sunk with the treasure on it and see what I could find out about the gold that had been found.

I continued to walk through the picturesque streets. Around me, the village was coming to life. I saw shop windows opening, neighbours chatting outside their doors, other people walking their dogs. On the hill above me, I could see cars going by in a steady flow and saw that the car park, which had been full last night, was now half empty where residents had taken their cars to drive to work. I also spotted a couple more of the yellow warning signs tacked to front doors but didn't stop to read them.

Then I came across another pub. The Star was a larger building than The Sea Pilgrim and, on a sign outside it boasted a beer garden and big screen television where all sporting matches could be watched. It didn't look as inviting as the Sea Pilgrim, but it was in good repair, so I had to assume it did sufficient trade for the owners to look after it.

I reached the harbour, where a small crowd had gathered. A tatty old boat was the centre of attention. There were boats moored either side of it and on the other side of the wooden jetty that formed a walkway to access them all. On many of the boats, I could see crew making ready to cast off and there were gaps at some mooring points where presumably other boats had already left for the day. Some of them were still visible, chugging out to sea.

I could hear conversation as I approached. There was a man standing on the deck of the tatty boat, poking it here and there. 'Honestly, Tilda,' I heard him say. 'The only thing you can do is scrap it. The engine still works but I don't know how. All the gear is held together with string and hope. It leaks. It smells. I couldn't sell it to a sailor if he was sinking.'

Through a gap in the assembled group on the jetty, I

saw who he was talking to. It was a woman in her late fifties, she was standing next to Gretchen and the pair were clearly sisters, they looked so alike.

'I'm not even slightly surprised, Norman,' said Tilda. 'Just take it away. I want it out of the harbour, but mostly I just never want to see it again.'

I was hanging around at the back of the group. A chap that was just in front of me noticed Bull sniffing his leg, looked down at the dogs, then looked up at me. 'What is going on?' I asked.

'Hmmm?' he said, as if not understanding the question. 'Oh, you mean the boat. It belonged to Philip Masonberg, the man that was murdered by the pirates on Saturday. That's his wife.' He pointed to the lady with Gretchen. 'She wants to be rid of the boat, but it's just an old wreck really. Norman there,' He pointed to the man on the boat, 'buys and sells boats. Nothing for him to do with that one but scrap it though. He was murdered on the boat, you know. Terrible thing to happen. Murdered by a ghost.'

I thanked the man and moved on, glancing back at the group as I left the jetty. Stopping to take a better look, I could see what looked like yellow crime scene tape fluttering on the boat. If the body had been found on the boat, then I wanted to have a look at it.

Ever more boats were leaving, sailing out to look for treasure. Whether there was treasure out there or not, the village of Cawsand, or at least the people that had businesses there, were seeing a boom in trade. I wondered about that as I left the jetty and stepped onto the rocky beach.

The dogs were very curious about the rock pools. I unclipped their leads and watched them scamper away across the rocks. I would come back later to have a look at the boat although I suspected I would need to do so soon, or I might find it had already been taken away. As the dogs scampered, I looked at the jetty – everyone was leaving far sooner than I had expected. I pretended not to watch as Norman climbed back off the boat. He was the last to leave and was talking on his phone while he did.

Would I be seen going on to the boat? Possibly. With most of the other boats gone there was very little between the shore and the tatty old boat itself to block the view so anyone looking out to sea from the village might see me. I thought about it for a moment but decided it was worth the risk. So, I herded the dogs back towards the jetty, clipped them onto their leads again, and with a quick glance to see if there was anyone obviously watching the area, I strode confidently towards the boat and jumped on board. To prevent the dogs from wandering off I hooked their leads over a handy cleat.

The yellow tape I had seen was indeed crime scene tape and there was dried blood visible on the wooden deck boards near the little cabin. Looking around, I had to agree that Norman had been right about the condition of the vessel; it was a wreck. Every part of it looked ruined and it really did smell. Like old rotting fish. There was a small below-deck compartment at the front where a couple of steps led down from the cabin. Inside I found old charts, a few items of nautical equipment and general detritus like a stained, old mug and a gas stove which I guessed he used for making tea.

I wasn't sure what I had hoped to find. Some evidence of a struggle perhaps. I had no time to dust for prints and had not brought my kit with me anyway. There was nothing here that I had not already seen and the longer I stayed poking around, the more likely I was to get caught where I ought not to be. With that thought in mind, I grabbed the handrail and pulled myself back up onto the deck.

'Good morning,' said the police officer looking at me from the jetty.

Bobbi the Bobby

'Good morning,' I tried jovially.

'I believe this is the point where I place you under arrest,' she said.

Bugger.

'I heard this was for sale. There was a chap here earlier saying it was nothing but scrap, so I wanted to check it out for myself, see if I thought I could do something with it.'

She eyed me dubiously. 'Are you aware that entering a boat without the owner's permission is still classed as piracy?'

Double bugger.

'I think you had best come with me, sir.' It was not a suggestion. I nodded and climbed off the boat. 'Will I need to cuff you?' she asked. She was staring right at me, but now she had a playful smile which confused me. Was I in trouble or not?

She was holding the dog leads, the two dogs standing next to her and looking at me. When I looked down at them, they wagged their tails, their expressions excited like

39

they were proudly claiming that they had found me a woman.

I wanted to say something cheeky or flirty, but I gawped at her brainlessly instead. She was a diminutive, little lady in what must have been the smallest police uniform they made. Barely more than five feet tall, my brain finally got out of neutral to provide me with the information it was sitting on. The lady police officer was John the chef's sister, which made her Gretchen's daughter, and she was the local Bobby.

'You are staying at the Sea Pilgrim, yes?' she asked. Well, she wasn't trying to cuff me or place me under arrest. I nodded. 'Let's go back there, shall we? Then you can try to come up with a more credible reason for being on my uncle's boat.'

'Right you are,' I replied. She offered me the dog leads and nodded her head back along the jetty to get me moving that direction. We walked in silence back to the pub with the people we passed looking at me suspiciously. At least, that was what my conscience was telling me they were doing. I was following the officer for most of the journey and about halfway there I worked out that it was her I had seen out jogging this morning. Her shapeless uniform was doing a good job of hiding the excellent shape beneath, so despite Mr. Wriggly's insistence that she must have a wonderfully shaped bottom from all the exercise, I stead-fastly avoided staring at it.

'So?' she asked, as we went through the front door of the Sea Pilgrim. 'Thought of a new story yet?' That playful edge was still there, tugging a smile at the corner of her mouth. I could not tell if she was amused because I was such an idiot, or if she was amusing herself by making me squirm.

The pub was empty and silent. No noise from the

kitchen and no smell of food being cooked, although the scent of bacon lingered a little from breakfast. She pointed to a chair by the bar indicating that I should sit. She went behind the bar and pulled out a kettle. 'Want a tea?' she asked.

Now I was curious. Just what was going on? With little option, I decided to come clean. 'My name is Tempest Michaels, and I'm a paranormal investigator.'

She raised an eyebrow in my direction as if trying to decide if that was an even bigger lie than my previous attempt.

'Oh, and yes please on the tea,' I added.

'How do you take it?' she asked reaching down to find two mugs.

'Julie Andrews, please,' I replied.

'Ex-military?' she enquired. I had used an old bit of army slang. Julie Andrews – white nun (milk with no sugar for my tea). That she had picked up on it made it very likely she had also been in the forces.

'Army,' I answered. 'You?'

'Navy. Six years.' The kettle began to bubble, hidden from sight somewhere behind the bar. 'The paranormal thing, that was the truth, wasn't it?' I nodded. 'Hmmm.' She poured hot water into the two mugs. 'I never met a person who did that before. Does it keep you busy?'

'Surprisingly busy in fact.'

'So, you came here to investigate our dead pirates.' It was a statement. She was adding two and two and reaching an obvious conclusion. I considered playing along, but the truth was always easier.

'Actually, no,' I replied. Her head came up from stirring the tea, her expression quizzical. 'I decided to take a few days off and came here on a whim,' I explained. 'I knew nothing about the ghosts or the treasure until last night. My plan was to spend the week walking the dogs and eating cream teas. The lure of the ghost story was too good to resist though. I thought I would poke around, ask a few questions and see if I could work out how they are doing it.'

'How who is doing what?' she asked, her brow furrowed in confusion.

'The ghosts are not real,' I said flatly. 'The ship they claim to have seen out to sea, the skeletal pirates that have scared people away from the town. None of it is real, so if there is something to see, it has to be a hoax, which means the real question to be answered is why, and then - who murdered your uncle?'

'You think that none of it is real but investigate the paranormal for a living?' she asked seeking confirmation.

'Yup.'

'That is… different,' she concluded, struggling to find a word that fitted. 'When they found my uncle's body, there were wet footprints leading out of his boat and back into the sea and he was stabbed with a rusty old cutlass. The coroner confirmed there were rust particles and traces of tiny marine organisms in the wound. The shape of the wound was consistent with an old cutlass type weapon. Some of the witness statements I have taken following ghost sightings were far too convincing for me to believe they are not real.' She handed me my cup of tea and took a cautious sip of her own. 'What about the treasure, do you believe in that?'

'I have no reason not to. Someone either found gold, or they didn't. A ship sank many centuries ago and may well have had something of value on board. Of course, it may not have, and the gold found recently is just a coincidence.'

'Goodness, you are a hard one to satisfy.'

No, I'm not. I ignored the voice from below my belt.

'Whatever your intentions, I need you to behave while you are here, Mr Michaels. If I find you on another boat that you have not been invited onto, or your poking around leads you to break into someone's property, I will arrest you, cuff you and cart you off to the station in Bodmin. Are we clear on that?'

'Perfectly.'

'Jolly good.' She seemed placated. I was not a fan of being berated but I had been trespassing so like it or not, she was just doing her job. 'Now, are you going to invite me out for dinner, or do I have to do all the work?'

The question caught me by surprise, making me choke on my tea. I had a drip hanging attractively from the end of my nose after I spluttered my mouthful back into the mug. I whipped out a handkerchief and wiped my face. She was chuckling, the playful smile once more tugging the corners of her mouth.

From three feet south, Mr Wriggly was calling me names for my total lack of cool.

'There are so few eligible or interesting men around here, Tempest,' she said with a sigh. 'I need some stimulating conversation that does not involve fish or fishing. Do you think you can manage that?'

I got my brain up to speed. 'I'm quite certain I can entertain you for an evening.' I gave her my best and most confident smile. I was a man in control of my life, someone for a woman to desire, at least I hoped that was what my face was portraying. I had never been happy about my smile, so she might be reading from it that I needed to go for a poo.

'The whole evening, huh? That opens up a few options.' Her eyes were dilating right in front of me. How was it that we had gone from threatening me with arrest to openly flirting in a few heartbeats?

'How about tonight?' I asked, calculating that since I was only here for a few days and that the lady was unlikely to fall into my bed after the first date, I would need to spend some time with her this week if there was to be any wonderful naked skin to skin action before I left on Friday. It was a pleasant concept, but I would need to get on with the romancing probably.

'Tonight is fine. I will collect you from here at seven o'clock. You can take me out in that fancy car of yours. I'll let you know where we are going later.' She finished her tea with a swig, put the mug down and picked up her hat. She was very much in charge and seemed to enjoy dominating me. 'Try to stay out of trouble please, Mr Michaels,' she shot over her shoulder as she headed for the door.

Staying out of Trouble

I finished my tea while wondering what had just happened. I appeared to have a date tonight and could not find a reason to be unhappy about it though I had to admit some confusion about how it had come about. I checked my watch: 1107hrs. Most of the morning was already gone. The dogs were certainly getting some exercise, and my plan was to go back out now and poke around some more, then look for some lunch when I got hungry.

Decision made, I placed the empty mug back on the bar, gathered the dogs and went back outside into the street. The first thing I noticed was a band of dark cloud hanging over the sea like a violent threat, but standing in front of the pub, facing out to watch the boats bobbing on the waves, I still had sunshine on my skin. The bank of cloud might pass us by or might not. Time would certainly tell.

To my right, there were four men in black outdoor gear coming towards me. They had just rounded the corner, their arms weighed down with heavy boxes, the hardened type that were made to carry expensive equipment. Just

45

behind them, I spotted a fifth person, smaller in stature than the previous four and slight of build, but also clearly the one in charge. She carried nothing but a phone.

They cut to their right before they reached me, walking down the concrete launching ramp to the beach where they began to dump the gear and open the boxes. The four men with the boxes looked like carbon copies of one another. They were all in good shape. One could argue in fact that their shape was great. Each of them clearly spent a good amount of time in the gym. Even with their fleece tops on I could see how broad their shoulders and backs were. Their afro hair was cut very short as if the team were a military unit, none of them had visible tattoos and they all wore exactly the same clothing. There was an emblem of some kind on the left breast of their tops, but I was too far away to read what it was.

The fifth person, the lady I believed to be in charge, didn't give any instructions as she arrived on the beach a few seconds after the men. They were all getting on with the tasks like a well-oiled and slick team. The lady noticed me watching. 'Not to worry, sir. Nothing to fear,' she offered her reassurance even though I was certain my face bore not the slightest trace of fear.

She wore the same outfit as the first four gentlemen but where they filled their clothing with muscle, she was petite, almost childlike in her measurements. Her long jet-black hair was tied into a bulbous ponytail that poked out of the hole in the back of the ballcap she was wearing. Like the men, I placed her age at somewhere around thirty. On her fleece top, the words Georgina Huntley Paranormal Sciences were embroidered in big clear letters.

Having spoken to me, I had been dismissed, she was getting on with whatever task they were performing. I flipped a mental coin on whether to leave her be but decided I was genuinely curious. The dogs started walking when I shifted my feet in the direction of the launch ramp, then dragged me down onto the beach when they reached it; the beach had lots of great smells to explore. Unclipped from their leads, they scampered away to look for dead fish and other interesting flotsam.

As I wandered towards them, the four men stood up and took a step in my direction to form a protective barrier between their equipment and me. Their faces all bore the same aggressive, warning look.

'Chaps. Chaps. This gentleman is merely curious. Go back to your tasks,' the lady said, finally showing her authority over them. Like robots, they immediately returned to their task, setting up the strange electronics they had taken from the boxes without sparing me a second glance. 'Georgina Huntley the Third,' the lady announced, offering me her hand as she stepped towards me. She was wearing no makeup, and her complexion was clear. Her nose, ears, eyes, and lips were all proportioned appropriately, and when she smiled in greeting it was not an unpleasant smile. The sparkle that one gets from some people was missing though, leaving her face a little forgettable.

'Tempest Michaels,' I replied, grasping her hand. She had a firm shake, which I have always believed to indicate positive things about a person. I was surprised though when her hand stopped moving suddenly.

'Tempest Michaels? The ghost hunter?' she asked still holding my hand but now looking at me with disbelief.

'Err, not exactly,' I replied. 'Tempest Michaels, the serial paranormal debunker. I don't hunt ghosts at all, but I do catch people that are pretending to be ghosts.' How on earth did she know who I was?

'Goodness,' she replied, the disbelief now firmly etched onto her face. 'You think that none of this is real?' she asked, waving her arm around to indicate the village. 'There are eyewitness reports, Mr Michaels.'

'They may have seen something, or perhaps they saw nothing. I cannot yet tell what they might have witnessed with their eyes, but there's no such thing as ghosts, so whatever it was, it wasn't dead pirates come back to collect their gold,' I said it as a fact because it was one.

She fixed me with a stony gaze. 'Well, I intend to prove you wrong, Mr Michaels. Tonight, if the ghosts come, I will record them.'

'Not going to attempt to capture one?' I asked, trying hard to keep any sense of sarcasm from my voice.

'Oi,' shouted one of the men. He was setting up his gear and Bull had just widdled up the leg of a rather expensive-looking tripod. Bull stood his ground but ducked out of the way when the chap tried to swat at him.

I moved to intercept, seeing the man's annoyance and predicting his move. The thing about dachshunds is that they are so damned low to the ground. When they run, they can turn on a penny and to catch them you have to get right down to the floor. So, as the chap swung his hand to scare off my dog and got low to the ground to do it, I took a single pace to close the distance and pushed on his shoulder lightly. His centre of gravity was already extended too far in his bid to reach the dog, so he fell forward onto the gravel of the beach and suddenly I had his three colleagues in my face.

'Stand down,' Georgina instructed them, the command delivered in a tone that was certain of compliance. The reluctance to obey was more palpable this time. They did it though, slowly returning to their tasks as the fourth man picked himself up. He locked eyes with me, and it was clear that he might not be acting upon it now, but my insult was not forgotten.

Don't mess with my dogs. I thought silently.

Georgina took up the conversation again, not noticing her employee's expression. 'No, Mr Michaels, I do not intend to catch a ghost. Such concepts border on the ridiculous, but I will be able to measure energy output and very possibly record the images.'

'To what end?' I wanted to know.

'To prove the existence of ghosts, Mr… Sorry, can I call you Tempest? Mr Michaels sounds so formal.'

'Of course, Georgina.'

'Gina, please.'

'So, you were telling me about proving the existence of ghosts,' I prompted.

'Tempest, do you believe in black holes?' she asked.

'Black holes?' I repeated.

'There's as much scientific evidence to support the existence of ghosts as there is for black holes. Pictures purporting to be of what are called black holes exist. Black holes can be detected not by seeing them, but by observing the effect they have on their surrounding environment, such as objects moving through space. Black holes are readily accepted as a feature of the universe, but no-one has managed to prove it. Yet. This is because the cause of the perceived presence of black holes is subject to many theories - each claiming to be correct. Ghosts are in the same category. There's a lot of evidence to suggest that they exist, but nothing substantial. Yet. I intend to change that.'

I nodded. It was the most rational explanation I had heard for a person to invest time in the supernatural sciences. 'I have another question. How do you know me?'

'That one is more easily answered. You're relatively well known in the supernatural investigation community. Your successful slaying of the vampire in Maidstone got everyone's attention. Vermont Wensdale wrote about you in very respectful tones.'

Did he really?

She went on to say, 'I must confess I'm a little shocked to hear that you're not a believer. Am I to assume that you are here specifically to prove the ghostly pirate sightings are not real?'

I wanted to move the conversation away from me, I would learn nothing from talking about myself. I pointed to the hi-tech equipment the goon-squad were setting up. 'What is all your gear going to do?'

'This?' she asked, her interest level instantly peaking. 'Much of this is my own design and thus very secret, so I cannot tell you much about it. However, I will say that it's going to monitor and measure on several different spectrums.

'Such as…?' I asked, trying to tease more information from her.

She smiled at me. She was clearly happy to talk about her pet subject. 'The premise of most theories concerning *ghosts* is that the human body contains energy and that after death this energy changes from one state to another. This is known scientifically as the First Law of Thermodynamics. So, what happens to that energy? It cannot be destroyed, so has to change state to something else. The energy identified in the human body is in the form of neurons. Neurons are electrically excitable cells that process and transmit information by electrical and chemical signals. They are at the core of the nervous system. Identified as energy, the First Law of Thermodynamics seems to support the idea that the energy changes from one state to another following death. In other words, science provides an explanation to the paranormal theory of electromagnetism and *ghosts*.'

She paused and touched a finger to her lips before continuing. 'While you would happily posit that ghosts cannot exist, I would argue that the energy of the person recently deceased has to still exist and that it will manifest in different forms depending on how it interacts with the other forces around it. To support this, other fields of discovery lend their weight. Among them are bioelectricity and neuroscience. Bioelectricity examines electric potentials produced by living organisms, and this includes the human being. The field of neuroscience is an interdisciplinary study including biology, chemistry, medicine, psychology, etc. and is the study of the nervous system. Bioelectricity and neuroscience are closely related, and both provide an insight into how one might measure the energy remaining to interact with the living world after a person has died.'

'I'm quite confident I will capture the evidence I seek when the dead pirates next come to shore.' She was smiling now, the expression altering her face pleasingly. My initial assessment of her looks had been unfair; she was quite pretty after all. Not that I gave myself enough credit to believe that she would care one jot what I thought about her features.

Before I replied, I called to the dogs. They were heading back towards the ramp that led off the beach already and I didn't wish for them to wander off. 'You present a convincing, logical and above all interesting argument, Gina. Will I see you around?' I asked as I turned to go. 'I might like to quiz you more deeply on this subject.'

'I expect so, Tempest.' She was smiling an engaging smile that suggested it might be nice to see her again. I bid her good day and went on my way. My stomach rumbled lightly to tell me I needed some lunch. I checked my watch: 1143hrs. Close enough to justify going for food. Patting my pocket to reassure myself that I had my car keys with me, I made a fast decision and walked to the car park. With the dogs on the passenger seat, I swung the car around in a wide arc and headed back up the hill out of Cawsand.

On the way in on Sunday, I spotted several places serving cream teas. For those that have never been to Cornwall, or have no idea what a cream tea is, the thing you are most missing out on is warm scones with clotted cream and jam. Served with a pot of tea, there's nothing like it. Whether such a thing was invented in Cornwall, or even in the West Country, I could not say. It's synonymous with the region though, and while clotted cream could be found elsewhere, it abounded in Cornwall and tea shops serving their interpretation of the traditional dish were everywhere.

Alien Spacecraft

Later, on the way back to Cawsand with my belly full after a large lunch and the first tendrils of post-lunch drowsiness starting to wind their way into me, I stopped to check a junction was clear then remained in place when I saw objects in the air ahead of me. I soon determined that they were not alien spacecraft, which my brain had been trying to insist they were, instead they were large drones. There were two of them, hovering in the air some distance ahead of my car and both appeared to be observing me.

In turn, I sat for a moment and observed them. I had never used a drone, but it was my understanding that one could operate them using an app on one's phone. I suspected that this applied only to basic models which these did not appear to be. They were large objects, at least two feet across and fitted with cameras. They also looked to be modified with other electronic equipment that hung beneath the central body. I could only imagine what its purpose might be.

The stalemate lasted no more than a few seconds before

the drones rose into the air as one and headed back towards the shore. I could not be certain, but if my mental compass was right, they were heading directly to Cawsand. I found their behaviour a little suspicious.

Staring through the top of the windscreen to keep an eye on their heading, I pulled forward to a horn blast from a Blue BMW 5 series whipping along the road in front of me. It shot past, swerving into the other lane to avoid clipping my car, the driver's face an angry mask caught for a half second as it went by.

My heartrate spiked briefly from the surprise. I checked the road was clear this time and pulled out. The drones were lost from sight, but I told myself to ignore them. They were just drones, most likely being flown by enthusiasts and their presence in front of me nothing more than coincidence. It was 1421hrs, I had enjoyed a full day already and most of it had been relaxing. That I somehow had a date tonight still felt strange, as if I had dreamt or imagined the sequence of events that had caused it. Nevertheless, I needed to find time to make myself ready for an evening with an attractive woman and would thus need to curtail my afternoon activities early enough to ensure I was ready on time.

The phone rang in the car, breaking my train of thought just as I passed the sign telling me I was entering Cawsand. I thumbed the answer button to connect Jane. 'Hi, Jane. Do you have information for me?'

'Yes and no. I need more time to pull together a worthwhile list of those that have reported witnessing the ghosts in Cawsand, but I have just emailed you a report on the ship that is currently being searched for. It's quite the story.' As she finished speaking my phone pinged with an incoming email.

'Thank you, Jane. When should I expect the witness report?'

'Another couple of hours hopefully. I will send you what I have before I finish for the day anyway.'

'Jane, you finish at lunchtime.' I pointed out. Her normal hours were 0900hrs to 1300hrs with the option of overtime if it suited both parties.

'This is interesting, fun research and with you away there needs to be someone here to answer the phone, doesn't there?' she argued.

She made a valid point. 'Jane, thank you. I don't know what I would do without you. I shall look forward to getting the witness list through.'

We said goodbye and disconnected. The call had taken longer than driving the remaining distance to Cawsand, so I remained in my car in the car park to finish it. Had I not done so I would have missed the two drones coming into land. They came in over my head, high above the houses. From the car park's elevated position above most of the village, I could see rows of roofs running in different directions. The drones were following one another and heading away from me. They appeared from the right, at least one hundred yards from me so there was no reason to believe they had followed me back to the village if they had indeed been following me earlier. Perhaps they were returning home. I continued to watch from my car, attempting to estimate which street they were coming down on.

As they sunk slowly from the sky, I exited the car. Doing so quickly to gain the few feet of elevation I needed to work out which two rows of houses they had descended between. I was so focused on the drones though that I had forgotten the dogs, who, upon seeing the open driver's door, hopped across the centre armrest, plopped onto the floor outside and took off after a cat that had been lazing under a nearby Ford Mondeo.

Daft little dog brains wired to chase anything that ran away, I knew with absolute certainty that if I didn't catch them soon, they would be lost somewhere in the back streets of Cawsand, and I would most likely spend the whole afternoon looking for them.

Yelling their names was as pointless as asking Paris Hilton to make sense, but I did it anyway, attracting the attention of anyone within earshot. Naturally, I sounded like a madman running through Cawsand shouting BULL-DOZER with as much volume as I could muster.

The cat did what cats generally do to evade a dog and went vertical. Its climbing medium of choice was a garden fence. I arrived a few seconds later to collect my two sausage-shaped idiots as they jumped and barked more than five feet below the ginger-haired cat as it sat atop the fence idly washing a paw and delighting in ignoring their efforts.

I didn't bother to berate them. They were dogs acting as dogs after all. I did clip them to their leads though and curse myself for I had lost sight of the drones, and they were gone.

On the way back to the pub, I took a few side streets in the general direction I had seen the drones go. My search proved fruitless though, all the houses looked the same and none had a big sign outside to tell me the occupants loved drones.

I let myself into my room, let the dogs go and flopped onto the bed. I was seriously considering an afternoon snooze. Then I remembered the email Jane had sent me and grabbed my phone.

The email read:

On the 23rd September 1641 the Merchant Royal, nicknamed the 'Eldorado of the seas' and skippered by well-respected captain John Limbrey, was returning home to Plymouth after two years transporting goods between trade points for the Spanish government, culminating in a voyage to Mexico alongside Spain's treasure fleet. Such were the successes of her expeditions that her holds were loaded with a rich cargo including 500 bars of gold bullion, 400 silver ingots, half a million silver coins and countless rubies, diamonds, emeralds, and pearls, not to mention many pieces of heavy jewellery. It was reported at the time that nearing her home port of Plymouth and only a few miles off the coast of Cawsand, a plank in the ship's hull sprung allowing water to rush in. Her crew hurried to pump it out but tragically their pumping equipment failed, and the ship was committed to a salty grave, along with her 58 crew and passengers.

However, there is much evidence and conjecture regarding the Merchant Royal being chased down and looted by pirates who emptied the hold before scuppering it and killing all the crew. The ship was returning from the East Indies and passed the Scilly Isles whereupon it met with three Royal Navy Frigates. A fog bank described in a Midshipman's journal as being of "unusual density" hid the Merchant Royal from the Naval escort which allowed the pirates to commit their raid. When the fog lifted, they found flotsam and dead bodies. The three Frigates sailed hard for the English coast and cornered the pirate ship near Cawsand where they exchanged cannon fire and crippled them before they could slip away.

There are conflicting reports regarding all the detail, but it seems likely that the pirates knew they would be shown no mercy so scuppered their own ship and rode it to the bottom.

Okay, so what did that actually tell me? That a pirate ship possibly did sink not far from Cawsand and may have indeed contained treasure. So, what?

The question never got an answer as I fell asleep, fully

clothed and on my back, probably snoring like a warthog with sore balls. It was 1642hrs when Dozer woke me up nudging the edge of the bed. It was getting close to their appointed dinner time, and he wanted to be fed.

Coming awake, I realised that I needed to get moving. I had to get clean, walk the dogs, and have a shave because I had a date tonight.

Date at the Jolly Roger Inn

Just as I was about to open the door to go down and wait for Roberta in the bar there was a polite and gentle knock on the door. The dogs started barking and leapt from their position on the bed behind me to repel the invader behind the door. My hand was mere inches from the knob, so I grasped and turned it almost before the person outside could stop knocking.

The dogs were running across the floor but skidded to a halt as I turned to them and crouched down. I fielded them both, certain that behind me was Roberta and she would be nicely dressed for dinner out and unwelcoming of stupid sausages climbing her legs.

'I was just coming down.' I started to say as I turned around holding the dogs, but the words mostly died on my lips because Roberta was dressed as a slightly slutty pirate. I say slightly slutty because her boobs were still in her dress, yet they could not have been shoved further up towards her chin without hanging her upside down.

Her costume consisted of a pair of thigh-length, black

59

leather boots with big shiny buckles stuck to them, a tight bodice that was doing the job of lifting her chest, a short skirt and a long, floating shirt that was open to reveal her cleavage. To accessorise the outfit, she had included a convincing looking cutlass, and an old flintlock pistol tucked into a wide belt that went around her tiny waist.

Stand by to be boarded. Arrrr! Cried Mr. Wriggly. I was expecting him to make a comment about cannon balls next.

'It's Halloween, Tempest,' she said to my confused expression. 'I brought an outfit for you as well. We are going to a party. I needed a date.' She held out her right hand, which had a bag of clothing in it. 'Quick, get changed or we will be late.'

Dumbfounded, or at last unable to form a coherent response, I plopped the dogs back onto the floor and took the clothes from her. The dogs fussed around her feet as I wandered to the bed taking the clothes from the bag.

I could sense my ire rising and was trying to quell it. Not a fan of being told what to do, her willingness to do exactly that, even in a playful, flirtatious manner was getting to me. I shoved the clothes back in the bag and turned around to face the door once more. She was coming in now though with the dogs following her.

'Quickly, Tempest,' she instructed, which was more or less the last straw. Then, just when I was opening my mouth to tell her I was not interested in dressing up, she started speaking again, 'I'm planning to see you naked later, so you might as well get changed in front of me now.'

Like a cutlass being raised for battle, Mr. Wriggly was instantly awake and ready to do harm. My protest died on my lips.

'I'll tell you what, I will turn around to protect your modesty while you change.' She was making a big joke of it, all the while smiling at me. I had already placed the bag of clothes on the bed and untucked my shirt. Now she crossed the rest of the room, kissed me lightly on the lips, then went to the window and made a show of not watching me undress.

Getting some gumption back, I tore off my clothes, telling Mr. Wriggly to shut up and go back to sleep. He begrudgingly obeyed. Pulling off my shirt, I could see that Roberta was watching me change in the reflection from the window, which was fine and formed a sort of early foreplay, but when I got to my trousers it seemed better to turn around and hide the semi-erect penis still struggling to come up to snorkelling depth. He, in turn, assured me that just one glance at his magnificence would have her back across the room demanding that he be set free. The costume, it turned out, was a Mr. Smeed outfit from Peter Pan. I was going to look very much like an utter twat.

A minute later I was dressed, and she was applying finishing touches to my outfit – a clip-on earring, a touch of eyeliner. I asked her where we were going and got advised that it was a secret. There was something a little unsettling about her dominance in our relationship. She was making all the decisions, telling me what to do, telling me what to wear. I wondered if she was going to pay for dinner, show me a great night out then expect sex and leave me some money in the morning so I could buy myself something pretty. I was telling myself it wasn't like that though and what I was witness to, was a woman with a mind of her own and the confidence to go after what she wanted. Right now, that was me, so I should play my part and enjoy my brief interaction with her.

Nevertheless, once she decided I was ready to be seen at her Halloween party, wherever or whatever it might be, I

STEVE HIGGS

stood up from where she had me sitting on the bed to apply my makeup. I towered over her at almost exactly six feet. She tilted her head right back to look at me, so I grasped her gently but firmly around her tiny waist and lifted her into the air to kiss her. The move instantly reversed the roles. I gave the kiss all I had. It was a proper kiss, deep and slow and with lots of suggestion of passion to follow. Helpless in my arms she returned the kiss with equal hunger, but I put her down again when I was done.

'Come on, let's go,' I said, taking her hand and pulling her towards the door.

'Hey, who's in charge around here?' she asked, laughing as we went out and left the dogs slumbering on the bed.

The one with the vagina is, said Mr. Wriggly. Always.

Our destination was The Jolly Roger public house on Finnygook lane in Portwrinkle. They had there a Halloween extravaganza, which it turned out meant they had decorated the place and laid on a buffet of beige food. The place was packed though with people in fancy dress. I was glad she had found me a costume, even if it was a bit crap, because at least by wearing it I didn't stick out as the only person in the room without one.

During the short drive, I breathed in the scent of her perfume and revelled in how delicate her body seemed. Her neck was slender and graceful, not to mention flawless and it led down to her chest, which heaved each time she breathed simply because her boobs were basically sitting on top of her outfit like it was a shelf. I realised then that this was the first time in a month that I had looked at a woman and not immediately compared her to Amanda.

I had been besotted by Amanda from the moment I met her. Amanda was exactly what I would wish for if chaps were allowed to design their dream woman. She oozed sex appeal but did nothing to flaunt it, she smelled great, her laughter was like listening to angels singing. I could go on, but you get the point. She had shown me barely the slightest interest and was dating a multi-millionaire playboy, so I could lust after her all I wanted, but I stood no chance of getting anywhere.

Now though, with no reason to believe that the interaction with Roberta was going anywhere, even though she had already intimated that it would, I was thinking about her and about how attracted to her I was right now. Like a spell had been broken, freeing me from my heart aching attraction to Amanda, I was now perhaps ready to move on.

The party was a limp affair, which Roberta seemed to quite enjoy, nevertheless. There were people there that she knew, she introduced me to each of them in turn and I made professional small talk as one does. My evening certainly wasn't terrible. Roberta was quite tactile, touching me on my arm or leg, cupping my buttock several times and commenting on the firmness she found. She was playing to my ego of course, but it was working.

By the time I was driving her back to Cawsand at 2230hrs, she was a little squiffy from drinking wine and was looking at me from the passenger's seat like I was a kebab she planned to eat. You can imagine my surprise then when we arrived at the carpark and she announced she had to get to bed because she had a shift in the morning. Her Superintendent was visiting to see how the investigation into the murder was going. She was not involved, of course, she explained, but had been assigned specific tasks in conjunction with the case which she could not tell me about.

Less sure of herself suddenly, she asked, 'Would you like to see me again while you're here?' It was the first time she had asked my opinion about anything.

I mulled her question over for a moment before answering. 'My dear Roberta. I can think of nothing I would like more.' Mr. Wriggly had of course been hoping for some action, not least because of the overtly flirtatious manner in which she had been acting this evening. I was a bit more realistic. Naked entanglement might occur this week, but it would be her decision not mine and few girls dive directly into bed a few hours after meeting a man.

All too few. Said the voice in my pants.

My evening had been different than I had imagined, but it had also been fun, and I got to spend it in the company of an attractive lady. Despite her decision to head home and get an early night, we were still sitting in my car, the cramped space ensuring there was very little room between us. She swivelled in her chair, then leaned across the centre transmission tunnel to kiss me, deeply and passionately.

She reached behind herself to open the door before she broke the kiss, then as the cool air swirled around us, she took her lips away. 'I'll see you soon, Tempest Michaels,' she said in parting, and she was gone, stolen away by the darkness that enveloped the streets.

I needed to get back to the dogs, so I wasted no further time in the car. With nothing else to do now, I was going up to the headland where I would spend a couple of hours looking for the spectral ship myself. There would be other people up there to mingle with, so by immersing myself in their activities, I might learn something new, even though I doubted there would be anything to see.

Back in my room, the dogs were pleased to see me of course and ready go out for a quick walk. It was cool out now, the sky clear and the temperature, which had not made it into double figures in daylight, was now hovering not far from zero. It would be too cold to take the dogs with me, and I had to wonder how determined the spook sleuths and others were and whether they would have already decided it was too cold and given up.

The dogs relieved themselves on several stationary objects and were then quite happy to head back inside. The pub was still open and still busy, making me change my mind about heading directly upstairs. I caught Gretchen's eye.

'What can I get you, Love?' she asked.

'Would you have a thermos flask I could use please?'

Her face showed surprise and confusion in response to my question. 'Oh, err. Yes, somewhere. You want me to have it ready for breakfast? Planning a day out somewhere?'

'I could do with it now if you can locate it,' I replied. 'I'm going up to the headland to watch for the supposed ghost ship. I have a few hunches about what is going on and might look into the odd ghostly events myself. Maybe even poke around the village a little to see if the pirates show up.'

Mostly I was joking but her face displayed a worried expression. It was only there for a very brief moment before she recovered, but I had definitely seen what I believed to be her natural reaction to the news. 'Oh, that sounds like a waste of time, love. You should stay in the warm and get a good night's sleep,' she advised, sounding an awful lot like my mother.

I didn't reply and a second passed while she continued looking at me, then she turned and vanished through the hole that led away from the bar. In less than a minute, she returned with a small thermos flask adorned with a red and green tartan pattern. 'While this do, Love?' she asked, offering me the object.

I said, 'Perfect, thank you,' as I took it and headed back to the room. Upstairs, I settled the two dogs in the bed I brought for them despite knowing they would leave it and get into my bed as soon as I fell asleep. I was tired. I needed some sleep, and experience had taught me that I was better off to get a couple of hours now, then have an alarm wake me for my night-time adventure.

As I settled down to sleep, my drowsy thoughts were focused on the tranquillity of this pretty village and whether there was any actual danger here. I dozed off soon enough, glad that thoughts of getting up soon weren't keeping me awake.

At some point after falling asleep but before the alarm went off, I came suddenly awake, adrenalin driving me to alertness. The sound of a creaking floorboard outside had brought me from deep slumber to some kind of semi-alert but still asleep state. But then the sound of a key slowly and quietly being turned in my lock brought me all the way back to reality.

Things That Go Bump in the Night

Another shot of adrenalin hit my bloodstream just as the door started to open. The two dogs were awake as well, their natural defensive posture manifesting in an explosion of barking in the silence of the night. They leapt from the bed before I could stop them.

There was no time for me to grab clothes, so I snagged a table lamp and ran towards the danger coming through the door.

'Christ, dogs! Shut up,' Roberta said from the doorway, her voice a hushed insistence. I was still running towards the door when I realised the person letting themselves into my room probably had intentions other than to harm me. I was about to stop myself, but before the message from my brain reached my legs, the cable from the table lamp reached full stretch and my right arm stopped moving. My legs hadn't stopped soon enough though, so I flipped upside down in mid-air and landed in a naked lump on the floor.

I looked up. Both dogs and Roberta were staring down at me.

'Err, hi,' I said, weakly.

'I didn't think this through very well, did I?' she said to herself. 'Of course, the dogs would make a noise.' She closed the door behind her, stepped over me, then grabbed the two dogs and placed them both on the bed.

I began to get up, but she said, 'Stay there, Tempest. I won't be a moment.' I turned a few degrees, so I could see her. She had already taken off her coat and top and was unfastening her bra. I swear I felt my testicles give each other a high five.

Or would that be a high one?

Moments later she joined me on the rug I had come to rest on. She didn't speak, she just started kissing me and I will happily admit I resisted not one bit.

A few seconds later my phone beeped its alarm to tell me it was time to get up. My plan to explore Cawsand at night and look for the pirate ship was dismissed though in favour of staying exactly where I was.

World's Best Granola

The room was drenched in sunlight when I opened my eyes. I turned over to check the other side of the bed but could tell before I looked that I was alone in the room. Roberta had left at some point after I had fallen asleep. She turned up, shagged me and left.

Brilliant!

Mr. Wriggly was doing a victory dance for one. My stomach rumbled to remind me that dinner was a long time ago and that by now I would normally have been up for a while and eaten. I rolled out of bed and headed to the bathroom. I needed to pee, but Mr. Wriggly was still doing his victory dance, so I busied myself by brushing my teeth, hoping he would calm down soon enough.

Ten minutes later, clean and with a thankfully empty bladder, I came back into the bedroom towelling my hair dry. The dogs had spent the night on the fold down bed once Roberta and I had moved them off the four-poster to make room for ourselves. She had been passionate and enthusiastic, and her diminutive size coupled with my ability to lift heavy stuff from regular hours in the gym had made the event very new and interesting. I estimated that she weighed no more than forty-five kilos: I could bicep curl more.

Thinking about it now was causing Mr. Wriggly to stir again. I needed a distraction and luckily it arrived in the form of two daft and lazy sausage dogs. They plopped onto the floor looking meaningfully between me and their food bowls.

Getting dressed while they crunched through their kibble, I remembered the amazing granola I had eaten yesterday morning. The thought of it made me want food to the extent that I considered leaving the task of walking the dogs until after my breakfast. So, it was with some reluctance, that I clipped on their collars and leads and took them for a walk.

It was cooler outside this morning. The clear sky above me must have come in during the night, allowing any warm air from yesterday to dissipate. The dogs didn't seem to notice. I took them on a circuit along the seafront to the edge of the village, then doubled back along a higher route to bring me out by the carpark once more. I was navigating by luck more than anything else, taking left and right turns as they appeared while keeping an eye on the position of the sun.

The car was still where I had left it, not that I expected it to have been vandalised or stolen, but it was reassuring to see it waiting patiently for me, nevertheless. The final part of our walk took us back down to the seafront where a left turn brought us back to the pub.

Twenty-two pleasant minutes had elapsed, but I was really hungry now and looking forward to my healthy granola for breakfast. I tried to eat healthily every day, and at every meal, accepting that I would not always be able to and knowing that I didn't always need to. My selection of food ensured I stayed the shape I wanted to be, but I thought it a bonus to be able to eat a healthy breakfast that also tasted as good as the granola did.

The pub restaurant area was just as packed as yesterday and filled with many of the same faces. It might have been all the same faces, but I had not paid enough attention yesterday to have committed every face to memory. As I walked through the room, I became aware that the chatter was all to do with the ghosts.

There had been another attack last night.

At the table with the tea urn on it, I selected a mug and a tea bag and waited for the chap already filling his mug with hot water to finish. He glanced at me as he released the tap to indicate he was done.

'Did you hear about the incident last night?' I asked him.

'What? Oh, you mean the pirates attacking that couple?' he confirmed.

In reply, I said, 'Actually, I don't know what I mean. I heard that there was a sighting or an attack last night and hoped you knew more than me.' Perhaps the pirate attack was why Roberta had left in the night.

'You by yourself?' the man asked, looking around to see if I had a wife or partner with me. 'Come and join us if you like. 'Ryan knows about it.' He indicated across the room to what I guessed was his table where two seats out of four were already occupied.

'Sure. Thanks,' I replied as he headed in that direction. I helped myself to a large bowl of granola as my tea bag steeped, then wove my way back across the room to join his table. The chaps at his table all wore clothing suitable for seafaring activities, which I soon learned was exactly what they had in store for the day. They were treasure hunters or at least part of a crew that served on a vessel that was here for treasure hunting. They were big men, each of them easily as tall and as broad as I, but far more weathered and a good decade older. Their haircuts were functional in that they were neat, but short and contained no trace of product to tame them. Their hands were calloused, and their faces bore a sun, wind, and rain etched hardness that made them look like men with tough jobs.

After introductions were made, the man I met at the tea urn, whose name was Harry, urged Ryan to explain what he knew about the ghostly incident of the previous night.

Ryan, who was sitting opposite me, took a large mouthful of bacon and eggs to chew while he considered what he wanted to say. Finally clearing it, he said, 'I went for a walk down to the jetty this morning. I always check on the boat and the weather charts before breakfast, so I can plan the day while I eat.' He forked in another mouthful. 'Well, it looks like there's a squall coming in from the south this afternoon. Should get here a little after lunch, maybe as late as three o'clock.'

'The ghosts,' Harry prompted.

'Oh, yeah.' Another forkful went in followed by a bite of toast and a swig of his tea. 'There was a police car parked outside a shop down towards the jetty next to the Asian place that sells pastries. It was easy to spot because the light inside the car was on. This was almost an hour ago, so the sun was still trying to come up and it was mostly dark. There was no one about, but on the way back there was an old fella walking his dog and he was talking to a tiny police lady.

Roberta.

72

'I heard her telling the chap that the ghosts had shown up in the middle of the night and that they had been trying to force their way into the property. Making all kinds of noise until they were seen, at which point they vanished. She also said it was not the first time they have targeted that particular property.' He paused once more to shovel some more breakfast in, but when he failed to restart his narrative, I took it that he had nothing more to say.

I would have to check out his report later, maybe ask Roberta what she could tell me. If ghosts have no physical form, how is it that they find themselves stuck outside a property trying to force their way in? There was something going on in Cawsand, and it felt grounded in unpleasantness to me.

Before I could finish my granola, the three chaps reached the end of their breakfasts and politely excused themselves; they had a busy day ahead. Alone at the table, I considered the pirate ghosts and who stood to gain from the pretence. My immediate assumption was that someone was dressing up, maybe it was more than one person, but whoever it was they had to be doing it for a reason. There had to be something to gain from it.

I had no plan for my time in Cornwall other than to walk the dogs and relax. The relaxing part was supposed to involve reading a few books and overindulging with food and alcohol. Instead, I was going to spend more time poking around in the village. It would still be relaxing, I told myself. I would take the dogs with me, and I would mostly be wandering around, taking in the sights while asking a few questions. Besides, I didn't have Roberta's number yet and quite fancied another bout of nocturnal activity for which I would need to try to accidentally bump into her.

I flashed to a memory of her last night, kneeling on the

chaise lounge and gripping the back of it. In my head, her pert little bottom was pointed towards me as she grinned coquettishly over one shoulder and beckoned me.

Okay, the genie is awake! How would you like to give the lamp a damned good rub?

I spent the next minute concentrating really hard on trying to divide a large number by seventeen. Mr. Wriggly gave up and went back to sleep.

A short while later, with breakfast behind me and the day ahead, I went out the front door of the pub with the dogs pulling me onward. On the beach, directly in front of the pub were Gina's spectral science team from yesterday.

I walked over to the railing to say hello, but Gina had already spotted me. She waved and said, 'Good morning, Tempest. Did you hear there was more paranormal activity last night?'

'I did. Was your equipment able to capture anything?' I asked, quite certain that it had not.

'Not this time,' she replied, her smile still in place. 'One of the big problems is where to site it. I wish I could set up in a dozen locations but that would require more equipment than is practical to carry and a lot more money. It seems they came ashore elsewhere last night.'

'How did you get into all this paranormal science?' I was making conversation as much as anything, but I was also genuinely interested to hear how an intelligent woman found herself committing time and money to such a pointless pursuit.

Gina handed a piece of electronic something to the man nearest to her. None of the men had paid me any attention thus far save for the douchebag from yesterday who offered me a basic hard stare when he managed to catch my eye. I wondered if I was going to have a problem with him, but I turned to look at Gina again. Her hands now empty, she came right up to the railing, rubbing them together against the cold.

'I grew up in a large house as an only child and like many children without siblings, I had an imaginary friend. The difference between my imaginary friend and that of others though is that I did not imagine mine. I must have been three when Emily first visited me. At first, I was too young to understand what she was. It was only when my parents, my grandparents, my nanny and everyone else refused to see her that I came to understand that she was a ghost and that only I could see her.' Gina had a wistful, but earnest look to her eyes, making me believe that she believed what she was telling me. 'Emily visited me day or night for years. When I was old enough to understand, I asked her how she had died and why she was still here. Her answer was that she was murdered by her drunken father and her body was buried in the grounds of the house in an unmarked grave. Now, I know you don't believe me, Tempest.'

I gave no comment and tried to keep my face emotionless.

'However, when I was nine, my father's men started digging ground works for a new extension to the east wing of the house. About three feet down, they found the skeletal remains of a little girl. The police and the coroner came and days later confirmed the little girl had died from a broken neck, most likely deliberate. Emily vanished the day they found the body and I never saw her again. My parents wasted countless thousands on therapy, always convinced they could make me see reason. I knew though. I knew what Emily was and one day I will prove it.'

It was quite the story. Told around a darkened campfire

with some marshmallows to toast it would get a round of applause. I had my explanation though; Gina was convinced from her own experience that ghosts existed and had dedicated her time and money to prove it. I had no idea what I was supposed to say at this point. The silence stretched out while Gina waited for me to say something. 'Do you, err... have you met others with similar experiences?' I asked finally.

'Yes, Tempest. There are thousands of us. Emily is just one example. Ghosts are everywhere and the behaviour the pirates are displaying is typical of a malevolent spirit anchored here by events in their life that prevent them from departing.' When I still said nothing, she shrugged. 'Look, Tempest. It's okay to not believe what I'm telling you, a lot of people don't. That's why it's so important for me to use science to prove it. I only ask that when I present irrefutable evidence, you accept it.' She smiled at me.

I smiled in return. 'Gina, I wish you luck.' I was certain that luck was not a factor but wondered if she had really thought her plan through. If she produced scientific evidence, she would most like spend the rest of her life defending it, not immediately be hailed as the next Nobel prize winner. The world was not ready to hear that their dear departed parents were still hanging around in ghostly form. And what would form irrefutable evidence anyway? She would need to have a ghost in captivity. The chap that found the Platypus had to bring back a live one before the scientific community he was showing it to would believe it was real.

'Thank you, Tempest,' Gina replied. 'I have plenty of work to do here, checking over the equipment and resetting it for tonight... but perhaps we can chat some more later?'

It suddenly occurred to me that Gina was flirting with

me. I knew that I was dumb when it came to recognising that a woman was interested. I always had been, but she was smiling more than the situation required and her eyes were sparkling at me. Now that I thought about it, when I had seen her before she had not been wearing any make-up and now her features were delicately highlighted with a swipe of this and that. My first reaction was to wonder why. My sister and others have told me that, like a person with body-dysmorphia, I don't see the real me when I look in the mirror and that I'm in fact far more attractive than I believe myself to be. I have accepted what they are telling me but still cannot see it.

Nevertheless, the cute, but tiny, cocoa-skinned lady in front of me appeared to be taking an interest. With Roberta having already thrown herself at me in the last twenty-four hours I was having a good week. It felt utterly wrong though to encourage Gina's advances if that is what they were since Roberta was probably less than a quarter mile from my current location and may yet plan to see me again. My old army buddy, Big Ben would have bedded them both at the same time of course and from below my waistline, Mr. Wriggly was yelling instructions that I was steadfastly ignoring.

'Gina…' I started, unsure about what I wanted to say. My silent internal debate continued to rage, but she was waiting for me to say something, and I concluded that meeting for a chat was harmless enough. I didn't have to sleep with her and perhaps that was not her intention anyway. 'Gina, I'm staying in the Sea Pilgrim.' I pointed to the pub behind me. 'You can find me there whenever you wish.' Then I wondered if what I had just said sounded like an invitation to come find my bed. I probably worried too much. 'I expect to be there most nights for dinner if you have free time and wish to spend it with me.' I fished in my pocket for my wallet and produced a business card. 'Here's my number should you need it.' I handed it down through the railing to her.

Gina inspected the card, holding it in her tiny hands.

She looked back with a big smile. 'I will be sure to call, Tempest.' Then she yawned, covering her mouth and turning away. 'Sorry,' she laughed. 'We always have someone with the equipment at night. It can be temperamental, and it's expensive, so I don't want to just leave it unattended. I could do with more sleep than I'm getting though.' She looked like she wanted to say something else and was debating it. Big Ben would say something outrageous like offer to help her out with her sleeping arrangements, but I would just mess it up and come off as idiotic instead of cool. The moment passed.

I shot my cuff to check my watch: 1012hrs. As if on cue the dogs tugged at their leads, pulling me away. 'I will see you later, lovely Gina,' I called as I let them drag me away from the beach.

Walking back up the hill out of Cawsand and nearing the carpark, I acknowledged that I had no plan for the day. Driving down here on Sunday, I thought only about being away from my home and that environment for a few days. Now unexpectedly embroiled in a ghostly mystery, I was faced with alternative activities to those I had previously planned. My mental diary had intended for me to go to Bodmin Moor today where the dogs and I would have bought an Ordnance Survey map and vanished into the wilderness for a few hours. Instead, I took a circuitous route around Cawsand to arrive at the eastern edge of the village where it joined the coast once more. I was going to find the Asian pastry shop they had talked about this morning.

Before I found it though I bumped into the couple themselves. As I turned onto the seafront, I spotted a moving van with items going into it rather than coming out: someone was leaving. Walking towards it, I saw a lady in a burka, then a man whose tan skin and dark hair could make him a descendant from one of a lot of different Muslim nations, yet the overriding feature on his face was fear. Their movements were hurried as if they were desperate to get away.

I stopped by the van as I saw the couple struggling out with a sofa, hooked the dog leads around a lamppost and offered to help the lady. 'Please, let me,' I insisted. She allowed me to take her end of the bulky item and they both thanked me as it went into the back of the van with ease.

'Is everything alright?' I asked. 'You seem to be in something of a hurry.'

'We just want to be gone. To leave this awful place behind,' the man replied.

Awful place?

'I'm a tourist here, but the village seems wonderful,' I replied with a deliberately leading statement.

He took the bait. 'It looks wonderful, yes. Do you believe in ghosts?'

I shook my head with a wry smile.

'Nor do I. Our shop has been targeted by the *ghosts*,' He did the quote fingers in the air thing when he said ghosts. 'Three times in the last two weeks. We are not wanted here, that is the bottom line. We have seen them outside our window – I will admit they look real enough. Damned scary in fact, and we have had four, no five of Tilda's council warning messages to make the shop appear more in keeping with the tone of the village.'

'How can she impose that?' I asked, truly curious.

'She cannot. But that does not stop her from trying and the village council believes she's the best thing to ever happen to the village. Under her leadership, all the less desirable properties have been brought up to match the standard of the others, the beach is always clean, the streets are spotless and the businesses in the village are all doing so much better than they were.'

'So, what was wrong with your business that she wanted you to change?' I asked.

'We sold pastries.' That seemed harmless enough. 'But not traditional Cornish pastries. We sold Muslim pastries, things like Iftar and Kunafa. I believed that by diversifying from what everyone else was selling we would capture a segment of the market not catered to by others and there are plenty of Muslim tourists that come here.'

'Not that we sold only to Muslims.' His wife spoke for the first time. 'We gave out samples to all the locals several times to create interest. The shop did a steady trade all year round.'

The man took up the narrative again. 'Three years we have been here, but the last six months have been hard with Tilda pushing us to change the name of the store and to put the Muslim food to the back and away from the window so that we could display more *regular*,' he did the quote fingers thing again. 'Cornish food instead.' He slumped his shoulders defeated. 'The shop is with an agent to sell. After the murder, I'm worried they might target us next. We are moving back to Manchester with my brother for now.'

There seemed to be little more to say. I wished them good luck and left them to pack the rest of their belongings. It was quite troubling. The familiar tug of the unsolved mystery was back. There was something rotten at the heart of this village if a nice Muslim couple was being forced to flee.

Further along the path, I came across a bench facing out to sea. There were a number of them dotted along the shoreline for tourists, or locals I supposed, to use. I picked up the two dogs and settled them either side of me.

In my head, I was trying to work out how to connect all the bits of the puzzle. The ghosts, the ghost ship at night, the treasure. Were they all linked? Was none of it linked? What about the business owners and others that had been forced to flee and the man that had been murdered? My simple assumption was that one thing was being used to cover up or draw attention away from another thing. Someone murdered the man on the boat since he had not stabbed himself with a cutlass and then hidden it. That it had been blamed on the ghosts indicated that someone was creating a story to misdirect the blame. The same ghosts had allegedly attacked the Muslim couple I just met. They had seen them, and I was willing to bet that some of the other witnesses would also report that the ghosts looked real. So, what were they seeing?

I sat on the bench until the cool air began to penetrate my clothing and make me feel cold. 'Come on, chaps.' I said, scooping the dogs from their happy slumber nestled either side of me.

Without checking my watch, I estimated that it was close to noon. The granola I ate for breakfast had burned off, leaving me with the first pangs of hunger. I knew the pub served drinks at lunchtime and their bar menu included some sandwiches that sounded enticing. Heading there, I spotted Thirty-Three coming out of a building ahead of me.

'Hello,' I said in greeting as I went past him. In turn, he

said nothing, giving me a blank look and holding it. I might have thought it rude from anyone else but told myself it was in keeping with his general demeanour.

Thirty-Three was dirty, or at least his clothes and hands were. He looked sweaty as if he had been grafting hard at a manual task for some time. The muscles in his arms, which were bare despite the cold, were shiny with sweat and the veins running over them were pronounced – an effect I only see on myself after a hard session in the gym. Did he have a set of weights inside the building that he had access to? It would certainly explain his huge muscles.

Following the dogs, I soon left the man behind me and arrived back at the pub where I found Gretchen behind the bar once more. Charlie was, as always, in his usual chair with a newspaper folded out on his lap. There was a half-drunk pint of Guinness on the bar next to him and his glasses were perched at the end of his nose. Two stools along from him was Tilda. I recognised her from the jetty and next to her was Roberta. She was in civilian clothes rather than uniform.

'Hello, ladies, Charlie,' I called as I crossed the room.

Roberta and Tilda turned to see who it was, Charlie looked up briefly, nodded his head ever so slightly and went back to reading the paper. Gretchen stood up from leaning on the bar in readiness to pour me a drink.

'I have to go,' Roberta said to her mother and Aunt as she slid from her stool. I flashed a smile at her. I wanted to accidentally run into her as I didn't have her phone number and didn't wish to ask her mother for it. Another date would be nice, especially since the first one had ended so pleasingly. She ducked past me though, heading for the door. 'Sorry, Tempest. I must dash. We shall have to catch up later.' A little deflated, I watched the door shut behind her, reaffixed my smile and turned back to the two older ladies.

'Might I buy a round of drinks?' I asked spontaneously. Getting laid last night made me feel generous. Unsurprisingly my offer was not turned down, although Gretchen was good enough to make sure she poured my beverage first. I sucked down a good third of the pint in my first swig.

With my back to the door, I heard it open once more but didn't turn to see who it was. Instead, I perused the bar menu, looking over my option while my stomach gave a faint grumble of emptiness. My idle musings were interrupted when, from behind me, a familiar voice caused my blood to freeze.

A Rude Surprise

I turned slowly, desperately hoping my senses were playing a cruel trick on me. They weren't though and there, standing in the doorway, was my mother.

Bother.

She said, 'Hello, Tempest. We decided to join you and have a little break.' She wore a beaming smile like she was delivering the best possible news that I could hope to hear. The dogs had seen her and were straining against their leads, so I lifted the chair leg I had trapped them under and watched as the pair shot across the room.

'Where's dad,' I asked.

'He's just bringing the suitcases from the car.'

'Where are you staying?' I asked, thankful that there were no rooms available in the pub.

'The landlady agreed to let us share your room,' she replied, once again delivering her answer like it was the best ever.

I spat out the mouthful of beer I was drinking, but my

84

mother was moving to the bar oblivious to my reaction. 'Excuse me, mother. You plan to stay where?'

'In your room with you. It will be nice and cosy, just like the last time we stayed here in the eighties. I even think it's the same room.' She spotted my horrified face finally and paused for a second. 'That's why you invited us down isn't it?'

'Mother, dear. I didn't invite you. I had no idea you were coming and there's only one bed. How do you propose to manage the sleeping arrangements?'

'Gretchen said there was a fold-down bed in the room as well and that the room is designed to sleep four.'

'That's right,' said Gretchen. 'That's okay, isn't it, Tempest?' she asked.

Honestly, I didn't know why I was arguing. Changing my mother's mind once it had settled upon an idea was like trying to change the course of a super tanker by farting in its general direction. I would try to find alternate accommodation for myself. It seemed the simpler option.

'I didn't know that we had ever stayed here before,' was what I finally said in reply.

'Oh, yes. We had a lovely week here back then. You and your sister shared the fold-down bed – you were only three at the time and we went all over the place exploring the caves on the shoreline, visiting tea rooms and enjoying the sunshine.' That I had been so young explained why I had no clear memory of it, just a few half-captured images. 'Don't you remember the dog they had here?' she asked. I didn't and shook my head. 'It was a dachshund. A little black and tan one like yours. Of course, the place has changed hands since then, possibly more than once.' Mother continued to ramble on as I heard the sound of someone struggling as the came into the pub. I put my pint down and went to help whoever it was.

Sure enough though, I had guessed right and found my father coming through the door, loaded down with bags and suitcases and other bits.

'Wotcha, kid,' he offered with an out of breath smile.

'Let me give you a hand.' I grabbed a bag that was looped around his neck and another that was sandwiched under his right arm.

'That's better,' he said, flexing his neck as if to loosen it.

'Is this all of it?' I asked.

'Don't be daft, son.' he replied with a chuckle. 'Your mum packed everything but the neighbour's cat.'

I shot my eyebrows in response. 'Come on, the room is just up here,' I said as I started toward the stairs. The stairs were just inside and to the right of the entrance, so as we turned up them, we could see mum now chatting with Gretchen at the bar. I placed a silent bet with myself that mother would have a large glass of wine in front of her by the time we got back down.

I was wrong though. In the two minutes it had taken us to get into the room, put the cases on the bed, which had thankfully been remade with clean sheets, and come back down, the glass in front of her was already empty.

'How much is left in the car, Dad?' I asked.

'A few more bags, your mum's knitting, that sort of thing,' he replied while hungrily eyeing up the bar.

'Enough for one to carry?' I didn't wait for an answer. 'Give me the keys, you go get a beer.' It was daylight, so dad had probably driven for at least the last five hours and had then lugged his body weight in bags through the streets of the village. His forehead was covered in a light sheen of sweat from the effort and he was a little out of breath. He would never admit it, and I would never say it, but he was getting old.

He handed the keys over thankfully. 'We parked right next to your car.'

Walking up through the village to the carpark, I searched for *accommodation near me* on my phone. There was a reasonable list within a couple of miles as there were other villages along the coastline in both directions and hotels or public houses with rooms dotted about randomly between them. During the ten-minute walk, I exhausted most of them though. They were all full of treasure hunters or ghost hunters and I was regaled several times by different persons exclaiming joyfully that they had never had such a late boom to the year.

After the tenth call, I gave up. I had reached the carpark anyway, so I needed my hands to empty the car, and it looked like my choices were to sleep in the car or sleep on the fold-down bed in the same room as my parents listening to my mother saw wood in her sleep.

Perhaps Roberta will invite you to bunk with her. Mr. Wriggly suggested. I performed magnificently last night after all.

He made a valid point. If Roberta had any further intention to spend naked alone time with me, it would have to be at hers and not in my hotel room. I would not ask her, but I felt certain I could carefully slip into the conversation that my parents were now in the room with me and perhaps she already knew since her mum owned the pub.

There were four different bags to carry but they weren't heavy, so I hooked two in each hand and started walking. The round trip out to the car and back with their luggage had taken no more than twenty minutes, but it was enough time for mother to settle into holiday mode; I could hear her cackling at the bar as pushed the pub's door open. I turned sideways to get inside with the bags and dropped them all in a small alcove before joining my parents in the bar.

Old Ladies Together

My mother was still sitting in the same place at the bar; she hadn't moved since she arrived. There was a half-drained glass of white wine in front of her which I hoped was the second one and not the third or fourth, but she had a healthy glow to her cheeks already and was getting to know the locals. Gretchen was leaning on the bar and to my mother's right was Tilda still. She too had a glass of wine in front of her, and the three old ladies were deep in conversation about something. My dad was sitting off to one side, reading a book and probably quite content. As I watched, his right arm left the book to grasp his glass of beer, he took a small mouthful and set it back down, all without taking his eyes from the pages in front of him.

The three women burst into loud cackles of laughter; one of them had said something funny. Looking across, I noticed that the dogs were no longer beneath mum's seat where I left them. They had been rescued from the floor and were in the laps of the two ladies sitting at the bar. Mum had Dozer which meant the black and tan bottom I could see beneath Tilda's arm belonged to Bull. Both were lying on their backs being cradled like babies.

I sat myself down opposite dad. He lifted a finger, asking for a moment's patience while he finished the passage he was reading. That done, a moment later, he closed the book and set it down. 'How are you feeling, kid?' he asked, serious for once. He knew about my tussle with the Klowns last week and about Deadface's death, although I had not told him that the man's death was at my hands.

'I'm fine, Dad. My ribs are still a little sore, I won't be lifting weights any time soon but otherwise, I'm fine. I felt like taking a break. It felt overdue.'

He nodded, accepting what I was telling him. 'I thought maybe you came here because of the ghosts.'

'You knew about them?' I raised my eyebrows.

'It has been on the news. I saw the first article a couple of weeks ago when the chap found the gold, then there came reports of a spectral ship and the ghosts of dead seamen coming to shore. On Sunday morning they were reporting a murder that had been wrought by a ghost and less than twenty-four hours later we hear from you saying you're already in Cawsand. Your mother convinced herself that you wanted us to join you, so here we are.'

'Here you are,' I repeated. 'Well, I will not say that you're not welcome. The room is going to be a little cramped now though. If I could find alternative accommodation I would, but the draw of treasure and ghosts has filled every room for miles around.'

'Yeah, sorry about that. Good thing you're not here with a lady,' he said. Then he saw my expression and understood that their intrusion was exactly that. 'Oh, err. Perhaps your mother and I should think about staying somewhere else.'

I waved him into silence. I had no future mapped out

with Roberta. We had a night of fun, I had no idea how it had come about, what smooth things I might have accidentally said for her to have fallen so willingly into my bed, but it was done, and I had no good reason to believe that there would be a second night. 'There are no rooms, Dad. I'm looking into the ghosts though. If you don't have any plans, maybe you can help with that.'

'Sounds like a great idea,' he replied. Then my phone pinged with an email to interrupt us, and dad took another sip of his beer while I rooted around in my pocket. As I was starting to read the message, John the chef appeared with two plates of food: my parents had ordered lunch. I left my seat so that mum could sit down with dad. The rosy glow was spreading across her cheeks and her eyes looked heavy. I predicted she would most likely want a nap once she had eaten, so maybe dad and I would take the dogs and explore some more.

'You won't believe all the things I have found out, Tempest,' announced my mother as she was sprinkling salt on her chips. 'There's a multi-millionaire gentleman who has bought a huge plot of land just outside the village and he's planning to build a huge hotel and run cruise ships through here. He's that chap on the Television, the one that had the show at night about being a top businessman.'

'Julien Hogg?' I clarified.

'Yes, that's him,' she confirmed. 'The Whole Hogg. That was his motto when he started out selling white goods back in the seventies. That was how he made his money initially.'

'How do you suddenly know all this?' asked my dad.

'Gretchen and Tilda, my new friends, told me all about it. Tilda is the local parish councillor, so she knows all about what land deals are going on.' Mother was talking between mouthfuls of food as she hungrily devoured her fish and chips with mushy peas, the obligatory lemon wedge ignored at the side of her plate. She lapsed into silence though, either having exhausted her repository of new information or deciding that she would rather eat than talk. I went back to reading the email from *Jane*.

> *Boss,*
>
> *I have attached a spreadsheet with names, addresses and phone numbers for the people I could find that have reported seeing the ghost ship or the ghosts themselves. I have indicated in column G which they saw and when it was in column H. I have not spoken with any of them.*
>
> *The newspaper and online reports correlate well; one of the things you always tell me to look out for. The reports all claim the same details regarding what they saw, how it manifested etcetera.*
>
> *The first sighting was the day after the gold was first spotted and was reported by a couple in their sixties from Scarborough who were in Cawsand on holiday. There are many other tourists that have claimed to have seen skeletal pirates walking the streets of Cawsand, plus several people living there. Some of them report that they are too scared to stay in the village after the pirates told them to leave. There have been no other physical attacks or injuries that I can find other than the murder two days ago.*
>
> *Good luck with the investigation. If you need anything else, please ask.*
>
> *Jane*
>
> *PS. I tried to open the patio door but could not work out how to open it. Is there a trick to it?*

I had forgotten to show my assistant how to open the back door. It was a little sticky, nothing more, and required a hefty shove to get it moving. The information about the witnesses would be interesting though. If they had all reported the same thing, then it was likely they had all seen something. I would need to meet the villagers who reported seeing the ghosts. I should have quizzed the Muslim couple.

I sent an email back to Jane:

Jane,

I have a new search for you to perform when you are finished with other tasks. Please look into Julien Hogg and any information pertaining to a proposed purchase of a large piece of land near Cawsand, or planning permission for a hotel or anything to do with cruise ships coming near the area with tourists.

The tourist cruise ship thing sounded erroneous. 'Mother, how many passengers on a cruise ship?' I asked. My parents had taken several cruises over the years.

'Depends on the size of the ship,' she replied between mouthfuls of food.

'Ballpark for one of the ships you went on.'

'Three thousand or thereabouts I think.'

I tried to put three thousand people into the tiny village of Cawsand. They just wouldn't fit.

I switched my phone to emails again:

Jane,

Can you please also investigate property and land ownership in Cawsand? See if anyone has been buying businesses or selling businesses recently. Just let me know if you find anything anomalous, please. As usual, I do not know what I'm looking for, so can offer no better guidance.

A reply from Jane pinged back to my phone seconds later to confirm she would get on it straight away. I tapped my phone to my forehead in thought. There was something lurking beneath the tranquil, idyllic surface of this little village. I could not tell what it was, but I intended to find out.

Next to me, my mother burped, then said, 'Excuse me.' Which she followed with a stifled yawn. 'I'm quite full and quite tired now,' she announced with another yawn, waving her almost empty wine glass around as she stretched. 'I think I might have a nap. All that driving has taken it out of me.'

'But I drove, Mary,' pointed out my father.

'But I navigated, Michael. That is the hard part. Especially the way you drive,' she countered snippily.

He frowned as he replied. 'Mary we already knew how to get here. You sat with the map on your lap and told me what I was doing wrong for five hours. If your jaw burns calories, then I'm not surprised you're exhausted.'

Mum looked like she was considering throwing the last of her wine at him but changed her mind and drank it instead. 'Knickers to you. You daft old git,' she said, pushing back her chair. 'I'm going for a nap. You should go and find something to entertain yourself with for the afternoon.'

My father didn't bother to protest and neither one of us offered a comment. She collected her handbag and tottered off in the direction of the stairs, swaying slightly as she went. I held up the key to the room and opened my mouth only to have my father reach forward and put his hand over it to prevent me from speaking.

It was an old building, so with only dad and I in the bar and no ambient noise, we could easily hear mum clomp up the wooden staircase and, via the squeaks of the floorboards, hear her move along the corridor towards the room. There was a pause, an audible swearword and the squeaks began moving back along the corridor toward the stairs once more.

Dad's grin was as wide as the Cheshire Cat's. 'My vengeance shall be subtle, but oh so sweet,' he delivered with a vaudevillian sneer while rising from his chair and taking the key. He arrived at the foot of the stairs just as his wife reach the bottom, playing the part of the loving husband so she could not berate him further. 'Here you are, dear. You will need the key to get into the room.' She eyed him suspiciously, but took the key, turned around and began clomping back up the stairs once more.

'Serves her right, the grumpy old bat,' he laughed coming back to the table. I wasn't fooled. My parents had always traded insults and banter, but they loved each other very much. 'What shall we do then, kid?' he asked. 'Solve a mystery? Catch a ghost? Find some treasure?'

'All of the above perhaps,' I replied as I stood up, an action which prompted the dogs to move also. They stretched in place, like a dog or cat always does before going anywhere. However, if you have never witnessed it when a dachshund stretches, it's a sight to behold. Since they are basically a long sausage with legs and tail at one end and legs and a head at the other, they manage to elongate themselves to unbelievable proportions when they stretch. Their warmup complete, they started for the door, not waiting to see if I was going with them. 'I want to poke around the village some more,' I said as my dad and I headed after the dogs. 'There are a few odd things going on.'

As we walked, I told him about the drones I had seen, about the Muslim couple, and about the yellow signs. I also told him about Roberta, not that she had visited me in the night, but that she had caught me on the boat then invited me on a date with her. He nodded but said little.

Using the map function on my phone, I navigated us to the shop the Muslim couple had been running. There was a closed sign in the window but beyond it, in the shop, there were still goods on the shelves and not just packets of things, there were pastries still on display. They had left so suddenly, and with such fear, that they had abandoned everything.

'This is not normal behaviour,' remarked my father when I explained what we were looking at.

On the door to the shop itself were no fewer than four yellow warning notices. I was seeing them now as harassment. They advised the couple that they needed to remove all ethnic cuisine from their shop and serve approved Cornish cuisine. The polite notices were all from the last couple of days.

Was it racially motivated?

It certainly looked like it was, and Gretchen's comment yesterday hinted that it could be. It made me feel a bit sick. But was this linked in any way to the pirates? Or the treasure? Or the murder?

'There are more of these about,' I commented. 'I read one yesterday that was all about tidying up the front façade of the house it was pinned to.'

'Did it need to be tidied?' dad asked.

'Need would be a hard word to justify, but if one were looking at the houses around it, then it failed to compare favourably. It was minor stuff though. A quick lick of paint, a few hours of DIY and it would pass muster.' When I put it like that, the notices sounded quite justified. Make the village nicer, not only for tourists but for the residents also. It was broaching a social boundary somewhere though, people had a right to be slobs, even if it annoyed other people and the notices on the shop in front of us were aiming at a completely different target.

'Let's move on,' I suggested.

Walking along Garrett Street to join Market Street, we passed the point where the border between Cornwall and Devon used to lie. A sign painted on the side of a house called Devon Corn showed visitors where the border was until 1844. It was then moved to the river Plym, but the point marked where the village of Cawsand ended and the village of Kingsand began. Without the sign, one would never know the street joined two villages as there was not so much as a break in the houses.

We kept walking. Yesterday morning, I spotted a small business near the seafront on Market Street that appeared to be under renovation, and I wanted a closer look at it now. Sure enough, there was activity again there today. The business had a good location, looking out to sea on a route that visitors were bound to walk along. The large floor-to-ceiling windows sitting on either side of the door were white-washed to obscure the activity inside. I tried peering around the edge of it where the paint had not made it all the way to the frame but could not quite make out what was going on inside.

'It's going to be a pasty shop,' said a voice from across the street. My father and I turned to find the voice belonged to an elderly gentleman walking his dog.

'What was it before?' I asked.

'Oh, err. An Indian restaurant,' he said after dredging his memory for a second. 'It had been there for a few years. It was a chip shop before that. Nice couple that ran it. Then suddenly a couple of weeks ago it closed, and they were gone.'

Dad had a question, 'Did you ever see a yellow notice stuck to the door before they left?'

The gentleman thought about that for a moment, but

nodded, yes. He believed he may have seen a yellow sign on the door. I asked if he remembered the name of the business, but he did not. I figured it would take me seconds to find out for myself, and I was right as it was still listed. Dad watched with fascination as I retrieved the name of the business, then the names of the owners, all within a minute by looking at Companies House using my phone. I wanted to find out if the owners had been visited by the pirates before they elected to leave.

We continued all the way along to The Cleave where the road ended. At the shoreline, dad produced a set of binoculars from his pocket and looked out to sea with them. I wondered sometimes if he missed the sea. He was a sailor in the Royal Navy for years, from boyhood almost. It had dominated his life, but other than going on a cruise ship, I was not aware that he had ever been on a ship since the day he took off the uniform. I didn't ask him about it, because if he did miss it, I would just be bringing the emotion to the surface.

'How do you think they are making the pirate ship appear?' he asked, still looking out to sea.

'That is a very good question. If they use an actual ship, they would have to hide it and would then need to sail it into position.'

'That would take a lot of effort and a lot of people,' he pointed out.

'Exactly, so I have to assume there's no physical ship. If there was, I cannot see how they could keep it secret. Also, how would it be visible from the shore at night?'

'It wouldn't be. Even if they put lights on it, the only thing people on the shore would see would be the lights.' Dad had taken his binoculars away from his eyes and was looking at me now. 'So, if there's no boat, and we assume that people have seen something ...'

'... is it a trick of the light or has someone deliberately created an illusion,' I finished his sentence.

'Then the question really is, how would they do that?' Dad nailed it. I was willing to believe that at least some of the persons reporting seeing a moonlit ancient pirate ship rising from the waves to dispatch its crew of dead pirates onto the shore, had seen something. I could not, however, believe that it was a ghost ship. How though would a person create such an illusion? It's one thing to make something like that look real in a movie, but altogether different to have it sailing along the Cornish coastline.

'I would not mind getting out on the water and having a look along the coast. If there is a vessel from which they are somehow projecting an illusion, then it must be moored somewhere.'

'It could be in a boathouse if it's small enough,' dad pointed out.

I checked my watch: 1612hrs. 'We should probably head back towards the pub. We can check out some of the buildings on the shoreline as we go.' Dad nodded but lingered for a moment looking once more at the distant boats. So far as I knew, they were all treasure hunters. I wondered if there was anything to find and whether it would be found if there was.

The harbour with its wooden jetties was the first thing we came to. We lost sight of it as we followed the path around the coastline because of the houses that sit on the seaward side of it in places. When it came back into view, it looked to be mostly devoid of people. There were a few chaps moving about on their boats in places but none paying any attention to us. On the shoreline to the east of the jetty were several wooden buildings, each of which had a slipway down into the water. If a person wanted to launch a boat at night and use it to create the pirate ship illusion, then these were an obvious place to hide that boat. I had no idea if the image of the pirate ship was coming from a boat, but it felt like an obvious place to start looking.

'Dad.'

'Yes, kid?'

'Let's check some of these buildings. There are a few gaps in the woodwork to look through, so we should not have to break or enter to see what is inside.'

'Okay. What are we looking for?'

'Anything that looks out of place in a sleepy fishing village,' I answered with a shrug. 'If there's something creating the pirate ship illusion, I would expect to see a boat fitted out with a ton of odd-looking electronic gear or something.'

'Roger.'

The old buildings were sturdy looking. I guess they had to be to weather the winter storms, but they also had holes in them where panels had come loose and not yet been repaired. These made looking inside easier than I expected. We crept along the side of one building, then moved to the next, all the while trying to look like we belonged where we were. The dachshunds continued to sniff around at my feet.

'What are you gentlemen doing?' asked a lady's voice from behind us.

We both turned to find Roberta with her arms folded and an annoyed expression on her face. She was in uniform again but this time she was flanked by two more police officers, both women and both more senior to her. If my knowledge of police insignia was to be trusted the lady to Roberta's right was a superintendent. The third lady was a sergeant with a face that reminded me of a bulldog. It was not Roberta's voice I had heard, although I could not tell which of the other two might have spoken.

'Hello, ladies,' said my dad, switching to charming mode. 'Allow me to introduce myself. I'm Michael Storm-cloud Michaels, and this is my son Tempest Danger Michaels.' He advanced on them with his hand outstretched for shaking. He was heading for the superintendent, but the sergeant stepped in his way, holding up a warning hand for him to stop.

'Stop,' she commanded. It was the same voice that had asked us what we were doing. 'I doubt there's a good reason for you to be poking around here, gentlemen. It's time to move on.'

Behind her, Roberta was speaking to the superintendent, her lips moving but no sound carrying. I could see her gesture in my direction though and the older woman's eyes swing to look at me. 'Paranormal investigators?' the older woman commented. 'Not met one of those before.'

At the sound of her superior's voice, the sergeant dropped her arm and took a step back. 'I'm afraid the question has not changed though. What are you doing here?' she repeated.

The question was aimed at both of us, but she was staring at me, so I answered. 'Just poking around.' I wanted to say that we were not doing anything illegal and that our activities were harmless, but expected that were I to do, so she would simply retort that it was her job to decide the legality or otherwise of our activities.

'You will have to do better than that unless you fancy a trip back to the station.' She had a cold stare, devoid of mirth. I kept my gaze away from Roberta, it would be unfair to expect anything helpful from her in these circumstances. But my father and I had not trespassed anywhere and were guilty of no crime that I could perceive.

Tempted to tell the Sergeant to get stuffed, I suspected it would result in our arrest regardless of whether we had done anything wrong. Instead, I played along. Ignoring the sergeant, I spoke to the senior officer, 'Superintendent...?' I let the space after the rank hang.

'Charters,' she provided.

'Superintendent Charters. Thank you. My father and I have been very careful to avoid trespassing where we ought not to be and have not entered, nor attempted to enter any premises. We are however looking for the vessel that is creating the pirate ship illusion that has been reported many times now. These buildings, with their slipways...' she waved me to silence.

'You think the pirate ship is an illusion?'

'You think it's real?' my father asked.

'I have seen the pictures for myself, Mr. Michaels. I have no doubt that it's real,' she retorted.

This was curious. That members of the general populace had bought into the daftness of the reports was completely usual. It fitted with my experience. However, the police I have dealt with in the past were never drawn in by the same paranormal nonsense. I said, 'Then by simple extrapolation, I assume you also believe the recent murder victim was run through by a pirate that drowned at sea several centuries ago.'

'The details of our investigations are not open for discussion,' she snapped.

'Listen, kitten,' my dad interrupted. He had reverted to acting in a laddish manner, something that often happened when he was away from my mother. In response to his sentence opener, three sets of eyebrows went up. 'There's no ghost at the end of your investigation, no creatures returned from hell to reclaim the treasure they died for. But don't worry your pretty, little heads,' Their heads looked about ready to burst, 'Tempest and I are here to save the day.'

The superintendent took a pace towards him, getting right into his personal space. 'Mr. Michaels, I find you offensive.'

'I was aiming for cheeky scamp,' he retorted with a smile, not making things better for himself.

As if to ward off his smile, she scowled at him. 'If I have cause to arrest you while you are here, I will do so gladly and will then most likely forget where I have put you. Do not break any laws, Mr. Michaels, you're already on thin ice.'

He hit her with his most sincere expression. 'Dear lady, has anyone ever told you that you are quite beautiful?'

The question caught her off guard, her face confused about what it wanted to do. Obviously, she had no interest in the pensioner in front of her, but she loved getting a compliment the same as the next person. The only problem was that it was not a compliment, it was a trap door that my father was patiently waiting for her to step on.

In the end, she smiled, the corners of her mouth tugging up slightly. 'Well, no...' she started.

'I find that not the least surprising,' dad cut in. The trap door was sprung and her smiled dropped along with her jaw which was flapping up and down with no words coming out.

He smiled pleasantly right at her face, and I wondered for a moment if she was going to arrest us both just for the fun of it. Thankfully, she turned and started to walk away. The sergeant, however, remained where she was, staring at us with gleeful displeasure etched onto her face. 'I shall escort you back to your lodgings, gentlemen. Far safer for all concerned if you're not out wandering where you ought not to be.'

I tilted my head while I considered that. 'Do you have the authority to escort us anywhere? What if I decide I do not wish to return to my lodgings? What is there to compel me to stay at my lodgings if I were to allow you to accompany me there?' Since my father and I had not committed a crime there was no good reason for any further interaction with the police. The sergeant seemed to be overstepping her bounds by a considerable margin and was doing so quite willingly.

She took a threatening step towards me. Instinctively, I moved into a defensive posture, her eyes widened at my reaction, and she whipped her baton from her belt and flicked it out to its full length. I was shocked at the escalation; the situation was going downhill fast.

Coming to the rescue, Roberta stepped between us. 'I will escort them and ensure they go inside, Sergeant Andrews,' she said quickly. I could not see her face as she had her back to me, but over the top of her head, I could see the sergeant's. It looked like thunder. The lady had some anger issues.

'Sergeant Andrews,' called the Superintendent in a tone that demanded compliance. 'Come along.'

Sergeant Andrews cut her eyes to me one last time, then to my father, then with what looked like great difficulty, she put the baton away and left us where we were.

'What the hell was that all about?' I asked Roberta.

'There's a lot of pressure on them to solve the murder. Murder is rare here and when there is one, it's solved within days because everyone knows everyone, everyone sees everything, and the killer is usually the spouse or business partner of the victim. Now they have supernatural deaths, the world is watching, and they don't know what to do about it.'

'And they genuinely believe there is a ghost ship and dead pirates at the centre of this?' I asked, stunned by the possibility.

Looking up at me, she said, 'Yes, Tempest. Too many people have seen the ship to deny its existence. The pirates likewise.' I studied her face; she was telling me the truth.

I nodded, wondering whether I was going to have to tread carefully around the police while I investigated. 'Come on, dad. Let's get back to the pub. Mum will wake up soon enough and will want more wine.'

Leaving the jetty, we came out from between the build-ings on the inland side. Ahead of us on the road where the jetty exited, the superintendent and her sergeant were just getting into a police car.

Beside me, Roberta blew out an audible sigh of relief. 'Boy, those two are so intense.'

'What are they actually doing to solve the case?' my father asked.

Roberta shrugged. 'Nothing much. It's not like they can arrest the dead pirates.'

I shook my head in wonder. 'Where are they from anyway, clearly not from Cawsand. Where is the nearest police headquarters?'

'In Liskeard. It's about thirty minutes away by car. I don't remember the last time anyone came from HQ to visit me in Cawsand though. Not until the body was found anyway. What do you plan to do tonight?' she asked changing the subject.

'Father?' I passed the baton as I had no idea what he planned to do.

'That will depend on your mother, but I would assume

her plan will be to consume her body weight in wine and eat some dinner while simultaneously moaning at me for something and sitting on her fat backside. She does like to multi-task.'

'Then I guess we will largely be in the pub tonight,' I concluded to Roberta.

She smiled at me. Whether she was pleased that I would be in the pub or was smiling for some other reason I did not know. However, Mr. Wriggly was convinced she had plans to come and find him later and now knew where he would be. He might even be right for once. 'You don't need me to take you all the way back to the pub, gents. So, I'm going to head off. I have other things to attend to. I'm going this way,' she said, pointing to a side street.

'I just need a second,' I said to my dad. I caught hold of Roberta's arm just as she was moving away from us. 'Roberta, it seems pertinent to let you know that my parents are now sleeping in my room, leaving me on the fold out bed. I would move elsewhere but there are no rooms available for miles with all the treasure hunters and ghost watchers.' She was looking at me expectantly, waiting for me to say something more. 'I just didn't want you to try to sneak into my room again.' She was still looking at me as if I was supposed to keep talking. 'Actually, if you don't have plans tonight...'

'Sorry, Tempest,' she replied instantly. I guess I had finally arrived at the bit she had been waiting for. 'I'm working tonight.' She didn't elaborate, and I was certain I had no place to ask her what she was doing.

'Ok. Well... see you later then?' I said, trying to not sound too hopeful.

'Yes,' she said like she was grabbing hold of an opportu-

nity to escape. She was already backing off towards the side street she had indicated. 'See you later.'

Hmmm. Her attitude towards me had changed quite remarkably in the last few hours. She was gone though, and I still didn't have her phone number and might never see her again.

'Come on, Dad,' I said, berating myself for thinking about the girl. 'Let's get back to the pub. I believe they will have a couple of pints with our names on them.'

'Damned fine idea, boy,' he replied.

We were speed walking back along Market Street heading for Garrett Street. The pub was ten minutes away when it started to rain. It was instant, like someone had turned on a tap. Caught out in it, we exchanged glances and started to jog. We didn't get far though before a shout pulled us up.

'Oi, wanker.' The voice came from behind us. We both stopped and turned towards the sound. Two men were coming out of a fish and chip shop. They were two of Gina's crew.

'You know them?' Dad asked.

'I want a word with you.' The man speaking was the one I had pushed over when he tried to swat my dog. The chap with him was one of the other men in the team.

He was coming right for me, his intentions uncertain, but he either wanted to issue some threats and attempt to make me apologise, or he planned to dispense with all that nonsense and just hit me.

'Be ready,' I whispered to dad as I quickly looked around. I had the dogs in my right hand, and they would be in the way in no time. The rain helped me though. dachshunds hate it. At least mine do, so all I needed to do was let go of their leads and nudge them with my boot and they both ran to find cover under the awning of a shop.

The man was almost upon me, his colleague two paces behind. He was bigger than me in every direction and a few years younger. As he closed the final few feet, he raised his right hand with a finger extended towards me. I estimated that his intention was indeed to threaten and berate, so I punched him in the throat.

I hadn't really planned to, I just did it. He went down, gagging and holding his throat. Whatever message he had planned to deliver went unspoken. With my lips curling in barely contained anger, I stepped over the man and came at his colleague with my arms up and loose, ready to strike. My father was just to my right and looking just as ready for action. In front of us, the man's eyes were wide, panicked. Whatever it was he had envisaged happening, this wasn't it.

'Shall we leave it at that?' I asked him before anything else could happen. 'My father and I are on holiday. Tell your friend he will be best served to leave me alone.' He was disinclined to argue with me or even the score for his fallen comrade, so dad and I let him be and went on our way. The dogs were only a few feet away, cowering from the rain near a shop door. There were faces inside the shop gawping out at us as we took the dogs and continued jogging back to the pub.

We arrived with our hair, clothing and the dog's fur completely soaked; the rain had been coming hard by the time we slipped inside the dry of the Sea Pilgrim. In our room, mum was awake and sitting in a corner chair by the window humming hymns to herself while knitting. Countdown was showing on the television: It was a numbers round.

'Did you get caught in the rain?' she asked as dad shut

the room door behind us. Dad and I exchanged glances. Rainwater was dripping from our hair, our ears, and our clothing and making the floorboards visibly wet, but mother was staring at the television and had not bothered to look at us yet.

'No, Love,' dad said. 'There was a freak wave and the pair of us were washed out to sea, but we swam back to shore carrying the dogs above our heads, fought a giant squid thingy on the way and still had time to learn the secret art to making the perfect Cornish pasty from a mermaid on the way.'

'That's nice, dear,' she replied, still staring straight ahead, her fingers and knitting needles a blur.

I walked in front of her, crossing the room to get an old towel I used for the dogs. They had short fur and would dry out soon enough but would jump on the bed or furniture unconcerned about their sopping wet coats if I didn't deal with them quickly.

Dad was stripping off his wet outer layer by the door, while I towelled the hounds as dry as I could get them. The room, which had seemed cavernous when it was just me, was cramped now. The extra suitcases and bags, as well as the two extra full-sized adults, meant there was too little room to move about. Worse yet, I wanted to get a shower and change, which before I would have just done.

Huffing to myself, I saw the best solution was to sort myself out and leave the room to them. I let dad know my plan, grabbed some clothes for the evening and locked myself in the bathroom.

An Evening in the Pub

TUESDAY, NOVEMBER 1ST 1850HRS

At 1752hrs when I took a seat in one of the upholstered chairs in the corner of the pub nearest the open fire, the fire itself was already lit. It gave the air in the room an enticing smoky smell that reminded me of winter evenings in country pubs back home. The fire was low though, not putting out much heat and I was the only person in the room so it was too cool for the shirt and thin sweater I wore; it would be much warmer once the pub was full of people. Knowing the bar would be closed, I had prudently brought a cup of tea down from the room with me and to further ward off the cool autumn air I plopped Dozer on my lap. With no more room on my lap, Bull stretched his lead as far as it would go, turned around three times and settled in front of the fire to sleep.

That was an hour ago and now the bar was open and most of the tables were filled with people ordering food or already eating. I was staring at the list of notes on the pad in front of me, notes which came about after talking to the people that had witnessed the ghosts – the list Jane had sent me.

Jane, being super-efficient, had provided me with names, addresses, mobile and home phone numbers plus information regarding what they had seen and when. I started at the top of the chronological list and worked down. A couple in Scarborough were the first one I got through to. The conversation went like this:

'Hello.' A man's voice.

'Good evening. My name is Tempest Michaels. I'm hoping to talk to you about the ghosts in Cawsand.'

'Hello.'

'Hello?' I repeated, wondering if the man could hear me.

'Hello.'

'Yes, hello. My name is Tempest Michaels and I'm hoping to speak to you about the ghost you saw in Cornwall.' The voice at the other end was elderly. The age of the witness was the one item of information Jane had left out.

Then I could hear the person at the other end talking to someone else. 'Well, I don't know, do I. Someone called Temple Smichael.' A pause. 'No, about the ghosts we saw.' A pause. 'Alright, alright, I'll ask him.' Then finally, he aimed his attention back at me. 'Are you a reporter?'

'No, sir,' I replied. 'I'm an investigator looking into the murder of Philip Masonberg in Cawsand.'

'A murder?' he blurted. There was further muttering in the background, a couple of heated words, then a woman's voice replaced the man's.

'What do you want?' she snapped.

'Good evening, madam.' I liked to address people politely. 'I hoped to ask you a few questions about the ghosts you saw.'

'Oh, right. What do you want to know?' she asked. I suspected the lady I was talking to was the elderly gentleman's wife, but she sounded less aged than her partner if it was.

I was still alone in the bar, so my phone was switched to speaker, leaving my hands free to take notes. 'Can you describe what you saw please, giving me as much detail as possible?'

I had to explain who I was again and why I wanted the information, but she was happy enough to launch into a long-winded description of the scene. She saw two skeletal figures with tattered clothing, each brandishing a cutlass. The couple were staying in a local B&B and had ventured down to Cawsand because they heard about a fantastic pub there – The Sea Pilgrim, had I heard of it? I had to steer her back onto the subject of the ghosts as she was telling me all about the menu at the pub and laying it on thick about how amazing it was. It wasn't. It was nice, but the food was not about to win Michelin stars. I had her describe the ghosts in detail, which she did with what I felt was too much embellishment about how scary they were. She had lots of detail to provide though. One of the skeletons had a gold tooth in place of his upper right incisor and his left incisor was missing. Who on earth recorded that much detail while being terrified?

I got through to six more people that claimed to have seen the ship or the skeletons. They were dotted all over the country but had all been in Cawsand in the last week or so. Each of them described the skeletons in a very similar way to the first lady, but not similar enough for me to cry foul and declare that they were reading from a script. The reports, or rather the descriptions weren't all the same. Where tourists had seen the ghosts, they reported that they glowed with an inner light and described them as nothing more than skin and bone; much like the first description I had listened to.

I also managed, after several attempts, to get through to the Indian family that fled their restaurant. Their tale was much the same as that of the Muslim couple. Their description of the ghosts differed though from that of the tourists. The man I spoke to, Rajesh Patel, was the owner of the restaurant and still very upset about having to leave it. He described the ghosts he saw as skeletal, much like everyone else, but then said that they also looked like they were well fed. He could see their bones, but they also filled their clothing well. They were tall also, around six feet he estimated, which did not align with what I knew about average height in the 17th century.

I was staring at my notepad on which several notes were underlined or circled. The gold tooth was a central theme to every description of the ghosts. It was all too neat, too polished for me to believe. The descriptions of the ghost ship were different though, they felt more genuine, as if the people I was speaking with had indeed seen something and could not determine what it was. Most of them weren't convinced it was a ghost ship but could offer no better explanation of what it was that they had seen.

I was still staring at the notes when a firm hand came to rest on my shoulder. 'What you up to, kid?' asked my father as he settled opposite me.

'I'll get my own chair, shall I?' mother said snippily as dad failed to draw her chair out for her.

'Watch it can take your weight first, love,' he replied, then quickly held up both hands to defend his head from her attack.

'Gobby old git. Go get me some wine,' she demanded.

My parents were a lot of fun to be around. They had been married for a long time and had fallen into a sort of comedy double act routine they never seemed to grow bored of. Their arrival on my holiday had annoyed me to start with, although I had not voiced my thoughts, but perhaps this evening was going to be fun after all.

'A pint of pear Rattler,' I said as dad inclined his head to me in question.

'What have you been up to down here?' mum asked, leaning over to look at my notepad. 'Gold tooth,' she read. It was the first thing anyone would see on the page as I had underlined it twice, drawn a circle around it and linked it to other bits of the description I had written down.

'I was talking to the people that have claimed to have seen the pirates or the pirate ship,' I explained.

'What did you learn?' she asked, taking an interest for once.

'Hard to say. It feels as if some people are making it all up, but others must have seen something, and the reports are conflicting. I have to assume someone is dressing up.'

'Why would someone go to the trouble of doing that?' she asked, one eyebrow raised quizzically.

'My question too. I don't have an answer for it though. If I knew that I would probably be able to solve the case right now.'

Dad arrived back with three drinks clustered together as one between his meaty hands. The cider had spilled slightly and was running down his arm to wet his cuff. Mother reached over to snag her wine then took a mighty glug from it.

'That's better,' she announced.

'Have you seen the size of the guy behind the bar?' dad asked.

Both mum and I swung our gaze to the bar where Thirty-Three was looking dumb and not doing anything. He wasn't serving drinks, but he was holding a tray, so he was probably going to be taking food out and collecting glasses again shortly.

'Yes, he's quite a size, isn't he?' I replied. 'They call him Thirty-Three,' I explained and then had to explain why. Dad sniggered.

'Shall we order food?' mum asked. 'I'm starving.'

There were menus on the table next to us. I stretched across, snagged them and handed them out. It was the same menu I had ordered from on Sunday, so I knew what choices I could select from. I settled on sausage and mash with onion gravy and mushy peas served in a giant Yorkshire pudding. It didn't sound like food I should be eating, but it did sound tasty.

Mother bustled off to the bar to order our food, leaving dad and me to chat. 'The ghost ship, Dad,' I started.

'Yes, son.'

'I think someone is creating an illusion of some kind. I spoke to some of the people that have reported seeing it and I believe they saw something. I don't know what they saw, but their descriptions were all convincing. The ones that reported seeing the pirates though had varying descriptions, but I still cannot decide if I think they are lying or not. The accounts were... disconnected somehow, as if some had seen one thing and others had seen something different.'

'So, what is it they are seeing?' asked my dad. We spit-balled a few ideas but could not come up with anything tangible. There were a few possibilities though, such as a dummy ship hung from a helicopter with a light shining on to it to make it visible. Turn the light off and it vanishes. Or a yacht with a shaped spinnaker sail. Again, a light can be shone onto it making it visible from the land and then turned off again to make it vanish. The only problem with both of these or any other theories was that people had already gone to sea at night to search for the ghost ship. They would notice a helicopter hovering above them and while a small yacht might slip around unnoticed it would need to be a big ship to hold a spinnaker large enough to be seen from the shore.

'What is keeping your mother?' Dad asked, turning in his chair to look towards the bar. Mum was still at the bar but was nattering with Tilda and Gretchen again. They were all a similar age and had hit it off. Next to mum though, were all four of the supernatural science squad. Gina was absent, so they were once again off the leash. They were all staring at me. The chap I had knocked to the ground twice now, smiled at me and made a big show of counting the four of them. One, two, three, four he mouthed silently while pointing at each man in turn. Then he pointed at my father and I and counted two in the same manner. Dad stiffened and made to rise from his chair. I placed my hand on his forearm to stop him. He looked at me quizzically. He wanted to deal with the blatant threat now.

'Later,' I told him. 'Let them have a few first.' The four men were drinking pints. A few drinks would dull their senses, weaken the reactions and impair their balance. Dad and I would need to hold off drinking ours to gain the advantage, but it seemed a small price to pay.

Oblivious to the interaction, mother returned bearing another large glass of wine. 'Food will be ten minutes.'

'Ten minutes from when you ordered it ten minutes ago, or ten minutes from now?' asked dad for clarification.

'Never mind. Here it is,' I said. Thirty-Three was

making his way through the crowd towards us bearing three plates. I could see my huge Yorkshire pudding towering over the surface of the plate in his huge left hand. I was ready for some food, but as he put the plates down, I saw that it was going to have to wait. The four guys from Gina's crew were coming our way.

They threaded their way through the bar, full of false bravado and probably egged on by one another. Had peer pressure pushed the man to come at me for the third time?

I stood up and moved away from the table. The inside of a pub was not the place to have a fight as too many other people could get hurt as inevitably, most fights end up on the floor. With the tables so close to one another, we would knock drinks over, bash into people and no matter what, we would make an unwelcome mess. Seeing me stand and tracking my gaze, my dad turned to see the four men arrive. I planned to invite them outside where the matter could be settled without any innocent bystanders getting their evening ruined.

'Hello again, wanker,' the man said. Before I could reply, my father came out of his chair, the back of which was against where the man was now standing. In a single motion, he stood, turned and delivered an uppercut to the man's jaw. I knew my dad had boxed when he was in the Navy, it was a regular thing to do in the forces, but I had personally never seen him hit anyone before.

There was a momentary stunned silence which my dad broke by saying. 'Language. There are ladies present.' The man was on the floor, not unconscious but looking quite dazed. My father's hands had gone back to resting at his sides, making him look like a wizened old Jedi Master that had just dispensed a lesson in humility. I was grinning from ear to ear. All hope of going outside was gone, but with the ringleader on the floor, the remaining three men seemed confused about what was supposed to happen next.

'Oi,' came a screech across the pub. 'There will be none of that in here.' It was Gretchen, who appeared to have somehow grown a foot or more, so must have been standing on something behind the bar to see over the crowd. Thirty-Three and John the chef were both heading our way and I worried for a second that we would all be turfed out.

Thankfully the supernatural science squad knew they had overstayed their welcome and were already apologising to my parents and the people around us for the fuss. Under the watchful gaze of the huge, lumbering Thirty-Three, they made their way to the pub door, dragging the man dad had punched with them. As they left, a middle-aged lady at the table next to us began clapping, then someone else did and seconds later my father was getting a standing ovation. I joined in.

'Goodness, Michael,' my mother said. 'That was ever so impressive.'

My father was sitting himself back at the table and collecting his knife and fork. 'Let's eat, shall we?' he replied, tucking in. He was doing a great job of being cool.

The food was hot and tasty, and it was a big portion. Big enough that I declined dessert, which Gretchen assured us was on the house. She was full of apologies for what had happened. I could not see how it was her fault, but it was her establishment, and she probably wanted to protect its name. She made a comment about knowing better than to let their kind in as she was departing. It sounded like another racist slur, but she was gone and no one else seemed to have heard it.

The clock ticked on and all too soon I started to yawn. I checked the clock on the wall. It was 2116hrs. I was such a lightweight. With three pints of cider in me and a day of adventure that had included two fights behind me, I was ready for my bed. I was tired. Mum and dad wanted to stay for a brandy, so I bid them goodnight and went outside to walk the dogs.

The rain had stopped, but the ground was wet still and there were puddles for the dogs to avoid. I looked around for Gina's men, but thankfully they weren't waiting for me across the street or around a corner. On the beach though I could see Gina. She was fiddling with the array of gadgets there and appeared to be alone, so I led the dogs to the ramp and let them off their leads. They scampered off across the pebbles to dig in the sand, probably glad of the exercise after spending the evening being shared between our laps and being fed crisps as treats.

Gina said, 'Hi, Tempest,' as I approached. She turned her head to me as she said it then went back to whatever it was that she was doing. 'I'm just checking everything still works,' she told me. 'The rain always seems to mess with the equipment.'

'Still hoping to photograph that ghost?' I made sure my voice carried no sarcasm or amusement.

'As always,' she replied as she slid a draw closed.

'Where are your team?' I wanted to know.

'I don't know actually. I gave them the night off. I think they were going to the pub, but I haven't heard from them since. Did you see them in there?'

'Yes. I saw them,' I replied with an ironic smile she didn't see.

'Well, I hope they were behaving. They can be idiots when they want to be. Like most men,' she commented, then realised what she had said. 'Oh! Sorry, no offense intended.'

'None taken.' I wondered if stories of their exploits tonight would find their way back to Gina's ears. The dogs reappeared at my feet when I called them, and it felt like a good time to get to bed. I bid Gina goodnight and headed back into the warmth of the pub. It felt like the day had been a long one and I was tired.

Things That Go Bump in the Night
Part 2

The fold-out bed was not comfortable, nor was it so uncomfortable that I felt a need to get up and try to improve it. I had fallen into bed with the two dogs cuddled in next to me. I could have placed them back on the floor, but they would have just returned as soon as I started snoring.

Sleep came easily, the fatigue of the day catching up with me, but I awoke at the sound of my parents coming to bed. They were moving around quietly, whispering to each other with only a single table lamp on to illuminate the room. They bumped into a few things but were getting into bed just a few minutes after entering the room. I had not moved, and I expected to fall asleep again in no time.

The light went out and I relaxed back into the pillow. The whispering from the bed continued though. My eyes were shut but my ears were working.

'Do you think he's asleep?' I heard my mother ask.

'I can't tell, love. Why?' asked my dad in reply.

My mother whispered her answer, 'Would you like to play ride the wild pony?'

I'M AWAKE!

I was out of bed and grabbing my clothes. The dogs looked a little bewildered as I scooped them from the bed, then thought better of it and put them back inside the warm covers. About eight seconds elapsed and I was outside in the corridor wearing only my undershorts, holding my bundled clothes and hoping that I had everything I needed.

Phone!

I opened the door a crack and reached in with my arm. The phone was on top of the cabinet next to the door, my hand finally finding it after scrabbling around unseeing for a few seconds. In the cool air of the corridor, I hurriedly dressed. My parents had not called after me, so were probably glad I was gone. *Play ride the wild pony* was going to stick with me for years.

Suddenly without a place to sleep, I figured it was the perfect time to wander up to the headland where the students and probably others were watching for the ghost ship to appear.

There were boats beyond the harbour, visible because of their pilot lights and probably out there for no reason other than to try to see the ghost ship if it appeared. It struck me as strange that people were willing to believe in such guff, but stranger still that having convinced themselves there were killer ghosts around, they then go looking for them. What happens if they are right and they meet with the killer ghosts? Or had they not thought it through that far?

The climb up the path to the headland was demanding even though I had to go slow in deference to the dark. Nearing the top, I could hear the voices of the persons already gathered on the headland before I could see them, the noise travelling far further at night than it would in the day. I crested the top of the path, bringing into view the people that went with the voices. The headland itself was a piece of land high above the village where signs had been erected warning of the cliff ahead. It was a picnic spot despite the danger and there were places to pull off the road and park a car. There were three cars parked on the grass, all older models and just on the safe side of the warning signs were the two chaps I had met in the bar on the first night. I wracked my brains to remember their names, finally coming up with Tarquin and something. The other chap's name would come to me probably. They were accompanied by another couple of chaps, both of whom were much older and had beards. I estimated their age at somewhere close to fifty. Also present were three girls about the same age as Tarquin and his friend. Every single one of them were looking out to sea and had clustered around several expensive looking cameras mounted on tripods. They were cold, that much I could tell instantly from their body language, but had I needed more clues about how they felt, I didn't have to wait long.

A voice rang out from the crowd. 'It's cold, Maxine. I'm going back to the car.' One of the girls broke off from the pack and trudged away, swiftly followed by another one of the young ladies. Whether it was Maxine that had followed her or if the pair had left Maxine behind, I could not tell.

'Evening, chaps,' I hallooed as I got within a few yards and had not been noticed.

'Arrrrrh!' squealed Tarquin, jumping out of his skin as my voice unexpectedly pierced the silence of the night air a few feet from his head. Geoffrey – I remembered his name finally, laughed at his friend's reaction. The others all laughed along as well.

'Welcome aboard,' said one of the older men jovially, but his attention was not focused on me for long. He went straight back to staring out to sea. The other mature chap next to him was using binoculars to get a better view.

'Anything out there?' I asked, the question aimed at anyone that wanted to answer it.

It was Geoffrey that replied, 'Not yet.'

I joined them all in looking out to sea. On the exposed edge of the land, there was no hiding from the cool breeze coming ashore. It was only a light breeze, and had it been stronger I would have wanted far more clothing than I was wearing. Even with that observation, I knew I would not stay out for very long. I intended to kill a couple of hours before returning to find my parents asleep. It was that, or sleep in the car – not a proposition I considered practical given the two tiny bucket seats it contained.

I have never previously had reason to watch the sea for the possible emergence of a ghostly pirate ship, but I can honestly report now that it's boring. An hour passed slowly, I checked my watch only when the girl that had not headed back to the car finally caved, admitting that she was too cold to stay out any longer. I got the impression she was there because she fancied Geoffrey, and the boys had sold the girls the idea that this would be a fun thing to do. With her departing due to the cold, I decided I could start my walk back to the pub. The climb up here had made me nice and warm; the return trip might do the same.

As I turned to leave though, I heard a suppressed squeal of excitement from one of the older chaps. Then the camera shutters were going like mad as they tried to capture as many pictures as possible of the ghost ship that was rising from the water in front of the headland.

I stood open mouthed and watched as an ethereal image of a centuries-old wooden sail ship emerged from the inky black waves prow first to settle on the surface. It was shining with a ghostly light of its own making. The sails were tattered but were blowing about in the breeze. It was too distant to pick out fine details but acknowledging that I could not see it very well, I also accepted that I was looking at a ghost ship.

I'm looking at a ghost ship.

I didn't know how else to classify it. No wonder everyone else that saw it had said the same thing. It was utterly convincing. It was sailing west towards Cawsand itself. There were a handful of other ships in the water, visible only by the lights on them, which were all now converging on the line it was taking. Before any of them could reach it though, the nose dipped once more, and it vanished back beneath the waves, leaving nothing to show it had ever been there.

Next to me, there were whoops and cheers from the very excited spook sleuths and the bearded gentlemen. They were all high fiving and checking the camera gear to see what they had captured.

'We are going to be famous!' Geoffrey shouted.

I worried that he might be right, then shook myself, a physical act to shift the foolishness. Whatever it was that I had seen, it was not a ghost ship being sailed by dead pirates. But now I had to find out what it was. I started back towards the village. The path down from the headland was not exactly treacherous, but neither was it even and it was steep in places. I wanted to run but prudently I kept my pace to a hastened walk. As the path descended, I still had a view out over the bay in front of Cawsand, so I saw the ship rise again no more than a few hundred yards from the shore. I kept going, losing sight of the ship a few seconds later as the path descended further and bushes obscured my view.

Two minutes later, I was getting close to the village when a scream pierced the air.

Dead Pirates

It was a man's voice, no doubt about it and if my knowledge of screams was to be believed, the man was in pain. What worried me though was how suddenly the scream had been cut off. I started running.

I was still on the path, hemmed in on both sides by thick gorse bushes and in almost total darkness. The clear sky provided a view of the top of the bushes, but no light was penetrating to where my feet were going. Inevitably I tripped on something. It might have been a root or a rock, but I stumbled, arms cartwheeling and as I fell heavily to the dirt.

I propelled myself back up, barely allowing the fall to arrest my forward motion and moments later I burst from the bushes back at the spot between two houses where the path started. Now there was streetlight, and I could run with confidence. Thankfully, I didn't have far to go, running downhill and turning left or right through the winding narrow streets until I emerged on the seafront. I stopped to listen, unsure which way I needed to turn. The scream had been loud and had come from the shore so far as I could tell, but the village was quiet again, making me worry that no one else had heard it.

I held my breath so that the sound of my laboured breathing would not rob me of the chance to pinpoint where the person was, but there was no sound to hear. I exhaled and guessed, turning right and heading back towards the pub rather than turning left towards the jetty.

Jogging swiftly along the road that bordered the shore, I questioned who would be out at this time. The pub was long shut, there were no other businesses open, and it was too late for anyone to be out walking a dog.

Then it hit me.

Gina's men.

There was always one of them with the equipment. Earlier it had been Gina, was it still her and I was mistaken about the scream coming from a man? Or had the next chap on rotation replaced her? I pressed on, getting breathless from the effort by the time I rounded the last bend to bring the pub into view. It was on my right, fifty yards ahead, the beach to my left already.

In the dark, I could only just about make out the weird electronic gear sited there. I grabbed the railing and vaulted over it to drop almost three yards to the dark ground below. The pebbles of the beach crunched beneath my feet as I hit them, the invisible ground shocking my legs despite knowing it was down there somewhere. There was no sign of the person I expected to be monitoring/guarding the equipment. I stopped once more to listen.

Nothing.

'Anyone here?' I called out. Then I cursed my stupidity, pulled my phone from my pocket and turned the torch on. The bright white light illuminated all around me in whatever direction I shone it. Finding the body took me less than a second.

It was ten feet away, spread out on the pebbles by a piece of equipment Gina had told me the name of but which I could not now remember. I swung the light around three hundred and sixty degrees to make sure I was alone as I crossed the distance.

I saw immediately that it was the douchebag that kept picking fights with me. His head was a mess. There was a large gouge starting just before his hairline on the left side of his head which extended back over the crown of his skull. It must have been ten inches long and looked like he been hacked at with a machete. I could see the bone of his skull where the skin had peeled back from it. He was breathing though, so he was alive despite the blood loss. Head wounds always bleed profusely and often look worse than they are, but I believed the man needed urgent care.

He needed to get to a hospital, that was for sure and there was little I could do for him; I didn't even want to roll him into the recovery position for fear he might have other injuries. He was unconscious but that didn't worry me, he was better off like that for now and were he to encounter breathing difficulty I was here to react should I need to.

Using my phone, I called an ambulance, though I realised after disconnecting that I had not asked for an ETA and had no idea how long it would take them to get to this remote point or where they were coming from.

Then, for the first time since I found him, the man stirred slightly. 'Pirates,' he mumbled, still not really conscious. He would go on to say it several more times before the ambulance finally found us thirty minutes later. I was getting pretty damned cold by then as I had stripped off my coat and fleece liner to wrap around him. I was able to move about to fight against hypothermia, he was not, and he was laying on the cold sand and pebbles of the beach which would further rob him od body heat.

The paramedics asked me what had happened. If they were sceptical about my involvement, they didn't offer an opinion on the matter. Instead, they accepted that I had found him in his current condition and got on with treating him. His pulse was steady, but I knew that already from my own ministrations. It was also weak though which indicated that he had lost a decent percentage of his blood. I suspected that he was in no real danger now that they were treating him, an IV line was connected minutes after they arrived to replenish his system, and they found no other injuries save for the one to his head. He was going to have quite the scar.

The flashing lights of the ambulance attracted the attention of local residents that were either light sleepers or were already awake for some reason. Faces appeared at windows, then a few emerged from their houses, curiosity drawing them into the cold night air. I checked my watch: 0159hrs. I expected to see one of the fool's colleagues at any moment. Typical night-time shift rotation would have the team switching over every couple of hours as there was no way a person could stave off the cold or the boredom for much longer than that. As if on cue, one of them appeared.

'Son of a bitch!' he yelled as he saw me still kneeling close to his bloodied teammate. He thought I was to blame and was coming for me. It was the same chap that had accompanied the fallen man when he left the pasty shop to attack me yesterday. He looked uncertain about his intentions then but didn't now. He came running at me, his fists up and ready to fight.

'Stop,' commanded Roberta. She was coming down the

ramp that led onto the beach. It was where the ambulance was parked, its back doors open and light flooding out to illuminate her. She was wearing whatever clothes she had found to throw on, a pair of jeans that needed ironing and a Northface jacket. Bereft of make-up she was still cute.

The man ignored her instruction and launched himself at me. I moved back to meet his leap, timing his attack so I could catch him around the torso. I converted his motion by spinning off my back foot so that he landed on his back with me on top of him. It gave Roberta time to close the remaining distance and shove her police ID in his face. The fight left him instantly.

'I didn't do it.' I said, now that I thought he might listen. He looked sceptical but didn't argue, instead, he turned his head to look at his friend. Just a few feet away the paramedics were getting ready to move him. He was strapped to a gurney and his head was bandaged, the white gauze going around and around his skull and over his face to cover much of it. He was still unconscious but looked to be coming around.

'Pirates,' he murmured, his eyes coming open for a second. Roberta went to him, flashing her badge at the medics as they were about to lift him.

'We need to get him to hospital,' one said. 'He's going to need surgery.'

'One question,' she insisted and as they paused, she took his hand, her tiny digits lost in his meaty paw. Then she leaned down so that she was directly above his face. Opening her mouth to speak she paused and swung her head back in my direction. It was not me she wanted though but his colleague. 'His name?'

'Err, Matthew Todd,' he replied.

'Matthew,' Roberta called softly. 'Matthew.' His eyes

opened, one of which half covered by bandages. 'What happened?' Who did this?' she demanded.

'Pirates,' he stammered, fear in his voice at the memory. 'Their skin was hanging off. I could see their bones.' His voice had carried to the onlookers, the stillness of the night allowing it to reach their ears clearly.

'We saw the ghost ship,' announced Tarquin. I looked up to see both he and Geoffrey leaning over the railings. Perhaps the lights of the ambulance had drawn them down the path from the headland to investigate. Or perhaps they had their photographs now and wanted to show people.

Murmurs were spreading through the crowd.

'Dead pirates,' Matthew the moron said again, more subdued this time like it was a terrible memory he could not escape.

'We need to go,' insisted the paramedic and with that, the pair of them grabbed either side of the gurney again and were loading him into the ambulance two seconds later.

As the strobe lights flickered back up the hill through the village and disappeared, the beach was plunged back into darkness, the gentle crashing of waves the only noise.

'I need to tell Gina,' I heard the man beside me say to himself. He wandered off; his ear illuminated by the screen light from the phone he was holding. On the road in front of the pub, Geoffrey and Tarquin were showing their photographs to anyone that would listen and everyone but the spectators who had left their houses, were all drifting back inside, and lights were going off again.

I was still on the beach, still cold and feeling very much in need of a hot shower and a stiff drink. 'Tempest, I need a statement from you,' said Roberta, as she came towards me.

'Can we make it quick?' I asked.

'That depends what you have to tell me,' she replied. 'It

may be necessary to get a more detailed statement from you at the station in Liskeard tomorrow. For now, please just give me a chronological sequence of what happened and what you saw.' She was all business, playing the role of police officer again. I took no issue with that. Yes, I wanted to get her naked again, but I was too tired and too cold and too covered in someone else's blood to consider it a desirable proposition right now.

As she flipped open her notebook, I told her about hearing the scream and finding the man lying on the beach. I left nothing out but also didn't add any details as I wanted to be done with the task and get to bed. Roberta asked me several times whether I had seen the ghosts myself or if I had seen anyone at all other than the man I found injured. Only when I had answered the same question the same way many times did she seem satisfied. I was surprised that she showed no warmth towards me when the necessary inter-view bit was done, we had slept together just twenty-four hours ago. As she thanked me for my help and turned to go, I held back from trying to elicit further conversation simply from fear of coming off as needy.

Left alone on the beach, I acknowledged that I was cold. That was the most pressing need I had to tackle. Having given up my coat and fleece I now had them back, but they were soaked with blood making them unpalatable for wear-ing. I had worn blood-soaked clothes before, many years back in Iraq. However, on that occasion, there had been no option to change into something clean. It was not my blood then either and I had put up with it for more than two days before I had been able to rotate back to a safe location where I could take the items off and burn them.

Now though, all I needed to do was wake my parents up. I crossed the road and went up to the room. Turning on the room's main light, I apologised for waking them and turned it off again a few seconds later once I had turned on the bathroom light. I locked myself in there and stripped off my clothes.

In the warmth of the shower, I reflected on what I had seen. Even knowing that the ship was not real, I could offer no explanation for what I had witnessed. The images captured by the photographers were compelling. They would most likely make it onto the front page of national papers if there were no more pressing stories to tell and net the men that had taken them a decent fee. The injured man, Matthew Todd, would recover from his injury in time. However, I wanted to know how the wound had been inflicted. He believed he had seen a dead pirate, had been attacked by a dead pirate. There were no other witnesses to corroborate or deny his version of events, that didn't matter though. He had not been attacked by a skeleton returned from a watery grave, he had been attacked by a person. Of that I was certain.

I had no idea why though.

I showered thoroughly for several minutes, getting the warmth back into my limbs and extremities. Then I took my fleece and coat and ran them under the water until it was no longer flowing away tinged with pink.

When I slipped into bed it was 0315hrs. I had achieved almost no sleep so far and had been pushing myself far harder than I had intended to or imagined I would have to when I got in the car three days ago.

Sleep took me in seconds.

Breakfast with Gina

I set no alarm. I rarely use one, but with my parents in the room and two dogs that would need to go out, I was confident I would be woken quite early enough.

As it was, the dogs woke me, or more specifically Bull did by standing on my chest until I woke up. His whiskers tickled my nose and as I opened my mouth to speak, he licked my upper incisors. I should have expected it, the move was not a new one, but in my sleepy haze, I had not considered what he might do.

Keeping my head to one side so he could not perform the same trick twice, I lifted him to the floor while yawning. He danced off across the rug in an excited manner, bumping into his brother which elicited a quick game of chase around the bedroom while they waited for me to find my clothes.

Less than a minute later I was outside in the cool morning air once more. On the beach was a white tent, in which I was sure I would find some kind of crime scene team. Roberta was probably not far away, but there was no sign of her now.

The dogs were trying to get me to take them on the beach. Crime scene tape blocked the access ramp but being dogs they were ignoring it and looking back over their shoulders at me to question why I was holding them back.

There were other sections of beach further along the coast, so I made them hold their bowels and bladders until we reached the next one. It was less than one hundred yards west and littered with seagulls, much to the delight of my two dogs who pounced on the chance to chase them all away barking madly while they did, though thankfully at nearly 0800hrs, I felt their noise would not wake too many people.

I watched them from the street, content that their only escape route was to swim out to sea and confident neither would do more than get their feet wet. I needed a cup of tea, needed one to the extent that I was willing the dogs to get on with their business, so I could get back to the pub and find some breakfast. Thinking of breakfast made me remember the granola. The wonderfully healthy granola I was going to tuck into again this morning.

I whistled for the boys, whistled again, then gave up and fetched them from the beach where they were inspecting a dead fish and probably deciding whether to eat it or not.

When I got back to the pub, the dining room was already full of people. The usual crowd I had been seeing for the last couple of days were there once more, the chatter today though was all about the pirate attack last night. I made my way through the pub turned restaurant to the hot water dispenser and helped myself to a mug of tea. It was too hot to drink, so with the dogs at my feet looking up hopefully in case I wanted to share, I sipped at it and listened.

Everyone in the room seemed to know that the ghost ship had been spotted last night and that the pirates had come ashore, attacked a man that was now in the hospital and vanished again. I looked about to see if there was a newspaper anywhere. I spotted one a couple of tables over. It was being read but as I began to turn my gaze away, I saw him fold it, place it on the table and get up to leave. The paper stayed on the table as he went, and I made a beeline for it.

Snatching it up, I was surprised to see nothing about the ghost ship on the front page. I flicked a few pages but found no reference to it at all. There was no other great news story that would have dominated the front page and pushed the ghost ship down the ranking. The front page, in fact, was covering a minor celebrity getting engaged. I placed the paper back down.

I thought about it for a second before the answer presented itself: time. That was why the paper had nothing in it. We were so far from the printing press in London that they could not get the late edition across the country in time for the people here to have it. Instead, they got the edition that was shipped late last night before the ghost ship showed itself. No doubt in London they were looking at the picture of the spectral ship right now. I only wanted to see what they had written about it. I could check it online easily enough.

Just then, I got the sense that I someone was looking at me and looked up to find Gina advancing on me across the restaurant.

'Tempest,' she said, wrapping me into a hug with her childlike arms. 'Thank you so much. You saved his life.' Her face was buried in my chest briefly, the warmth of her covering me in a very pleasant manner. 'Danny told me what Matthew had done. How he behaved towards you. I had no idea. And you saved him anyway.' She looked up, grabbed my face with both her hands and kissed my right cheek. 'Thank you,' she said again.

We were being watched by most of the people in the room, but as I looked around, they each returned their gaze to the food in front of them. John the chef emerged from the kitchen carrying two plates of food. He saw me and saw Gina hugging me and made a disappointed face.

Thankfully, Gina broke the hug just as it was getting personal. Looking down at her upturned face, I said, 'You are quite welcome.' It was all I could think of to say. I couldn't leave the man to die wounded on the beach no matter what he had done. Being a dick is not an actual crime. 'Are you planning to get some breakfast? Perhaps you would join me?'

Gina smiled up at me, her face radiant. 'That sounds lovely.'

There was a table next to us that had recently emptied, the dirty plates were still there so I stacked them and left them at the end to be collected. 'They have the best granola here. I know, I know.' I laughed when she looked at me curiously. 'Granola is not something you would expect a person to recommend. It's what I'm having. I expect everything here is good though.'

My tea had reached perfect drinking temperature, hot enough that it was really quite hot, but not so hot that it would scald my mouth. I downed it in three swallows then went to get some more and a cup for Gina. She wanted it sweet with three sugars. I shuddered at the thought but made it as she requested.

'Was your equipment damaged?' I asked her as I sat down again.

Her face was glum. 'Yeah. It looks trashed. The ghosts finally come ashore, but my equipment probably didn't capture anything useable at all.' I kept my mouth shut rather than comment on the ludicrous nature of her pursuits. 'I need to inspect it properly of course. I gave it a cursory once over last night in the dark to confirm none of it worked, but it may have recorded something before they broke it.'

John the chef came over to take our order. 'What can I get you?' he asked, his tone polite but I noticed he refused to make eye contact with me and seemed upset about something as if I had perpetrated some crime against him. Gina failed to notice, staring at her menu as she ordered smoked salmon and poached eggs on toast. I told John I would help myself to the cold buffet and thanked him, but he was already turning to leave as if keen to be elsewhere. I was itching to get to the granola, it was becoming an addiction, but I resisted, knowing that it would be rude to eat while Gina was waiting for her food to be cooked.

'Tempest, I feel I owe you a debt of gratitude. Will you let me take you out for dinner?' Gina asked.

I had not expected this. There was no need for her to do anything, there was no debt to repay to my mind. However, when an attractive woman wants to take you out, what possible reason could there be for saying no? Well, on this occasion probably timing. 'There's no need for you to feel any debt towards me, Gina. Dinner sounds great of course, but I leave on Friday.'

'So soon? Maybe you will have time to have a drink with me tonight?' she asked coyly, like meeting her for a drink was not what she was actually suggesting.

Before I could answer, my mother landed at the table. I say landed because the empty space next to Gina was suddenly and quite instantly filled with my mother's girthful hips as she plonked her knitting bag on the table. 'Good morning, Tempest. Who is this?' she enquired of me rather than introducing herself to Gina like a normal person might. She was staring down at Gina as one might a prize cow, taking in her attributes and trying to make a fast decision on whether said cow was worth buying.

'Good morning, mother,' I replied then turned my attention back to Gina. 'Gina, this is my mother. You could probably have guessed that though. Where's dad?' I asked, swinging my gaze back up to mum.

'Just coming. He was taking a dump and stunk out the room, so I left him there,' she announced with unnecessary detail.

Lovely.

Any hope of a conversation with Gina now lost, I offered to get my mother some tea. I could drop a hint the size of a house and she would not find a different table at which to eat her breakfast, so I might as well just get on with it. Mother settled into the chair next to Gina and finally introduced herself properly. Against my better judgement, I left them to chat while I fetched four fresh mugs of tea.

'Did you know Gina was rich?' my mother asked as I returned to the table. Quite how she had already established what Gina had in her bank account I didn't wish to know.

'It's of no consequence, mother,' I replied.

Like a steamroller, she ignored my reply and kept right on going. 'She's single and has no siblings and is very well educated,' she continued.

'I'm sorry, Gina,' I said glumly. 'My mother believes that I need to find a woman to marry. Right now, like by the weekend and I very definitely need to get her pregnant by the end of the honeymoon.'

'Are you interfering again, Mary?' my father asked, finally joining us, his bathroom ministrations seemingly complete.

'I'm helping, Michael,' she replied.

'You're really not,' I assured her as I offered dad the mug of tea I made for him. Gina's eyes were going back and forth like she was watching a tennis match.

'Michael, this is Gina. She and Tempest are friends.' She said the word 'friends' like it was secret code for about-to-go-shag somewhere.

'Good morning, Gina. Very pleased to meet you,' said my father while extending his hand to shake. He took a seat opposite her and next to me, then picked up the breakfast menu to inspect.

Thirty-Three appeared with Gina's breakfast on a warm plate which meant I could finally tuck into some granola. I took a generous portion, topped it with some yoghurt and fruit, then took an extra few spoons of the granola for good measure. I was looking forward to tucking into it and hoping that getting the healthy breakfast would combat some of the bloat I was feeling. Usually, I only get bloated when I eat a lot of carbohydrates – bread or pasta mostly, which I do not normally eat and had eaten very little of this week. Despite that, my trousers felt quite snug. You might argue that the granola is carbohydrate, and you would, of course, be correct, but it's little more than toasted clusters of oats in their rawest form – a very healthy and nutritious way to fuel one's body.

Anyway, I took the bowl back to the table to find my mother regaling Gina with stories about my childhood. '... and he was running around the house naked, covered in poop and refusing to let anyone get near him.' Gina looked like she wanted to eat her breakfast and not think about poop covered kids.

'Are your chaps checking over the equipment?' I asked her to change the direction of the conversation. Really, I was trying to divert my mother before she began talking about my penis and how it had been so tiny when I was a baby. That was probably the worst case, but who could guess what she might say next.

Gina flashed her eyes at me in gratitude for the chance to speak herself. 'They are, Tempest. Yes. I will check on them once I have eaten. If the equipment is not repairable, we will have to pack up and leave. It's all bespoke, so any parts I need will most likely have to be manufactured. Maybe I will get lucky, maybe if they can get it working, we will find it recorded something before it was broken.'

'What equipment?' asked my mother.

'Gina is trying to capture evidence of the ghosts reported here,' I filled in as Gina had just taken a mouthful of salmon and eggs.

'Tempest says that ghosts do not exist. The two of you should team up,' my mother suggested helpfully.

'To do what?' I asked. 'Constantly try to disprove one another?'

'No. You could help each other.' I almost asked her how but stopped myself. The easiest way out of that particular line of conversation was to just let it die.

'Gina. You mentioned dinner. Would Thursday suit you?' I was asking a woman out, a tactic which silenced my mother instantly.

She cleared her mouth to speak, 'Absolutely, that sounds great. If the kit is all broken, we will not leave before Friday anyway.'

'Are you going on a date?' asked mum, sticking her nose in as usual.

Just then one of Gina's crew came through the pub door looking around to find her. I saw him spot her sitting with me and begin to weave his way through the tables to cross the room. I didn't know his name, thus far I had only worked out Matthew and Danny.

'We've got something,' he said excitedly when Gina spotted him. He was still five yards away and had raised his voice so she would hear it. I guess everyone knew what Gina and her crew were up to as there were a lot of faces suddenly attuned to hear what the man had to say.

Gina, frozen for a nanosecond by the news, was suddenly moving. 'Show me,' she said as she left her chair, her breakfast abandoned and forgotten. AS she left the table, she glanced back at me, looking like she was about to apologise for running out, but I was already getting up to go with her. As I passed tables there were others getting up to follow us, their curiosity getting the better of them. I picked the dachshunds up to avoid having someone stand on them.

Outside, the temperature had gone up a bit compared with last night, but it was still cool. A light mist was hovering above the water of the bay. It was thick enough to obscure the view out beyond the headland rocks to our left and right and had spread inland, the tiny water molecules visible around us as we moved through them. We left the pub, crossed the road and fetched up against the railings that stopped people falling off the edge and down to the beach. The ramp one could walk down was still taped off to keep people out and the tent was still in place with people visibly moving around inside it. There was a uniformed police officer standing outside the tent who had most likely come along with the SOCO team to assist Roberta rather than leave her to do all the work. He nodded towards us, giving his permission to come down onto the beach. Ivan, (I overheard Gina address him by name) Gina and I climbed over the railing to drop down to the pebbles on the other side. Others tried to follow us but were ordered back by the police officer.

Ahead of us were the other two from Gina's crew, one of which was Danny from the pasty shop scuffle and the beach last night. They had cobbled together some wiring to attach a laptop to the largest piece of equipment. I tried to remember what Gina had told me it was called but the name eluded me. It was five feet tall, squat and heavy looking and appeared to be a mash of electronic gear all shoved together. I think that, in essence, that was exactly what it was. On the laptop, there was an image.

Danny was speaking, 'Most of it looks smashed, right? But we figured that it would have continued to record data right up until the moment when the power went off. That data would go onto the hard drive, which is pretty hard to get to, so unless the ghosts turned up with a huge magnet it would still be here.' He juggled the laptop a little so that Gina could see the screen better. 'Well, the spectroscope picked up nothing prior to going off, nor did the spectrum analyser or the IR camera. The IR camera was pointing out to sea but what if the pirates came to shore elsewhere and then found Matthew, right? So, I checked the standard video, which ought to not capture much at night but...' he drew the last word out for effect and clicked a key on the laptop. The screen started to play.

Real Ghosts

I had to get closer to the screen to be able to see anything then realised there was nothing to see. The video feed was pointing at the pub, or at least away from the shore, the ambient light allowing us to see shapes but not much else.

Then we all heard Matthew's voice, deeply panicked but very clear. 'Oh, my God!' A half second pause followed before he spoke again, this time clearly in terror. 'No. No. NO!' It was all off-screen, so we couldn't see him and the screen itself was still black. I got to listen to the sound of Matthew screaming in fear and then his voice suddenly cutting off. It was exactly what I heard last night and quite disturbing.

I was beginning to wonder what Ivan had been so excited about when a clearly dead figure, its skin sloughing from its face to reveal the bone beneath, walked right in front of the camera. It was followed by a second, which turned towards the camera whereupon the light from the moon glinted off a gold tooth. The lack of light made it hard to see detail, but the ghosts looked convincing to me.

145

Holding the laptop, Daniel performed a fist bump with Ivan while Gina stared intently at the final images. The skeletal figures moved out of shot, a clang was heard, and the feed went black.

'That's all we have,' announced Daniel.

In response, Gina said, 'Play it again.' She watched it three times through, her smile widening every time, then guiltily vanishing when she heard Matthew scream. I had moved away a few feet, running the footage through in my head. It was compelling. However, it was also utter nonsense. It had to be. I conceded that I could not explain what I had seen but I was more determined than ever now to find out what was going on.

Gina was distracted by her work, leaving me forgotten. I left her to it as I walked away towards the ramp back up to street level. The dogs were pulling me forwards, keen to get to wherever we were going as always. Motion to my left caught my eye and a glance revealed a police car sweeping down the hill towards me. It was the same police car from yesterday, the sergeant at the wheel, her angry expression still in place. I stepped through the crime scene tape as she was pulling to a halt. In the back of the car, I could see the superintendent which made me glad my father was still inside having breakfast. I wondered if the sergeant was going to question why I had been beyond the barrier tape but if she had any interest in me, she failed to show it, and I kept walking. Choosing to exercise the dogs while I considered the footage some more.

Thirty minutes later, I had completed a loop of the village and found myself back at the beach in front of the pub. My outer layer of clothes and my hair were damp from the mist. The dogs too were wet and would need to be dried off when we got back to the room.

As I approached the beach, I could see a van parked by the railings. It was distinctly marked with the logo for a major national television network and had several antennae and a satellite dish on the roof. The crew from it were deployed at the railing where a well-dressed woman with flowing ginger locks tied into a French braid was being filmed. Her back was to the beach, so the shot on television would contain the white tent in the background. As I drew close enough to hear, I paused to listen.

'… where last night another brutal attack took place. This unexplained series of attacks, each one reportedly perpetrated by the ghosts of pirates drowned near here in the 18th century has left this village in shock. Professional paranormal scientist Georgina Huntley the Third was here last night. Using specialist equipment of her own design, she was able to capture images of the ghosts.' The woman moved slightly to her side to reveal the diminutive Gina stood next to her. I hadn't noticed that she was there. Stepping to my right to gain a better view, I then had to apologise to the man next to me as I bumped him. The event was drawing quite a crowd.

The reporter continued. 'Georgina, please tell us about the footage we are about to see. I must first warn the viewers at home that this footage is not suitable for young children and has been edited to remove some of the audio content as it was not suitable for daytime airing.' She moved the microphone from her own mouth and thrust it towards Gina.

Looking both terrified, like a rabbit caught in headlights, and at the same time elated to be able to present her evidence, Gina began to talk. 'The equipment we deployed earlier this week in the hope that we would be able to capture evidence of the ghosts, records data in a number of different spectrums.' Gina then launched into a detailed explanation of the scientific research she was conducting which I'm certain was lost on everyone listening both here and at home.

The reporter asked a few qualifying questions as Gina spoke but mostly just let her talk freely for several minutes. As Gina reached a pause, the reporter cut in, 'Shall we show the folks at home the terrifying footage?' She didn't wait for an answer and kept the microphone to herself as she turned once more to face the camera directly. She issued the warning about the nature of the scene about to be shown once more, then visibly relaxed as I assume the television screens around the country switched from her face to Gina's video.

The footage was only a short burst lasting twenty or so seconds, so the ginger-haired reporter was soon lifting the microphone again. 'Georgina, that is a compelling piece of video. What can you tell us about it?'

Still looking nervous or uncomfortable, Gina said, 'Most of our equipment was broken when the pirates attacked, so that is all we have. Video footage is not enough to prove the existence of ghosts...'

The reporter cut her off. 'Experts from within the paranormal science community are heralding this as the greatest breakthrough of all time. Do you agree with them?'

'Well, yes that has been said I believe, but without any energy readings, I feel it's too open to interpretation for any scientist to claim it as irrefutable evidence of paranormal activity.' Gina was doing a great job of keeping her feet on the ground despite the reporter repeatedly trying to draw her into speculation.

'So, are you saying that those weren't ghosts?' It was a

leading question, the reporter stringing the news segment out as much as she could.

'Not exactly,' replied Gina, smiling at the camera though I could sense she was becoming frustrated. 'What I'm saying is that further evidence is required, and I will be continuing my studies while the phenomenon persists.'

Perhaps accepting her line of questions was not going to yield the result she wanted, the reporter switch tact. 'I understand that one of your employees was injured in the attack last night. Please tell us about that.'

'Matthew received a cut to the head and was taken to Plymouth general for surgery. I didn't see him and was only alerted to the event after he had been treated by the paramedics and taken away.'

'A cut to the head?' the reporter echoed. 'That sounds serious, but in the previous attack, the victim was killed. How did Matthew escape further injury?'

'I cannot answer that. Matthew himself will have to give an account of the event once he's able to do so. I can tell you that the wound was life-threatening and that his life was probably saved by the person that heard his cry for help and came to his assistance.'

The reporter's eyes lit up. She didn't know this bit of the story. 'A good Samaritan? What was he doing out at that time of the night?'

I took a step back to merge with the crowd, then another to place myself behind the front row of people watching the interview. Then I ducked my head and headed towards the pub. As I went, I could still hear what they were saying.

Gina replied to her latest question. 'You will have to ask him that yourself. I can tell you his name though.' I groaned internally. I was not a fan of the press. 'Oh.' I heard her exclaim. 'He was just across the street a moment ago.' My tactic of ducking out of the scene had been timed to perfection because now she was looking to point me out.

'You were about to give me the mystery man's name,' the reporter prompted.

Powerless to stop her, I cringed when Gina said, 'It's Tempest Michaels. He's here on holiday with his parents.'

'Oh, so it's a boy?' the reporter's voice was filled with excited surprise.

'No, no. He's a man. I don't think he planned to have his parents with him.' I slipped inside the pub and heard no more of the conversation. That the press might track me down was a very real concern. Not that I was particularly worried, I just saw no benefit in it and would rather avoid it if I could. I had been on camera before; I always hated the way my voice sounded and would always have a crumb of lunch stuck to my lapel or a piece of hair waving in the breeze to make me look ridiculous.

There was no sign of my parents in the restaurant, so I headed upstairs to the room where I found them watching the television. 'The ghost ship was spotted last night,' my mother told me before I was even in the room.

'I know,' I replied as I let the dogs off their leads.

'And the lady just said your name in her interview.'

'I know.'

'And a man was attacked by the dead pirates.'

'He knows that, Mary,' interjected my father. 'Tempest is the one that found him and called the ambulance.'

'Oh, yes. They just said that,' she replied without taking her eyes of the screen.

I dried the dogs on an old towel I kept for just that purpose, but I did so quickly because I could hear the reporter finishing her interview. An itch at the back of my head insisted that her next move was going to be to look for me. To avoid her, I needed to get out of the pub. But first, I needed to work out what to do with my day.

I sat at the desk and opened my notepad. What did I know?

- There have been violent attacks which are being blamed on ghosts
- Figures which look convincingly like dead pirates have been filmed and have been reported by several witnesses
- A ghost ship has also been seen and photographed. It also looks convincing
- Several persons have been scared from their homes and have fled the village
- Odd yellow warning notices from the parish councillor can be found on the abandoned properties. There may be no correlation
- I have no idea who is behind the attacks nor what the motivation for them is

The list was not even slightly helpful. If I continued to operate under the assumption that both the ghost ship and the pirates themselves are fake, then I only needed to work out how they were being faked. Doing that would most likely lead me to who and then why.

Then I remembered the drones and added them to the list. Their behaviour was odd, but yet again might have no correlation to the other events. My plan was to spend the day lifting the lid on the mystery of the dead pirates, but I was still looking for a start point.

I started a new list: Who gained from the activities?

I didn't get very far in writing the list though because I

could not yet come up with anyone that gained. A Muslim couple had been scared into moving, an Indian family had been scared into moving and their business was already being converted into something else. Who owned it?

I grabbed my phone and called Jane, launching into questions the moment she came on the line. 'Jane, hi. How did you get on with the search for businesses owned in Cawsand?'

'I'm just finishing that now. Give me half an hour?' she requested. Then asked, 'Is there anything else you need me to do?'

I didn't, not yet at least, but it occurred to me that I should act like a good boss for a moment and show some concern for my abandoned employee. 'How are things back there?'

'Quiet, I guess,' she replied. 'It's very different coming to work at your house instead of going to the office every day. I believe Mr. Jarvis has builders there about to start work though and Amanda handed her uniform back today plus we have several cases to look at.'

'Do tell,' I requested. I had not missed the business back home until now.

I heard Jane click the mouse. 'We have a client, two clients in fact that believe they have been cursed by a Haitian voodoo priest. Amanda started looking into that a couple of days ago.'

'A voodoo priest?' I repeated, a little surprised. We got all kinds of weird stuff, I guess we were asking for it, but a voodoo priest was unexpected. 'Well, that is our first one of those.'

'Yeah. It's really spooky. I mean more than normal,' Jane clarified. 'The way the client told her story freaked me out. I won't be going on holiday to Haiti any time soon.' We chatted for a minute before disconnecting. I was glad I made the call, but I was still waiting for her to furnish me with information, so I still didn't know what to do today or where to apply my effort.

There was a knock at the door. Dad got up from the bed, where he had been sitting to read a book. I grabbed his arm to stop him. 'Ask who it is, please. If it's the reporter or anything to do with the reporter, I'm not here.'

'Where are you then?' he asked, sounding mystified.

'Out, dad,' I said, exasperated. 'Nevermind, I've got it.' I got up and got to the door before mum could get bored and answer it.

'Who is it?' I asked loudly through the door.

'Rebecca Franks for Channel Six news. Can I come in?' The voice on the other side of the door was definitely the voice of the ginger-haired reporter I had seen outside.

'No,' I replied, certain that this would not cause her to give up and go away.

'I'm looking for Tempest Michaels. I need to speak to him please,' she called loudly, putting authority in her voice that suggested compliance was expected. The one thing I know about reporters and the press is that they are persistent. Miss Franks was not someone I knew, not that I watched Channel Six news, but I had not heard the name, so she was either new and thus trying to make her mark or she was not new, in which case she was really trying to make her mark. Either way, she was likely to hound me until she got her story. Thinking that I might as well get it over with, I turned the doorknob, then changed my mind and turned the key to lock the door instead.

I crossed the room and looked out the window on the seaward side of the building. Then crossed the room again to the bathroom. The window there opened out onto a courtyard at the back of the pub. It was a sash window that I could slide up. Having done so, I saw my escape route.

'What you up to, kid?' dad asked, his face a curious frown.

'Avoiding reporters hopefully. I won't get anything done while they are trying to get my story and I suspect that once they find out what I do for a living, they will get all excited. I can do without it, so I'm going out the window. Can you meet me along the street towards the car park in half an hour?'

'Do I bring the dogs?' he asked.

'Yes, please.' I grabbed my coat, checked my pockets, patted the dogs and went out the bathroom window. Without looking up as I went by, my mother sighed and muttered something about her friends not having sons that went out of windows.

Beneath the window was a ledge I could step onto and then climb across a few feet to lower myself down to the roof that covered the pub toilets. Once I was out on the ledge though, a door opened directly underneath me, and I had to freeze when I saw Gretchen and Tilda emerge. I doubted Gretchen would approve of me playing Spiderman outside her master suite.

'Did you tell them to do it?' Tilda asked.

'Quiet, Tilda,' insisted Gretchen in a hushed voice. 'We cannot talk about any of this in the open. We could be heard.'

They both lit cigarettes, the foul smoke twirling up to assail my nostrils. I tried to hold my breath even knowing that I could not hold it long enough. I wanted to cover my mouth and nose, to create a filter but could not let go my grip on the wall.

'It was your job to control them. That was what we agreed,' Tilda said while jabbing a finger at her sister.

'Well, we are not the only players in the game are we, Tilda? Saturday night was not their doing. It couldn't have been.'

'So, who was it?' asked Tilda, the question sounding more like an accusation.

Gretchen inhaled another lungful of smoke before answering. 'When? Last night or Saturday? Because the answer to either question is that it was the ghosts.'

I had no idea what I was listening to, they were annoyingly avoiding giving me any specific information. However, if I attempted to fill in the blanks, it sounded very much like they were guilty of something and were worried about someone overhearing what it was.

'Did you see the video footage?' Gretchen asked.

'Yes. They look very convincing, don't they?' The two women were talking about the ghosts, I was certain of it, but they were smirking about it like it was funny.

Gretchen said, 'He said they would. Anyway, I didn't tell them to act last night. They did it of their own volition. They know how I feel about my place being disrespected.'

'Especially by their kind,' agreed Tilda. Filling in the blanks and trying hard not to jump to conclusions, I was convinced that Gretchen and Tilda were somehow responsible for the ghosts, and they were currently talking about the attack on Matthew Todd being deserved. Was this really to do with racial hatred?

'I can't be undone now. The ghosts will get blamed for everything anyway,' said Tilda.

'Will they?' asked Gretchen, sounding less sure than her sister.

'Yes, Gretchen. They will. We have too much riding on it now.'

'I have to get back inside,' Gretchen replied, resignation in her voice. 'Your plan had better work.'

As Gretchen stubbed her cigarette out on the wall below me, Tilda said, 'It will Gretchen. The investors are already starting to bite.'

'They had better be. The sooner I get out of this damned place the better.' I saw Gretchen head back inside and heard the door swing shut once more, leaving Tilda outside by herself. Above her, my arms and legs were starting to shake from the effort of holding still on the tiny ledge and my fingertips were going numb from the cold stone I was holding onto. I didn't dare to move for fear of revealing my position. Tilda would go inside soon enough, and I would be able to climb down and then start poking around in their business. If they were up to something nefarious and were relying on the ghosts to take the blame for it, then were they also to blame for the appearance of the ghosts? It sure sounded that way.

A minute passed and just as I thought I was going to have to move anyway, Tilda dropped her cigarette, stamped on it to kill it, then gripped the door handle and went inside.

I started to move, discovered my fingers were too numb to grip the next handhold and lost contact with the wall.

I fell.

Digging deeper

I pushed off the wall as I went, twisting in mid-air to land heavily on the toilet roof. I was right in the middle of it, its weakest point. There was a faint cracking noise as I edged back to the main wall of the pub and sidled to the edge. If there was anyone in the toilets, they would have heard me land, so I wasted no time in getting down to the ground and leaving the premises.

Out on the street, I made sure I turned away from the direction of the news crew van. Then I jammed my hands into my pockets to warm them up and hurried away, but my mind was whirling with possible scenarios from the over-heard conversation. That Gretchen and Tilda were involved in the appearance of the dead pirates was a certainty as far as I was concerned. They were racists and appeared to be committing blatant racially motivated crimes. Was Roberta involved? I cast my mind back to the Halloween party she had taken me to. Several of her friends were Asian or Africa descent and she mingled with every race and orientation that evening without the slightest indication of bigotry.

Adding up what I knew, I dismissed the notion that Roberta was colluding with her mother; I doubted she even knew. The two older ladies had talked about last night and Saturday night, two nights on which violent ghost attacks had occurred. Were they also responsible for the murder? I recalled witnessing several television detectives state that it was always the wife when a man was murdered. Was there truth to the cliché this time?

Then I remembered the comment about investors. I needed to do some more digging, so spurred on by the notion that I might find out something pertinent, I jogged to the car, hoping the exercise would get my heart to pump some warm blood into my fingers. Once there, I got the engine running and called mum's mobile.

'Tempest, where are you?' she asked. 'Your father and I are just leaving.'

'Change of plans, mother. I need to check something out, so will be taking a drive. Can you have the dachshunds for a while? I will be back for lunch probably.'

'Yes, okay. Where are you going?'

'Bodmin. I learned some things in the fifteen minutes since you last saw me. I will tell you all about it when I get back.'

She sounded a little reluctant but acquiesced. I wanted to look at county records so would need a decent sized library that sat within the county lines. The biggest town within sensible driving distance was Bodmin, so I was going there. But as I turned the engine on, I wondered if I needed to go anywhere. I remembered that Jane promised sending me an email with a whole stack of property information on. My plan had been to go to the library because there I could access all kinds of records. I wanted to know about Tilda and Gretchen, about the different businesses in Cawsand

and I really wanted to find out if the rumour about Julien Hogg building a hotel near the village was true. I suspected though that the last item might be difficult to find that out.

The email was waiting on my phone and Jane, as always, had uncovered a goldmine of detail. Reading it on the tiny screen of my phone was less than ideal and likely to make my eyes go squinty after a while, but it was what I had, and I could make it work.

What I had was property deed records showing the purchase of land and businesses going back for almost two years. What became clear very quickly was that Tilda and Gretchen had bought almost everything that had come onto the market. Where the money for that came from, I didn't know. Borrowed I assumed, but they had bought houses, fisherman's huts, two restaurants nearby and a whole stack of land parcels that surrounded the village. What were they up to? The information was not giving me a solution to the many questions I had. It just added more questions. Maybe I would gain something from going to the county library after all.

I made the decision to go, but just as I put the car into gear, I spotted the drones again. They were coming down off the headland, high up in the sky. They were so high I would be able to see them even if I was moving through the narrow streets.

I made a snap decision, killed the engine and got out of the car. I knew roughly where they were going, assuming their destination was the same as the last time. I set off on foot, trying to track them in the sky, but every time I moved, I lost sight of them and had to stop to find them again. Between the roofs they were still visible, their trajectory taking them back to the same landing point I had been unable to follow them to two days ago.

I started running, stopping at each intersecting street to check where they were. I lost sight of them twice and had to move to a wider point to catch sight of them again. There was a distinct danger I was going to run into something or catch my foot in a drain or gutter as I ran with my face looking upwards, yet I managed to stay on my feet. The drones were getting lower, descending towards the houses and I would lose sight of them completely soon if I didn't find my way through to the street they were heading for. With only a rough idea where they were going, they inevitably they sank from sight behind a row of roofs before I could get to them. It would help if they weren't so damned quiet; there was no noise at all from them to indicate they were there. I wondered how many people they flew over that never noticed.

Defeated, I stopped running and tried to catch my breath. My route passed through one of the narrow alleys that ran between the houses and emerged into a street where two rows of terraces houses faced each other. The street between them barely big enough for a small car to traverse and never designed for one to do so. Opposite me was the row of houses that the drones had landed behind. I crossed the street and went down the next alley, trying to keep my breathing under control so that I could hear the drones because maybe their motors had not yet been shut off.

I could not hear their motors, of course, because there was almost no noise to hear. However, I could hear the two pilots, or whatever the correct term for them was, talking behind a garden fence. The fence was taller than me and I approached quietly enough that they had not heard me. If I hoped to glean something from them though, I was to be disappointed as they were discussing their lunch options.

'How about fish fingers?' the first voice asked.

'I fancy a McDonald's,' a second voice replied. Both voices were male, late teens or early twenties, I estimated. They had an educated, geeky edge to their voices and their accents were distinctly Bristol area. This told me that they weren't local at least.

'Mike, it's a forty-five-minute drive to the nearest McDonald's. Let's live in the real world. We are not allowed to leave the village, you know that,' the first voice complained.

'How's he going to find out?' the second voice asked.

'Have you not noticed that he knows everything?' the first voice said, he sounded exasperated and scared in the same breath. 'He makes out like he's stupid, but I reckon his IQ is off the chart. Plus, if you make him angry, he'll crush your head like a disposable coffee cup.'

Just like Gretchen and Tilda, they were talking as if they had major secrets to keep. They weren't allowed to leave the village, and they were working for some unnamed man that as far as one of the two was concerned might inflict violence as punishment for transgressing his rules. Give me a name, chaps, please give me a name, I begged mentally.

'He gives me the creeps, you know that?' the second voice said. 'What kind of a name is Edington Hungerford anyway? We should never have signed up to this.'

The first voice snapped an angry answer, 'Mike, you utter idiot! I told you not to take the deal! I told you repeatedly that this was a bad idea, but you insisted we were going to get rich.'

'We will get rich. He said he's nearly done,' the first voice whined.

'Well, he better be. I've been here too long. Stupid

STEVE HIGGS

Cornish village with its stupid people and their stupid accents.'

'Damned right. So, what do you want for lunch?' the first voice asked again. They were moving away from me and seconds later a door shut, and they were gone.

I still had not the faintest idea what was going on. There were two chaps flying drones, which was not a crime, but they appeared to be up to something just like Gretchen and her sister were. I wanted the two sets of odd activities to be connected, though I could not see how they were. I did have a name though: Edington Hungerford. It would be easy to look that up and find out who was controlling whatever nefarious activity the drone pilots were guilty of. I also had the first name of one of the drone pilots and the address of the house they were staying in, which were details I might be able to use.

There was nothing more that I could do here, so I turned to head back to the car, and that was when something hit me in the head. There was a very brief moment where I understood I had been hit with something that was far harder than my skull and the sensation of my eyesight shutting down.

Then nothing.

162

Roberta's House

I opened my eyes then shut them tightly against the searing pain that opening them had induced.

'Are you awake?' a woman's voice asked. I knew the voice although my brain was struggling to provide me with the name that belonged to it, and I opened my mouth to speak but discovered that doing so hurt prohibitively as well and lifted my arm instead to give the voice a thumbs up.

'How are you feeling?' she asked. My brain caught up finally, telling me it was Roberta I was hearing. I tried to open my eyes again but gave up no sooner than the first crack of light came past my eyelids.

'Can you close the curtains, please?' I asked

'Of course,' she replied, and I heard her crossing the room followed by the sound of curtains being pulled. The notion of light coming through the skin of my eyelids diminished, and I was able to open them a little.

'Where am I?' I asked.

'My place. You were found lying in the street by old Mrs. Colver. You have a head wound. It's not serious but you have a convincing lump. Do you remember what happened?'

I shifted a little on the bed I was lying on and reached up with my left hand to feel my head, finding that I did indeed have a lump on my skull. It was just into the hairline above my right temple. The skin was broken, probably from the initial impact, but it was not bleeding or discharging plasma.

'What is the time please?' I asked.

'Just after one,' came her answer. I had lost most of three hours somewhere. 'Do you remember what happened?' she asked again, and I was about to start speaking when I remembered that if I said much at all I was going to mention her mother. I didn't know how she might react to my suspicions, plus I had no idea what it was that I suspected.

'I got hit in the head,' I ventured. 'I didn't see who did it.' The effort of speaking was spiking my headache. 'Do you have any painkillers?'

'Somewhere, yes. How many would you like?' she asked. Even with my eyes closed, I could tell she had stood up and was starting to move across the room.

'All of them please.' There was a small snort of amusement as she left the room. Lying there alone, I slowly opened my eyes a crack and looked around. I was on a single bed, probably in a spare room. Under other circumstances, I would be excited to be at Roberta's house. As it was, there was little to be excited about.

I wiggled a little to get my hand into my pocket to retrieve my phone. I found myself mildly surprised I still had it, but it showed that the attack had not been a robbery and thus might well have been intended solely to slow me down or stop me from poking around. The obvious conclusion I drew from that was that someone knew I was doing it.

My phone showed fifteen missed calls because my mother thought persistence was a virtue. I had a couple of emails and text messages as well, but I could not commit to squinting at the screen right now.

Roberta came back into the room with a glass of water in one hand a packet in the other. She said, 'Help yourself,' as she put them down on the small bedside table.

I rolled gently to my side, popped eight of the four-hundred-milligram tablets out and took them all at once. They were ibuprofen, so would do a decent enough job, but would work much better if taken in conjunction with some paracetamol. I would try to get some when I left her house rather than inconvenience her any further.

I said, 'Thank you,' as I rolled onto my back once more. My head was pounding; I wanted to leave but I acknowledged that I was going nowhere yet. 'Can I ask you to let my parents know where I am, please? You can use my phone if that helps.' I held it out in case she wanted to take it. She didn't, but I sensed her leave the room and could hear her talking with someone in another room. She returned a minute later and took the phone from my hand.

'They are listed as mum and dad,' I told her just in case she had any trouble finding them. I continued to lay still with my eyes closed as she made the call. This was probably going to be fun.

'Hello, this is…'

Pause.

'Hello.'

Pause.

'No, I haven't kidnapped your son. This is…'

Pause. Roberta was being very polite. My mother was

almost impossible to talk to in person let alone on the phone. She would have seen my name come up as the caller on her phone so would have been expecting my voice and would now be getting quite agitated and refusing to listen to the rational voice at the other end.

'If you would just let me…'

Pause.

'Fine. Well, when you call the police, please ask for me.' The call ended. I chuckled but did so very carefully because the act of doing so hurt.

A different phone rang. It was not my ringtone and was answered instantly by Roberta. She said, 'Hello dispatch, what do you have for me?' and then there was silence while she listened.

'Please put her through.' I was just guessing, but my assumption was that a person dialling 999 here would get put through to a dispatch-unit miles away and they would then connect the caller to the local unit in whichever area that was.

'Mary Michaels?' I heard Roberta ask and then fall silent again while she listened. 'How do I know who is calling?' she asked. 'Because we just spoke on the phone. I called using your son's handset because he's laying injured on my spare bed.'

Another pause while she listened.

Then she said, 'Yes.' Which was followed by another pause before she spoke again. 'No. He has a bump to his forehead but will be fine when his headache dissipates. Are you at the pub?' Yet another pause while she listened. 'I will bring him to you.' There were a few more words and she disconnected. 'Goodness, your mother is worse than mine.' She commented.

I smiled, trying not to chuckle. My mother was worse

than everyone's mother. Then I felt Roberta sit on the edge of the bed. 'They are waiting for you at the pub,' she said. 'Your mother wanted me to tell you that the dogs have had a nice walk and that you need to get back and entertain your father for the afternoon because she's going out with my mother and my aunt.'

My smile froze at the news, which I quickly tried to hide by pretending to yawn. What do I tell Roberta at this point? Do I say there's odd stuff going on and I have a vague suspicion that her mother and aunt are involved? I had no evidence. Nothing but an overheard conversation or two and certainly nothing that would convince her.

'Are you sure you're able to move?' she asked. 'I have to go, more murder investigation work, I'm afraid. But you can stay here and rest if you want.' It was a generous offer, but I wanted to get back.

Sitting up almost split my head in two, but I did it anyway. I paused for a second on the edge of her bed, gathering myself, then slowly stood up, keeping my head low in case it started spinning. My vision went a little fuzzy and keeping my eyes open really hurt, yet I was determined to show the lady that I was tough and brave and quite able to deal with a little injury.

As Roberta put an arm around me to keep me upright, she said, 'I will need a statement from you later, Tempest. You got attacked in my town and that makes me responsible. Taking statements from you is starting to feel like a habit.'

I smiled, refraining from speaking unless I absolutely had to and gave her another thumbs up instead.

Headache

I borrowed a pair of sunglasses from Roberta when the sun outside in the street proved to be just too much for me to take. However, with the glare toned down a little, I was able to walk back to the pub with Roberta holding my arm. She did so by looping her arm through mine, the effect making us look like a couple out for a holiday stroll.

Roberta saw me into the pub where her mother, my mother, and her aunt were sitting at the bar drinking wine. I thanked her and let her get on her way. Her radio had been squawking with demands for her to report to Dan's Fishing Tackle and Bait shop where something suspicious had been found. I ought to have been interested enough to ask what it was, but the thumping in my head was sufficient to dissuade me from doing so.

'Such a fuss, Tempest,' my mother had said as I plonked down on a chair and quietly asked for some water. 'Gretchen, do either of your children ever get found unconscious in the street with head wounds?'

'No, Mary. No, they do not,' Gretchen answered most agreeably.

'Well, mine does. Tempest is always getting into bother of some kind.' I felt like throwing something at my mother, but the effort required was evading me. 'Just this morning, he went out the window of our room to avoid the press.'

I saw Gretchen stiffen. Tilda had her back to me, but Gretchen's eyes went directly to her sister's and widened. 'What time would that have been?' she asked.

Mum thought about it before she answered, 'Oh, about quarter past ten I suppose.'

Tilda slid off her bar stool as she said, 'Shall we go, ladies?'

'Where are you going?' I asked, politely enquiring about their intended activities and hoping I had managed to keep any hint of suspicion from my voice.

Mum turned to give me a big smile. 'The ladies have invited me out for a leisurely lunch at Mount Edgecombe.'

'The taxi might not wait if we don't get moving,' piped up Gretchen as she moved from behind the bar. Mother's wine glass was still half full, and she looked a little confused that she was suddenly being asked to finish it. It didn't exactly present a problem though so a heartbeat later she upended into her cavernous mouth.

'Don't let your father get into any trouble,' she called out as the three of them got to the door. Then she was gone. Out with two ladies that might be embroiled in murder, hate crimes and goodness knows what else. I wanted to speak, to tell her not to go with them and why. However, if I did so it would reveal my hand, and I really didn't know what it was that I knew yet.

Slowly, and with my head still pounding, I made my way

up the stairs to the bedroom where I found my father. He was sitting in an armchair happily reading a book with a dachshund on his lap. Both dogs came to greet me at the door whereupon I ruffled their fur. Dad looked up from his book to see me sign that I was going for a lie-down. I snagged my little pot of medicinal bits from the sideboard on my way through the room and chugged half a dozen of the paracetamol with a glass of stale tasting water I found on the bedside table.

The sheets of the big bed were cool and soft. I just needed enough time for the painkillers to do their magic.

Adventures with My Dad

It was the sound of the kettle boiling that woke me. I opened my eyes a crack and waited to see how my head felt. The pounding had receded to a dull ache, although it would be several minutes before I would become confident I could operate without it returning immediately.

'Are you making tea?' I asked the room assuming there was someone there. I had not yet rolled over to look around so was reassured when my father's voice replied in the affirmative. 'One for me as well, please,' I asked.

'How are you feeling?' he asked.

I sat up, prising two sleeping dachshunds from my legs as I moved. Having rested, they were ready for walkies, so both plopped onto the floor for a stretch and limber up as I answered dad's question. 'The headache is gone thankfully.' I performed my own series of stretches, mostly to see what hurt and what did not. All systems reported back that they were operational, if not necessarily one hundred percent. 'I'm okay,' I finally concluded as he poured hot water from the kettle.

Without turning to face me, he asked, 'Did you get a look at them?' Clearly, he meant whoever had hit me on the head.

I searched my memory again. 'No. At least, I don't think so. I cannot remember anything about them. I think it was their intention to strike the back of my head, but the blow landed just as I was turning around.'

'Any idea why?' It was a good question.

'Not yet. My gut tells me I was poking around and spooked someone. I heard a name though; Edington Hungerford.' I took the steaming cup as my father offered it and explained about the drones and about the conversation I managed to eavesdrop. While I was talking, I searched for Edington Hungerford on my phone search app. I expected to find him immediately. However, the unusual nature of the name failed to help: There were no results apart from a match against the name of a town. Disappointed, I put my phone down, then remembered the drone pilots and searched for them instead.

I didn't have much to go on. Drone pilots from maybe Bristol and one of them was called Mike, or Michael. Inevitably, I drew a blank on that as well. It was hope that there were competitions where drone pilots got to pit their skills against one another and might have pictures and names of past winners. It was a stretch though, really quite a stretch. However, I found there were such pictures and names though none of the search results helped.

I called Jane. 'Jane, can you find someone called Edington Hungerford for me. I cannot find a single listing for him.'

'Who is he?' she asked.

'I don't know,' I replied chuckling. 'Sorry, Jane. As usual, I don't really know what I'm doing, or what I'm looking for.

I overheard the name being spoken by two chaps I have reason to believe are involved in whatever is going on here. For that matter, I also need to find the identity of a couple of drone pilots. They might be associated with Mr. Hungerford, or they might have just met him. I don't have anything to go on other than they had Bristol accents and one of them is called Mike.'

'That's pretty thin, Boss,' she replied. I could imagine her staring wide eyed at her notes and wondering why I kept giving her impossible problems to solve. 'I'll do my best and let you know what I find.' She hung up.

I turned to my father. 'Dad, I think the landlady and her sister are caught up, or possibly even behind the events here.' His eyebrows went up at the news. 'I think mum is safe enough,' I said to reassure him. 'Actually, my theory is that they invited her out so they can pick her brains about me, find out what I know perhaps. I'm not sure how deep this goes, or to what extent they are involved, but it could be that Tilda murdered her own husband, and the ghosts are part of the cover-up. Or the ghosts have another purpose, and Tilda took the opportunity to murder her husband.'

'What about Roberta?' he asked. Dad always asked the best questions.

'I don't think she knows.' I hoped she didn't. 'She does not strike me as someone that would let a family tie affect her judgement.'

'How sure are you?' Dad was trying to make me consider that my theory might be clouded by my feelings regarding Roberta. He might even be right but thinking about what I knew as objectively as I could, I saw no behaviour from Roberta that suggested she knew what her mother and aunt were doing.

I shook my head. 'Let us assume she's innocent for now.'

Dad nodded his acceptance. 'Okay. So, what are they up to? Also, how are they making the pirates appear and what about the ghost ship?' These were great questions, but before I could answer them, someone knocked at the door and the dogs started barking, the sound cutting through the barrier imposed by the painkillers to once again take a saw to my brain.

Covering my ears to dull the sound out, I waited for dad to shush the daft pair of furry attack hounds, but with the ache in my head distracting me, I failed to call out for him to check who it was before he opened the door.

'Rebecca Franks, Channel Six News,' the reporter announced as she burst into the room, sweeping around my father and bringing a cameraman and a boom guy with her. She took a half second to take in the scene then walked directly across the room to where I was sitting on the bed. 'Tempest Michaels? Famed paranormal debunker? What can you tell us about the ghosts?'

The microphone was thrust under my nose. I had no desire to tell her anything and no wish to be interviewed. My worry, however, was that I was already being filmed and thus there would be footage of me no matter what I said, which they might run regardless to push me into a proper interview should I elect to eject them from the room now. Their invasion though was both rude and inconsiderate.

I gathered my thoughts and gave Rebecca my best smile. I was going to polite her into the ground. 'Miss Franks, why are you in my room? Do you not think it rude to just burst in on a chap? My father and I were enjoying a quiet cup of tea.'

Whatever response she had been expecting, this was not it. 'Tempest…' she began again.

'Tempest? I do not believe we have been acquainted,

yet you address me as if we are old friends. You have invaded the privacy... the sanctity of my parent's bedroom with nary a word of apology and demanded I answer your questions. Why are you still here? Be gone please.'

'Mr. Michaels,' she started again, catching on fast and certainly not put off yet. 'You're here to uncover the mystery of the Cawsand pirates and catch the killer. How is your investigation going so far?'

'Miss Franks. If you do not leave my parent's room right now and make an appointment to speak with me at a time that I find convenient, I will eject you and your colleagues. Using force if necessary.' As I added the final sentence, I dropped the polite tone and stood up. I was the tallest person in the room by a couple of inches and Rebecca was taller than the two men she had with her. My barely concealed threat hit home. She still had her microphone under my nose, but the boom guy had already backed out the door which my father was graciously holding open for them.

She allowed the microphone to drop to her side, looking back up with an imploring look. 'Tempest...'

I chastised her once more with my eyes. I had the upper hand against an attractive woman for once, so I was pressing the advantage home. Burst into my room? What was she thinking?

'Sorry. Mr. Michaels, I need this story. I apologise for the intrusion. I'm just a little desperate. If I don't get something juicy soon, they will put me back at a desk.'

So, it was career driving Miss Franks to be impolite. Perhaps she had her sights set on being the anchor in the studio one day and needed to be the bright star of the outside broadcast first. It was hardly my problem, but her desperation pulled at my pathetic need to come to a lady's aid.

Letting my glare slip, I said, 'Miss Franks. I'm here on vacation, nothing more. However, if I have a moment of inspired insight and can reveal what is happening here, I will let you know and give you an exclusive interview.' Her eyes lit up and she opened her mouth to start asking me questions again. I held up my hand to silence her. 'Not now, Miss Franks. Give me your card and I will call you when it's time.'

Meekly she complied, sliding a card from her handbag. I closed the door on her face as she stepped back over the threshold, then I slumped against it. I could hear the crew walk back along the corridor and start to make their way down the stairs. It was safe to speak.

'You're not a fan of the press then?' Dad asked.

'Not particularly. I don't like the way they think every-one's business should be available for public record. I prob-ably would have spoken to her if she hadn't barged into our room. Anyway, enough of that. Something occurred to me while she was being rude. Do you not have an old Navy buddy in Plymouth somewhere working in a library of some kind?'

'Old Warty Bartrum?'

'I could not tell you, Father. I only remember that he exists. Details such as names were never my strong point.'

'Well, I haven't spoken to him in some time,' Dad said while scratching his chin. 'But yes, when he retired, he took a job as head curator at the Royal Navy Archive in Plymouth and so far as I know, he's still there.'

'Got his number?'

The Royal Navy Archive

Plymouth was almost spitting distance from Cawsand if one ignored the body of sea that got between them. The road distance wasn't far either but in Cornwall, with its tight, winding roads, it took far longer than one might think to get from A to B. Dad drove because he worried the blow to my head might affect my reaction time, so I remained in the passenger's seat observing the countryside for once. I rarely got to look around as I was always driving.

The route took us along the coastline, where, through gaps in the trees, we could look across at Plymouth on the other side of the estuary. The sun was shining, although there was plenty of cloud about and Plymouth itself was bathed in bright light making the green open plain of the Hoe attractive. I could just about make out tiny dots of people walking their dogs or taking children to the swings and slides.

Once we passed over the Isambard Kingdom Brunel bridge and into Devon, dad began to recognise and point out landmarks that he remembered from being posted here several times in his Royal Navy career.

'Why Warty?' I asked. It had been bugging me since he said it.

'Hmmm?'

'The chap we are going to see, why is his name Warty? I'm guessing that it's a nickname and I probably don't wish to know its origin. Curiosity demands I ask.'

Dad chuckled and then explained. 'Young Oscar Bartrum caught a nasty case of genital warts in Singapore back when we were both Sub-Lieutenants. It stuck with him, at least among those of equal or higher rank. I doubt he gets called it very often now though. When I retired, he was already two ranks ahead of me. He got all the way to Rear Admiral before he got too old.'

The Royal Navy Archive was part of the Royal Navy Museum, where there was a car park that visitors didn't have to pay for. This seemed like a good deal since we weren't going to pay for entry to the museum either. There were passes waiting for us in reception, but they weren't at the desk. Instead, they were being held by a lady in a business suit who introduced herself at Lorna Sweetland. She was the Rear Admiral's granddaughter. Her hair was tied back into a very neat bun that had a pen sticking out of it and she smiled as she introduced herself to show off perfect white teeth. I guessed her age at twenty-one or twenty-two; her skin still had the flawless gift of youth, and she was vibrant in the way only a young person can be.

We shook hands and she led us through a portion of the museum before we came to an unmarked door. It opened with a large mortice key that disappeared back into the pocket it had appeared from as we went through it.

'Here we are, gentlemen,' she announced as we took a

right turn and arrived in a very large room that had book-shelves on every wall stretching up thirty feet. The room was circular and there were two ladders with wheels on the base that were set on opposite sides of the room for access to the upper shelves. Looking up, I saw an upper floor visible above the bookshelves.

Before I could take any more in there was a roar from across the room. 'Floppy!' A pensionable aged man appeared from a doorway to our left. Dominating his face was a moustache that would shame a walrus though there was barely a wisp of hair anywhere else on his head.

'Warty! You old bugger.' my father roared back as he crossed the room. The pair shook hands with the deep affection that only shared hardships can engender. I recog-nised it.

'Is this your boy?' Warty asked, peering around my father's shoulder.

I stepped forward, smiling, to shake his hand. 'Pleased to meet you.'

'Meet me? I used to bounce you on my knee. I don't think I could manage that anymore though; you got a good deal bigger. I understand you broke the family tradition and joined the army. The senior service not good enough for you?'

'Leave him alone, Warty,' chided my father. 'He served with honour and made me proud.' I half expected the senior service nonsense to come up; it was the only argu-ment the Navy had. I was well practiced at ignoring their goading.

'I dare say he did,' the old man said while nodding, then slapped me on the shoulder. 'Care for a drop of port?' The question was addressed to the whole room.

Lorna sighed, 'Grandfather, you know you're not supposed to drink.'

'Oh, nonsense, Lorna. A little port is good for the soul,' Warty argued.

'Well, none for me, thank you,' she replied.

I shook my head as well. 'Nor me. I doubt it will mix well with the drugs I took earlier.'

Warty nudged my father in the ribs with a conspiratorial elbow. 'All the more for us, eh, Floppy?' The two old comrades retreated to his office where I soon heard the glug, glug, glug of liquid leaving a decanter.

Once they departed, Lorna turned her attention to me. 'Grandfather said you wanted to look into the history of a battle in 1641? The Merchant Royal, isn't it? I got started already.'

'Oh, thanks,' I replied, surprised that some of the work had been done for me.

'What exactly are you looking for?' she asked.

I gave her an apologetic look. 'Honestly, I'm not sure. I want to learn whatever there is to learn about the treasure that was on board the ship, look for any information pertaining to the pirates that are alleged to have stolen it and try to work out what they might have done with it.'

'Is it for a research paper you are working on?' she asked as she led me to a computer table.

'Not exactly. I'm investigating the ghost pirates that are terrorising the village of Cawsand.'

She laughed politely, then paused. 'Oh, my God, you're serious.' Her mouth had formed a surprised O shape.

'I'm afraid so. But, just to be clear,' I added, 'I don't believe there are any dead pirates risen from the depths of the sea to attack the locals.'

'Well, I should think not,' she replied as she clicked the mouse to bring the computer to life, 'They were all hanged.'

Hanged?

'Show me please.'

Lorna had gathered several letters, a ship's log, and several historians' papers into a folder for me. One document was the diary of a midshipman from HMS Cruelty, a Class 2 Frigate that had been the lead ship pursuing the pirates. In his account, they were bound for Plymouth having recently returned from the Canary Islands where they had been engaged in a brief battle with a Portuguese warship. They required some minor repairs. The Merchant Royal was seen to their North, a mile to starboard but was soon lost to sight when a sudden squall blew in and forced all hands to re-rig the sails less the ship be further damaged by the sudden winds in her full sails. As they came out of the weather, they were confronted by flotsam and debris, then the forward lookout spotted a man in the water, clinging to both a barrel and his life. Rescued, he told the tail of the pirates' faster ship bearing down on them and barraging their ship with cannon fire until crippled, the crew of the Merchant Royale were forced to surrender. Despite the care they tried to give him, he died before he could complete his tale. The captain, knowing the likely cargo of the Merchant Royal, set course for the coast in a bid to trap the pirates and win back the stolen loot.

The crew was enthused, the promise of even the small share of bounty each would receive in comparison with the captain, sufficient to set their hearts ablaze with fighting fervour. They chased after the likely direction the pirates would have gone, the captain's guess proving accurate, but they arrived too late – the pirates had already made shore, near a small fishing village that bore no name. Unperturbed, the captain showed his determination and brilliance as he dispatched jolly boats bearing Royal Marines to the shore on either side of the village. In doing so, he created a three-pronged attack that pinned the pirates in place. It was too late for the village though; the pirates had arrived at night and murdered the priest and several others before HMS Cruelty and her two subordinate ships could make land and trap them.

The report went on to state that a short battle with the pirates resulted in two Royal Marines dead but the pirates all but annihilated. Those left alive were hanged while the villagers cheered on. Of the treasure, there was no sign, the pirates refusing to give up any information despite terrible torture to loosen their tongues. The only bounty gained was the value of the pirate ship itself. The Merchant Royal had sunk in deep water.

A rip of laughter from my father tore through the silence of the room, making both Lorna and I jump.

As my pulse settled, I said, 'This is great stuff, Lorna. What else have you got?' What she had turned out to be conflicting reports from other officers on HMS Cruelty and the two other ships involved. The captain's log gave yet another report of the event. All went along a similar theme of chasing the pirates to shore, fight with them and hang them but the story of the treasure and what might have happened to it varied in each retelling.

'Is it me? Or is this suspicious?' I asked Lorna. What I was reading made me want to believe they had found the treasure, kept it for themselves and lied about the whole thing.

She pursed her lips as she shuffled some more pages. 'I thought exactly the same, so I looked into some of the men aboard the ships at that time. Almost all hands onboard HMS Cruelty and the other two ships were killed less than six months later in a terrible storm in the Caribbean. There were some rich widows though. Even families of the lowly crewmen were able to move out of the inner-city slums.'

'So, you think they found the treasure,' I stated.

'Only some of it. At today's value, the full cargo would be worth around five hundred million pounds Stirling. If they did take the treasure, they only got a portion of it.'

'Then where is it?' I asked, but it was a rhetorical question that I answered myself. 'That is the question I think someone is still trying to answer. Either it went down with the Merchant Royal, or it came ashore and its location went to the pirates' grave along with their bodies.'

Another guffaw split the air. Both men were laughing hard, probably retelling old stories and having a great time. I needed to visit the smallest room, so I excused myself and went to check on my father while I was up. Crossing the room, I checked my watch: Over an hour had passed already.

The two chaps were sitting either side of a small table, a decanter of port on a walnut burr veneered tray between them. The tray held six crystal glasses that matched the decanter. Two were missing, positioned instead in the hands of the two old friends. On the body of the decanter was the name HMS Oberon. I recognised it as a boat my father had once served on. I also remembered I had to call it a boat because it was a submarine and thus not a ship, a differentiation that confused me but one that seemed important to him.

'Having a good time, chaps?' I enquired.

Warty turned to me, 'Tempest, my boy. Won't you join us for one?'

'I will.' I replied, taking up the offered glass. My headache was gone, and I felt it likely the painkillers were now mostly through my system.

'Lorna,' he called through to the main room. 'Lorna, won't you join us? The sun is across the yardarm.' I had no idea what that meant, but she appeared and also conceded to a glass of port.

Four glasses were held aloft. 'To our wives and girlfriends,' announced Warty in a loud toast, then dropped his voice to a surreptitious whisper. 'I hope mine never meet.'

'Oh, granddad. That's awful,' wailed Lorna as the two men dissolved into giggles.

The red liquid warmed my insides as it went down, its deep earthy taste at once refreshing and debasing, like it was something illegal I should not be doing. 'I'm going to leave you to it, I think. I still have research to do,' I announced on my way to the door. A few minutes later I was back at the computer, speed reading through the vast reams of information. The sun was already setting, taking no time at all to go from twilight to full dark at this time of year.

I read through as much as I could, stopping only to take screen breaks and to stretch. Lorna had busied herself elsewhere in the Archive but returned to let me know it was finishing time, 'I really must be getting home, Tempest.'

'Do you need me to leave?' I asked.

'No. But I do need to get grandfather home, and I expect I will catch hell from grandmother for letting him get this drunk.'

'Is he drunk?' I asked. I had no idea. They were being noisy in their little room, but I figured they were entertaining themselves with stories.

'They both are,' she replied with a sigh. I got up to investigate. The laughter of earlier had swung around to reminiscing about old or fallen colleagues, men they had known that either through natural causes or other events were no longer around. I felt happy that dad had enjoyed a pleasant afternoon with an old friend, but then I saw that the port was gone. My eyeballs almost popped clean out when I saw the empty decanter. It must have held a litre or more of the highly alcoholic liquid.

I said, 'Dear lord, dad. How are you feeling?'

'Sad, boy. Sad. Warty and I are a dying breed, son. So many of our cohort are gone now.' A single tear ran down his right cheek.

'I think that should about do it for the port portion of today then. Time to go home I'm afraid.' I would have put the stopper back in the decanter in a show that they were done with it, but there seemed no point.

'But Warty and I were going to go for a curry?' he said drunkenly, his words mingling in his mouth to come out as a regurgitated, slurry mess.

'Jolly good. I'll drive. Lorna, would you care to escort your grandfather out? I assume you have a car.'

We got the two men up and moving, their legs supporting them but their sense of balance and direction severely impaired. With my arm around him and his arm over my shoulders for support, I walked my father back to the desk, snagged some pages I'd printed and tottered out to the car. Lorna had a parking space in front of the building, so I left her there gently folding the Rear Admiral into her car, but not without exchanging business cards first in case I needed to ask her something later.

Dad was asleep in the passenger's seat before I left the car park. I had learned a lot this afternoon, information that was taking my notion of what might be going on in a new direction. I had yet more things I needed to check now.

However, I had a rough idea sketched out in my head, I just needed evidence. Driving back to Cawsand though, the biggest questions I had were whether mother was back from her trip with Gretchen and Tilda and whether I could sneak dad back to the room without her discovering just how drunk he was.

What Shall I Do with a Drunken Sailor?

While my father snored in the seat next to me and dribbled on the window, I did my best to lay out what I knew in my head. It was still a confusing jumble of clues that were refusing to coalesce into a cogent theory. I felt that I was getting there though. I just needed to confirm a few things. One element that was bothering me was the ghost ship. I could not work out how that was being done or by whom or even why.

When we arrived back in Cawsand, there was a spot in the carpark next to my own car, so I reversed into the space and killed the engine. My father came awake at the change in motion, blearily smacking his lips together.

'How are you feeling?' I asked.

'A little lightheaded. How much port did I drink?'

'All of it, dad. All of it.'

'What's the time?' he asked, pulling back his sleeve to squint at his watch in the dark. His watch was an old model with no light on it, so after twisting around and around to try to catch enough moonlight to see by, he gave up.

'It's 1821hrs,' I said, pointing to the still-lit clock on my dashboard very clearly stating the time. 'We should get back to the pub, I expect mother is waiting.'

'She can't be, son,' he replied with a knowing smile. 'If she were waiting, we would already know about it.'

Fair point. The phone had not rung to ask my whereabouts yet.

'I could do with something to eat,' dad announced, and I felt my stomach growl its concurrence. We both exited the car and headed downhill into the village. 'Warty's grand-daughter sure had some big tits on her,' my father declared without prompting.

'Good grief, dad,' I tutted, glancing around to see if there was anyone around to hear him.

'I'm just saying. You do not see a young woman with boobs that big very often.' I had, of course, noticed the size of Lorna's ample chest but had seen no reason to dwell on it.

My father wasn't done with the breast conversation though. 'I miss tits,' he announced.

Still drunk then.

I wanted to point out that he was married to a woman and therefore surely there were some tits to be had some-where but since it was my mother we were talking about, I decided to just stay quiet. Helpfully though, dad filled in my side of the conversation for me. 'Your mother had wonderful boobs when we met. Gravity-defying, they were.'

He fell silent again, making me hope he had exhausted the topic. He hadn't though. 'I could have married her just to get my hands on them.'

'Dad.'

'Of course, they don't look like that anymore.'

'Dad!'

He was on a roll now though and thoroughly entertaining himself. 'Now they are more like a spaniel's ears, and she has to roll them up to put them away.'

'DAD!'

'Alright. Alright,' he laughed at my discomfort. 'Here, can you spot an alleyway anywhere? I need a widdle.'

Good grief.

'Can you not hold it until we get back to the pub? It's only half a mile.'

'No chance, son. We stop, or you walk me through the pub with wet pants.'

I sighed.

'Over there,' I pointed. Then stood lookout while he relieved himself against the side of some unsuspecting person's house. He toppled forward as he tried to balance so his forehead came to rest on the brickwork.

'Much better,' he quipped as he hopped back out into the street zipping his fly closed.

'Tomorrow, we need to hire a boat, dad. I want to check out the coastline. Whatever they are using to create the illusion of the ghost ship must be launched from somewhere. It's a big piece of the puzzle, so I'm going to look for it.'

'Jolly good, kiddo. I'll be the first mate.' He sounded excited at the prospect, but I was feeling a little aggrieved at having to tow him drunk through the village.

'You'll be the cabin boy, you drunken halfwit,' I replied jokingly. We turned onto the front, the lights of the pub just ahead of us. The moon was a big glowing ball hovering over the sea. It was an impressive sight, and I realised as I thought that, that people should be here to see it. I had not seen another person since we arrived. Had the ghosts finally scared everyone inside at night? We had walked right through town without seeing a live body. If this had been their intention, then they could toast their success. But to what end? Gina and her ghost team, plus all their equipment were also missing, packed up and gone most likely now that most of the gear was broken.

I pushed my father towards the pub door and through it, the warm air a welcome relief against the coolness outside.

Upstairs, I tentatively tried the door handle, hoping it was unlocked and mother was inside asleep on the bed. I envisaged one of three scenarios. Either she was not here and that would worry me since I had last seen her leaving with two women I suspected might be guilty of murder, or she was here and asleep which was the favoured option. Or she was here and impatiently tapping her foot for us to return. I pushed the door open.

'Where the heck have you pair been?' she raged before I could even see her.

Option number three then.

'Good evening, mother,' I replied.

Dad elected to throw off my steadying hand now that we were in the safety of the room. 'Hey, love. Show us yer tits!' he called out joyously as he staggered a pace and caught hold of the wall to keep himself upright.

'Is he drunk?' mother demanded to know.

'Little bit,' I conceded with a sigh.

She stared at him as she asked me, 'Why the hell is he drunk?'

'Come on love, give us a kiss,' dad slurred as he flopped on the bed.

'We went to visit an old friend of his. They drank some port.'

'So, this is your fault,' my mother accused, pointing a finger at me and squinting angrily in my direction.

On the bed, dad farted. Loudly. Then giggled. Mother

picked up a pillow and wafted the air while taking a few steps away. 'Don't pick on the boy, Mary. He does not make my rules. Neither do you for that matter.' He was drunk enough to feel brave so was poking the bear with a stick and foolishly unconcerned about what it might do when it took offense.

Mother's temper could reach incandescent levels at times, and it was headed that way right now. Sensing the volcano creating vibrations beneath my feet, I decided that running away was the sensible option. Two backward steps carried me out the door and back into the corridor where her muffled voice was quite audibly blaming me, my father and anything else with a penis for existing. As I hurried towards the stairs something smashed against the door.

I retreated to the quiet sanctuary of the pub where I believed I would find a cold pint of beer that would be pleased to meet me.

'Good evening, Charlie,' I hallooed as I took a seat at the bar. As always, Charlie was halfway through a pint and reading the paper. I had never before witnessed someone spend so long doing the same thing. The level of scrutiny he gave the paper each day was remarkable. For that matter, I found it remarkable that he was always in the bar. There he was in the same seat every time I came in. I wondered how long ago he had started the practice and just how many hours he spent in that seat every week. There was a similar chap in the pub back home displaying the exact same habits. I wondered if every bar everywhere had a Charlie.

There was no sign of Gretchen or anyone else that might serve me a drink, so I took a seat next to Charlie and waited. Then, because there was no sound coming from behind the bar to indicate Gretchen was coming, I asked Charlie what he knew about Philip Masonberg.

'Philip Masonberg,' he repeated the name. 'Don't rightly know what I should tell you. He was a character that's for sure. Not one for being monogamous. He didn't drink here, not for years. Not since Gretchen bought the place.'

'When was that?' I asked.

'Just about two years ago, I think. Philip was always in here before then. He was rarely without company, if you know what I mean.'

I suspected that I did, but I needed him to confirm information, not hint at it. 'You're saying he met with women other than his wife.'

Charlie chuckled. 'That he did. The rest of us could never work out how he did it. He was never that much to look at, even when he was young. Most fellows would have the sense to reserve such activities for when they were further afield and less likely to get caught, but I don't think Philip cared. Of course, he cared enough to not try to do it under his sister-in-law's nose, I suppose.'

'What did he do for a living?' I asked, taking mental notes and wishing I had my bag with me.

'A living?' Charlie chuckled again. 'Philip Masonberg hardly did a decent day's work in his life. Tilda made all the money in that household. Philip was a fisherman. The worst one in the village. Probably the worst in the county. Most days he came back with just enough fish to feed himself.'

Tilda's husband was a lazy, philandering arse by the sound of it. She had a motive for murder, one might argue. Had she arranged a pirate ghost to kill him? Had the whole pirate ghost ruse been dreamt up to distract investigators from the cause of the murder? Make them think it was just another ghostly attack? I thanked Charlie for his time and made a mental note to buy him a drink when Gretchen appeared. I continued waiting for her and while I was waiting, I took my phone from my pocket and called Jane. Who says men cannot multi-task?

'Hi, boss. It's Jane,' Jane answered on the third ring.

'Good evening, Jane. How are things in Kent?'

'Getting interesting. The voodoo priest case is getting kinda scary.'

'Is Amanda in danger? Do I need to come back?' My nonchalant attitude toward the business back at home suddenly shifted and I was sitting bolt upright on my bar stool. If Amanda was in trouble I was going to leave immediately.

'She doesn't think so and she has Big Ben and Patience with her, so I expect she is fine.' Jane's tone was calm and unconcerned; enough so that I relaxed. If she had Big Ben with her, she was probably still in danger, but only in danger of being seduced and thoroughly bedded.

I would call her in a minute anyway, but first I had a question for my assistant. 'Do you have the name of the man that found the gold coins on the beach?'

'I do not,' she replied to the sound of a keyboard being typed on. 'And... now I do. Gary Wainwright.' There was more tapping. 'He lives in Kingsand. I just emailed you his address and phone number.'

Efficient as always. 'Thank you, Jane. My apologies for disturbing your evening.'

'No problem. When are you coming back?' she asked, sounding like she was keen to have me back.

'Hopefully soon,' I replied. 'I only rented the room until Friday.' I bid her a good evening once more and killed the call, dialling Amanda's number straight away. I got no answer though, so tried Big Ben next.

He answered immediately. 'Hey, dog's dick. How's the West Country?' Big Ben was a delight to talk to as usual.

'Not as relaxing as I had anticipated,' I replied honestly.

His voice turned serious for a moment. 'I heard.'

'I wanted to ask if Amanda needed any assistance.' Jane seemed concerned. 'So I'm really just calling to hear whether you think she's in any danger.'

'Mate, listen. Amanda's only problem right now is that she continues to resist me and thus is missing out on the shag of her life. Honestly, I don't know what is wrong with her. She swears she's not a lesbian but can spend all day with me and not feel the need to rip my clothes off. It's so weird.' I could not tell if he was joking or serious. 'Seriously though,' he continued, 'the voodoo thing is a bit creepy. I don't think there's any actual danger to her or anyone else, but we are being cautious. Don't go racing back here for no good reason. Stay there until you're ready to come back, mate.' His tone softened for the last sentence, sincerity creeping into his voice. We had both been in tough situations before, so he knew what I was feeling and why I had wanted to get away for a while. I thanked him and feeling less tense about the situation I left Amanda in, I disconnected.

'Would you like a drink, love?' Gretchen asked from right by my ear, scaring the life right out of me. I had been so focused on other events, I had not heard her approach. When my heart started beating again a second later, I pointed to the Rattler cider pump and gave her a thumbs up as she grabbed a glass and started pouring the clear liquid.

'Thank you,' I managed. As always, the drink was smooth, cold and utterly refreshing. However, now that my brain was working again, I remembered that Gretchen had

I got, 'Go to hell,' as a final comment just before the door slammed shut behind her.

'Smooth,' said Charlie from his bar stool.

All I could do was nod.

Thankfully, there was no one else to see my failure and confusion. Slumped on my bar stool, I sipped my beverage and read the email from Jane. It was a short note giving me the name, address and phone number of the man that found the gold coins on the beach. He might have nothing of importance to tell me, but I was still gathering information, so it felt necessary to ask him a couple of questions. He lived within walking distance as Kingsand and Cawsand were one and the same. They may have started out as separate places a few hundred years ago and were not exactly an urban sprawl now, but the two had joined at some point in the past and one could walk from the start of one to the end of the other in fifteen minutes.

I would call him when I was done with my drink, but as I thought that, my stomach started to rumble. I needed to consider what I would do about dinner. Mum and dad would see to themselves, assuming one had not yet killed the other, so I could please myself, so thinking about it, I considered that I might take a drive and find myself something different to pub food for a change. I was sure I had spotted a sign for an Indian place earlier today on the way back from Plymouth.

Then I remembered that my car keys were still upstairs. I was not going up for them. Pondering my options, the door to the pub opened again. I glanced first at the clock on the wall behind the bar: 1915hrs. Time for regulars and others to be arriving. It was quiet tonight compared with previous evenings in the village pub. Perhaps the effect of the ghost attack last night. Perhaps not.

I heard Roberta's voice behind me. 'Hi, Tempest.'

I swivelled to see her making a beeline for me. 'Good evening, Roberta. Lovely to see you.' Mr. Wriggly was instantly alert. She came right up to me and kissed me on the cheek in greeting, her left hand coming to rest on my left thigh about half an inch from where Mr. Wriggly had been dozing moments ago. Now he was trying to crawl across my leg to get to her as the warmth of her hand sent messages zinging through me.

'How is your head?' she asked.

'It appears to be okay,' I replied. 'I have a small lump still, but the headache is gone.'

'Oh good. I was hoping to catch you here tonight,' she said with a very definite sub-textual meaning. 'Do you have plans?'

'Nothing I cannot cancel.' I had no plan at all other than to get some food somewhere. What I told Gretchen I planned to do tonight was an outright lie. 'I need to eat, but that is about it.'

'Well, I have something for you to munch on.' The outrageously flirty reply was accompanied by her taking my hand and pulling it to convince me it was time to go. I had less than an inch of my pint remaining, so I downed it in one, slid from my stool and followed her out of the pub, her tiny hand holding mine.

It was cool out again. The clear skies of the afternoon were still in place, providing a blanket of stars across the inky black canopy and the huge moon hovered above the sea, bathing the village streets in silvery moonlight. All this was lost to me though because I was being dragged away for sex by a very willing and minxy young lady. I decided I was hungry as my tummy again growled its emptiness, but the protest was shouted into silence by Mr. Wriggly who felt his needs were currently more pressing. Had there been any doubt about her intention, it was swiftly quelled when she pushed me into the mouth of an alley as we passed it. She looped a hand behind my head so she could pull my lips down to hers and her other hand slid between my legs to find something other than my hand to hold. Just when I was beginning to wonder if round one would be in the alleyway, she let go and pulled me back into the street, so we could hurry onwards.

Roberta lived in one of the small terrace houses that was the dominant style in Cawsand. Judging distance, I placed her house at almost dead centre of the village, tucked up a small street called Green Lane. As the front door closed, our clothes were already spilling onto the floor.

Two for One?

WEDNESDAY, NOVEMBER 2ND 2115HRS

Over ninety minutes of sweating and smiling and rolling around ended in the shower because we both needed to get clean. I suspected she was not done yet, but my empty belly had protested loudly enough for her to suggest pizza.

A short while later, I was clothed and sitting on her sofa surfing channels while she fetched wine from the kitchen. There was a delivery service a couple of villages over that were due to bring us a large stuffed-crust meat feast any minute. I was ready for it and thankful I had cash in my wallet in preparation for the unknown this week since I rarely carry it. Somewhere deeper in the house, I heard a phone ring. I heard Roberta answer it, though I could not make out what she was saying. I could, however, hear enough to know that her muffled voice sounded displeased.

The short conversation ended moments before she joined me in her living room. She was carrying only one wine glass. 'I have to go out,' she said, annoyance etched on her delicate features. 'Work stuff,' she explained. 'Hopefully, I will not be long. Please make yourself comfortable, eat the pizza and if I don't get back before you get tired, please keep my bed warm until I do. I will make it worth your while,' she promised. Then she kissed me and rushed off to get changed.

I consoled myself with the thought of eating the pizza without having to share. It was more food than I needed but delaying dinner until almost bedtime had made me ravenous. Less than five minutes later, she reappeared in her uniform, swept back through the room to kiss me and was gone. Alone now, I was feeling a little out of place in someone else's house. Admittedly, I had been running around naked in the house not very long ago, yet now, it felt very quiet and alien.

Only a scant minute went by before I heard the front door open again. My assumption that Roberta had forgotten something vital proved incorrect though when John's head appeared around the doorframe. He seemed shocked to see me, clearly expecting his sister instead. A glance at the clock told me it was 2130hrs, so John had most likely served the last order of food at 2100hrs and was now done for the night. I didn't know he lived with his sister, but thinking back now to when I first arrived, he appeared from the dark that night right around this loca-tion to help me with my bags. Maybe he lived with his sister, or perhaps she lived with him, but whatever the case, we were staring at each other with neither speaking and my paranoid brain was worried the house smelled of sex.

I got up to shake his hand and explain my presence in his house. 'John, hi. Roberta invited me over for pizza, then had to duck out to deal with something. She expected to be back soon.'

'Really?' he said, sounding surprised. 'I just bumped

into her outside. She said she would most likely not be back tonight. She's out at night a lot lately.'

Curious.

'Well, the pizza is designed for two, so you're welcome to join me if you want to share. I ordered meat feast.' My disappointed belly took its cue to growl quite audibly.

'Meat feast?' he confirmed.

'Yes. I like … meat,' I said weakly by way of explanation.

John was biting his bottom lip as if in deep thought. 'Am I welcome to join you, Tempest?' he asked. He had an odd tone to his voice now and his cheeks were flushed. I wondered if he was alright.

'Yes. Of course. I just said so.'

'I, ah. I need a shower,' he replied though it seemed like an odd thing to say.

'Okay.'

'Yes, I'm very dirty. A dirty boy,' he explained.

I didn't really need to know about his hygiene habits.

'You might hear me singing because I never lock the bathroom door.'

'Okay.' I had no idea why I was getting so much information from him. On the television, Vin Diesel was about to drive a car off a bridge with Paul Walker on the back of it, I had wine and there was pizza coming. I couldn't care less about his singing.

'So, I'm going upstairs now. To get a shower. Because I'm a dirty boy. And the bathroom door will not be locked.' He paused in the doorway then bent over to tie his shoelace. He appeared to be watching the movie while doing so, staring back into the room to see the screen, his head upside down against his legs. Finally, he tore himself away. It was a great movie, so I expected him back soon enough. I only hoped the pizza was big enough for us both.

Another five minutes went by before the long-anticipated knock at the door came. I handed over notes that included a good tip before retreating to the sofa, the warm box held before me like a prize. I hoped it was acceptable etiquette in this house to eat pizza on the sofa. John still hadn't reappeared, so I couldn't ask him, and I didn't wish to go rooting around in the kitchen for a plate. With a shrug, I slid a slice out and devoured it hungrily.

John was taking forever in the shower, perhaps knowing how long pizza delivery takes at this end of the earth. I could hear him moving around upstairs now though. I peeked inside the box once more to assure myself there really was enough pizza to go around then closed it again. I had consumed one slice, and it felt polite to offer John some before I took another. If he didn't hurry up though I might reassess my pizza sharing protocols. Thankfully I could hear him on the stairs now.

'Warm pizza?' I asked, lifting the box towards the door with my left hand while keeping my eyes glued to the screen. When I got no reply, I turned to look.

I dropped the pizza box and only just caught it.

John didn't want pizza.

In the doorway, John was wearing a cowboy outfit that included imitation leather chaps with tassels running all the way down the outer seam of both legs. He also had on a matching fake leather waistcoat that was undone in the middle and had a sheriff's badge on the right breast. On his feet were cowboy boots and around his waist was a holster that carried two guns. I assumed they were also fake. Complementing everything else was a large Stetson hat, but the dominant feature of the ensemble was the surprisingly large and erect penis pointing in my direction.

'Howdy, pardner,' he said as he lounged against the doorway. 'You, ah. You might want to close that mouth unless you would like me to put something in it.'

Get me the hell out of here right now! Seriously, why are there not bits of glass stuck in you now from diving out of a window?

Mr. Wriggly had a point.

I could feel my lower jaw flapping as I tried to find a response. He pushed away from the door frame and came towards me, his move jolting me into action.

'Sorry, chap. I'm strictly butter side up.' I believe that I'm not in the slightest bit homophobic. I cared not that John was gay and have always assumed that a person is born with their sexuality already determined. You either were or you were not, or in some cases, I suppose you're both. I, however, was very much heterosexual and wondered when I would be able to get this image out of my head.

John looked desperately confused. 'But... but you said.'

'Sorry. Miscommunication,' I mumbled. I was off the sofa and stuffing my phone back into my pocket. I grabbed my jacket and went for the door. John was in my way though and it was the only exit from the small living room.

Trapped by a dick.

Thankfully he stepped to one side as I tried to get by him. I got the front door opened, remembered the pizza, tussled internally about whether I wanted it enough to squeeze back around the naked cowboy again and decided I was hungry enough to be brave one more time.

'Changed your mind?' he asked hopefully.

'No, John. I have not,' I assured him, trying to sound

neutral rather than apologetic. I rushed through the house with the pizza box held in front of me like a shield. In the tight confines of Roberta's house, I didn't wish to rub against the appendage still jutting out from John's waist.

A Discovery

Outside in the street, I wondered what to do with myself. It was dark and cold and getting late. The pizza would be cold in minutes. Still tasty, but cold pizza is not as nice as hot pizza in my opinion. I snuck a slice out by cracking the lid ever so slightly and did my best to gobble it down without the grease dripping onto my fingers.

As I chewed, I meandered slowly back towards the pub, the routes through Cawsand becoming familiar now as it was not a big place and I had been walking around it continually for the last three days. I was about to walk in front of the house I saw Thirty-Three come out of yesterday. Was that yesterday? I asked myself. The days were merging into one.

As I snagged another slice, the impatient demands of my empty belly now subsiding, I thought about all that had happened today. From climbing out of windows to getting whacked in the head. My father getting drunk and my disappointing conversation with Gina. I was so lost in thought that I almost missed the figure coming out of the door ahead of me.

I froze. When you want to not be noticed one of the easiest things to do is stop moving. The eye is drawn to movement more than anything else. Shapes that don't fit with the surroundings, silhouetting oneself against a skyline or a contrasting background, a shiny surface reflecting light as you move, all these things will give away your presence, but none more swiftly than movement. Moving only my eyes, I glanced around to make sure I was not illuminated by a streetlamp and held still.

Roberta was coming out of a door less than thirty yards ahead of me. There was no mistaking her shape, but light coming from inside the house showed me her face as she turned back towards the house. She spoke to someone unseen within then shut the door, turned away from me and hurried off.

I gave her a minute to leave the area then checked what I was already certain to be true: it was the same house Thirty-Three had come out of. I moved into a deep shadow on the other side of the street and watched the house. The property was as nondescript as any other in the street. They all looked the same, differing only in colour and other minor features such as whether it had a door knocker or whether the owner had hung flower baskets outside.

I stared at the house for forty-five minutes, until my feet and back began to get sore from the lack of movement and it seemed likely that there was nothing to watch. In a different part of the world, I would park a car across the road and watch the house. Since that was not possible here and I wanted sleep and comfort more than I wanted to see if anything happened, I gave up and walked away.

Where was I going though? Not back to Roberta's. The room at the pub didn't appeal much either. Then I remembered that I had my dad's car keys and that they always used to keep a blanket in the boot. I had endured far worse sleeping conditions on many occasions in the army, so with a shrug, I walked up the hill and out of the village to the car park.

Breakfast and Another Clue

I had been warm enough in the car with the blanket wrapped around me, but I was far longer than the car was wide, so upon waking I had been forced to perform a complicated series of stretches to uncrack my back, shoulders, and neck. I was not entirely happy about leaving left the dogs with my parents, the pair of dopey dachshunds were probably wondering where I was. Although provided someone had fed them, I doubted they fretted too much about my absence.

It had occurred to me as I fell asleep, that I had forgotten to call Gary Wainwright last night. By the time I remembered him, it was too late to call, and I felt that it was currently too early. After 0800hrs would be acceptable I hoped.

I walked through the early dawn light, embracing the cool air and feeling alive. Despite the brush with John and his cowboy dick last night, I had enjoyed a wonderful interlude with Roberta. The second time is generally better than the first in my opinion, a belief that had held true last night. I wanted to tell myself that once this week was over and I had departed, it would still be possible to see her again. It wasn't that far to come after all. I checked my phone. It was getting low on battery, I noticed, but I was checking to see what messages I received while I was sleeping. Had Roberta returned to her house late last night and tried to find out where I was? No such luck. Maybe she spoke with her brother and learned that he scared me off.

What I did have, was an email from Jane, sent just before midnight. She had not been able to find anyone called Edington Hungerford anywhere. Nor had she had any success finding two drone pilots from Bristol.

It was unusual for Jane to draw a blank and it made me wonder if I had heard the name correctly. I dismissed the notion that the man had changed his name as I found in a recent case. If this was either his new name or old name, Jane would have found him in seconds. I left the information to stew in my brain for a while as there were other needs to attend to right now. It was breakfast time, I was hungry, and the granola was calling once more. I still felt pudgy, like I was putting on weight despite all the exercise I was getting. I was drinking a couple of pints most days and had eaten a couple of meals that I might not have at home. Like the pizza last night which I had eaten most of all by myself. Other than that, I was being sensible about what I was eating, but I would start today right with a big bowl of the healthy stuff and carry that policy through the rest of the day. As my stomach rumbled its emptiness, I quickened my pace.

I was not the first one to arrive for breakfast. As usual, there were lots of the seafaring treasure hunters filling themselves with bacon, eggs, and toast. I went to the hot water dispenser first, made tea and then helped myself to a large bowl of the wonderous granola.

John came out from the kitchen to check on something, spotted me and when my gaze met his he whipped his head away and stomped back to where he had come from.

By the time my parents appeared, looking well rested and over the tiff they had last night, it was 0812hrs. I had been just about to go outside to call Mr. Wainwright, but since they were here, I postponed the task for a few more minutes.

My mother got to the table first. 'Good morning, Tempest,' she said, sitting down opposite to me. 'Where did you spend the night?' Her voice had a disapproving tone to it as if no matter what I had been doing it would be something she would not approve of.

'Leave the boy alone, Mary,' advised my father, joining the table with two mugs of steaming tea. He handed one to his wife and took a sip of his own. 'Sleep in the car?'

'I did, yes,' I replied, fishing their car keys from my pocket and handing them over.

'What did you do about dinner?' asked my mother. My parents were full of questions this morning.

'I was invited to Roberta's house for pizza.' I omitted all other details about my evening, most especially the bits involving various naked people.

'Oh, you didn't sleep with her did you, Tempest?' my mother whined, her face a mask of disappointment. 'She doesn't have the right body for childbearing. Hardly any breasts at all and her hips are so narrow.' My mother had very distinct ideas about what sort of woman I should be looking for and what facets should be on my tick list when selecting a wife. I was with her on the breast size thing, bigger is better and all that, but since I didn't speak to women based on whether they were ovulating or not, I hardly saw that any of it mattered. You might think my best ploy at this juncture would be to simply stay quiet. There was no need though as my mother was not done talking and had no real interest in anyone else's opinion anyway. For her, a good conversation was one where only she got to talk. 'I don't trust her for that matter. Her eyes are too beady.'

I sipped my tea. 'She's a police officer, mum. One might argue that historically it has been considered an honourable and trustworthy role.'

Mother scoffed at my response. 'Nonsense, Tempest. I bet there are bent cops everywhere. Why not here as well?'

'How was your afternoon with Gretchen and Tilda?' I asked, giving her a new topic to talk about. The tactic worked as she launched into a long-winded complaint about the two ladies. They had spent most of the afternoon asking her questions about me. Quizzing her about my investigation and what I had been able to find out. Had I told her who I thought was behind it all if the ghosts weren't real after all? Of course, they both believed wholeheartedly that they were real and wished I would stop my investigation for my own safety. In the end, I had to stop her. 'Mother, I think they are both involved.'

'Hmm, what's that, Love,' she asked, not really paying attention as she stirred sugar into her second cup of tea.

'Gretchen and Tilda. I think they are involved in the conspiracy,' I repeated.

Still only half listening, she asked, 'What conspiracy, love?'

'What is that you think is going on here, Mum? A man has been murdered and another one hacked almost to death. Someone is creating fake ghosts and a fake ghost ship and there is treasure here somewhere. I don't have all the parts worked out yet but there's a conspiracy to divert attention away from what is really going on and I'm fairly sure your two friends are at the heart of it.'

'Don't be daft, dear,' she chuckled. 'They are just two old ladies. Like me.'

It was foolish of me to think my mother would see reason. 'Just be careful around them please, mother. They were asking all those questions about me because they are worried I will work out what is going on and someone hit me on the head with an iron bar or a bat or something. I'm not entirely convinced I was supposed to survive the attack.' My mother didn't seem convinced, even when my father advised her to listen to me. I noted that he seemed no worse for his overindulged drinking yesterday.

Thirty-Three came to the table to take their food order. I had not seen him taking food orders before and didn't think he was trusted to do so as it had always been John before. Perhaps the chef was avoiding me after last night. My large bowl of granola was finished, and daylight was wasting, so I excused myself, said I would be back shortly and reminded dad that we needed a boat today to get around the coastline.

Outside the pub, I placed a call to Mr. Wainwright. He didn't answer. I tried again, letting the phone ring until it went to voicemail. Not to be defeated, I went back to the email from Jane to check his address, then set off for his house.

Gary Wainwright lived on Armada Road. I had the number but could not tell which way they ran. Were the low numbers at the top, furthest away from my position, or at the bottom, closest to me? I found out soon enough that he lived all the way at the top, where, it transpired, he had a fantastic view over the village and out to sea.

His house was impressive. Standing apart from the terrace houses below, his place overlooked the poor people as if it might once have been the Lord's house. It wasn't even part of Armada Road really; it was an addition built on a piece of land beyond the end of the road so that it faced directly down the street to allow an unencumbered view. There was an electronic gate with a communication panel, but the gate was already open, so I slipped inside to cross the gravel driveway and knock on the oversized front door.

A lady, most likely his wife, answered the door. She was thin in a healthy way and in her early fifties. It was early in the day, and she was dressed for sports in Lycra leggings, new looking sports shoes and a matching stretchy top that left her arms and shoulders exposed. It was a bit col for such an outfit, but her skin had a light sheen of perspiration on it so perhaps she had just been using a home gym.

I gave her an engaging smile. 'Good morning. My name is Tempest Michaels. I'm investigating the rather odd crimes that have occurred in the village recently and hoped I might have two minutes of your husband's time.'

'Are you the police?' she asked, her brow furrowed.

'No, ma'am. A private investigator.' She seemed confused by my presence. 'I simply wish to ask your husband about the gold coins he found. Where they were. What condition they were in.'

'Oh, well, in that case, please come in. He loves talking about the damned gold coins. I hope you have a while.' She let me into the house and led me through the large, vaulted lobby and along a short corridor to a kitchen. At one end of a marble, island in the middle of their expansive and well-appointed kitchen, a man sat with his back to us. Dressed in shirt and trousers, he wore house slippers on his feet.

'Copper fell another two points,' he announced angrily as he heard his wife approach.

'I told you not to short it,' she replied. So, he was into stocks and shares. It explained the expensive house.

'Gary, there's a man here to see you.' She turned to me. 'I'm sorry, I forgot your name.'

'Tempest Michaels,' I announced, moving past her to hand Gary a business card. I offered him my hand, which he shook while examining the card.

'Paranormal Investigations?' he asked, his face screwed up in disgust.

'Do you believe in ghosts, sir?' I asked. It was a leading question.

He looked at me like he was addressing an idiot. 'Of course not, man.'

'Neither do I. You may, however, have heard that a man was killed in Cawsand a few days ago. His death thus far has been blamed on dead pirates.'

'Of course, I heard. It's all the villagers are talking about,' snapped Gary, irritation showing.

I pressed on. 'And therein lies my purpose. There are no ghosts, so someone living is to blame and I intend to find out who that is.' He nodded, showing his understanding or agreement. 'Mr. Wainwright, I want to ask you about the gold coins you found. I believe there may be a connection between the gold and other events.' Out of sight behind me, Mrs. Wainwright decided she was bored and left us to it.

'Gold coins,' Mr Wainwright muttered. 'Those coins are mine. I found them.'

'Can I ask what happened?' I asked to tease more information out. I wanted to get him talking.

'I got over excited and told too many people. That is what happened,' Mr Wainwright raged, mostly at himself.

'Then the government sent a fellow from The British Museum Treasure Registry and all I have now is a receipt.' That he was not allowed to retain treasure found on a shoreline was no surprise to me. It could have significant cultural or historic importance or might be delicate and thus in need of specialists to handle it correctly. I believed the receipt had value though and that he may, because of his find, be entitled to a reward at some point in the future. Despite this, he seemed quite angry that he had been forced to hand it over.

He stopped speaking, so I asked another question. 'What can you tell me about the circumstances when you found it, please? What were the weather and light like? What time of the day was it? As much detail as possible please.'

'Why am I answering your questions again?' he asked, a wary look on his face.

'Because I can get you your coins back,' I lied.

His face looked stunned at the news but rather than ask me how I would perform that improbable miracle, he started talking instead. 'It was really early, maybe eight thirty.' His idea of early was decidedly different to mine. 'It must have been about that because it was still mostly dark out. I was walking the dog on the beach, which is my usual practice, and I spotted something on the sand. I almost stepped on it. It was the shape that drew my eye more than anything, I think. When I bent down to look, I knew immediately that it was an old gold coin. Then I spotted another and then another. Six in total.'

'Which piece of the beach was it?' I asked, making mental notes.

He looked out of the large panoramic window down toward the coast and pointed. 'In front of the Cleave.'

'The one with all the rock pools at low tide?' I confirmed.

He nodded. 'That's it. The first coin was about halfway down the beach with the remaining ones leading towards the water. They were in a line as if someone was leaving a breadcrumb trail. As in Hansel and Gretel. I thought there might be more in the water, so I pulled off my socks and shoes and waded in. I cut my foot on a rock before I found any though.'

'Was there anyone else around?' I asked.

'Not when I found them, but old Mr. Morris came along while I was wading back out of the water. He was walking his dog as usual and my dog bounded over to play. He stopped to ask what I was doing so I showed him the coins. Then another person showed up, a pretty, young woman out jogging. I had no idea she was the local police officer. Well, she tried to confiscate the coins right there and then. The next thing I knew there was a chap knocking on my door and the coins were confiscated anyway.'

'Did you take a picture of the coins? Or can you tell me what they were or what they looked like?' I didn't know if that would be important information, but I wanted to know everything there was to know. I could sift the details later.

'They were Spanish Escudos. A heavy coin by today's standards. I didn't take a picture though.'

I was running out of things to ask him. When he mentioned Roberta trying to confiscate the coins, I felt there was something untoward about her actions and intended to clarify exactly what happened. But now I wondered if he had perhaps embellished the event. It was something to consider but I doubted it was significant.

'Is there anything else you want to ask me?' Gary enquired. I couldn't think of anything, so I thanked him for his time and began making my way back to the front door. 'Do you really think you can get my coins back?' he called after me. 'Or better yet, if you find out where they are buried, maybe let me know.'

Buried?

'I'm sorry. You said buried?' I returned to the kitchen door to ask the question.

'They were covered in soil,' he explained. 'All of them. Quite dirty in fact.'

'You're sure of this?' My brain was spinning at high RPMs now.

'The dirt? Absolutely. All those idiots looking for them out to sea are looking in the wrong place. The ones I found had been dug up.' I searched his face as he spoke, then asked him who else he had spoken to about the dirt. When he claimed I was the first, I grilled him on it to be sure he was telling me the truth. The truth about who he had told, not about the dirt. I believed the bit about the dirt. Walking away from his house and back down toward the seafront of Cawsand, I wondered how big of a clue the dirt was. I had a couple of things I needed Jane to check. Or… maybe Lorna would be able to help.

I shot my cuff to look at my watch: 1002hrs. Plenty of day left. Pausing on the seafront, before I arrived back at the pub and forgot to do it, I sent an email to both Jane and Lorna asking them to resume the search for Edington Hungerford. Piecing bits of the puzzle together, I had arrived at a theory and wanted to see if it were true. I didn't like that it might be, as it would be personally disappointing to me. However, even though it felt like a stretch and highly unlikely, all the parts fitted. I set both girls on it because it felt more likely to yield a successful result that way, than Jane by herself and included a brief plea for Lorna's help as

I had no right to demand it; her Navy contacts might prove useful to the quest.

With the emails sent, I thought about what to do next. I was going sailing sometime soon, but most likely that would be after lunch which left a couple of hours to poke my nose in elsewhere. Getting whacked in the head yesterday had diverted my attention away from the drone pilots. I hadn't forgotten them though. Jane hadn't been able to turn up anything on them, so I was going to employ a different tactic.

The house I tracked them to was just off St Andrews Place. Crossing the village from one end to the other, I arrived at the house to see that it was a holiday let and that fit because the chaps seemed temporary yesterday when I listened to them. They were staying hidden and not leaving the village; a policy that could not be permanent.

I knocked loudly on the door and waited. Nothing happened for a while, then I could see movement inside, shadows moving and the curtain to the front window twitched. I hammered on the door and shouted that I had a parcel to deliver. I had been deliberately hiding my face in case they recognised me, but when the door opened, I walked through it, shoving the surprised young man out of my way.

'Hey,' he said, but I had already gone by him and was moving deeper into the house. 'What the hell, man?'

'Where is your colleague?' I asked.

'I'm calling the police,' he stated, pulling out his phone from a back pocket.

'Jolly good,' I replied without bothering to look at him. 'It will save me the bother. Be sure to tell them where Edington Hungerford is, won't you.' I was looking about for his friend still but I stopped for a moment so I could lock eyes with him. He paused, frozen to the spot and unsure what to do next. He held the phone in his hands, but he wasn't trying to call anyone. Then, I heard a toilet flush somewhere deeper in the house. The sound increased as the bathroom door opened, then diminished as it closed once more.

'We need more bog paper,' an unseen voice announced just before a second man came through a door to find himself the other side of me from his friend. He froze, like his friend had, his mouth hanging open in indecision.

Knowing that I had the upper hand, I said, 'I think we should have a little chat, chaps.' Then, I indicated through to the room at the front of the house where there was a pair of matching sofas. 'Shall we?' I prompted when neither man moved and demonstrated my confidence by leaving them to take a seat and wait. Presently they joined me, both sitting on the other sofa. They knew who I was, or, at least, I assumed they did because they had been watching me with their drones.

Neither spoke. So, I did. 'Chaps, the pirate thing is about to unravel.' It was a leading sentence, but I left it at that because I wanted them to fill in the blanks. They didn't know how much of the full picture I was still guessing. I was sure they were involved; I just couldn't yet determine how or why.

'What pirate thing?' asked the chap on the left. Both men were twenty or maybe twenty-one years old by my esti-mate. They were both skinny and tall, perhaps two or three inches taller than me and both wore glasses. The one on the left had a strip of tape holding the frame of his glasses together.

'Which of you is Mike?' I asked. Neither spoke. They were savvier than I expected and were giving nothing away when I expected them to cave in seconds. I looked from one to the other, fixing them with a steely, hard-faced glare. 'Okay, chaps,' I conceded. 'I cannot force you to talk but be warned: people are going to jail. When I crack this case, you will want to be nowhere near it.'

'No idea what you're talking about, mister,' said the one on the left.

'I will remind you of that later,' I replied, making sure it sounded like a promise.

I got up from the sofa in a sudden motion. Both men instinctively cowered backward away from me, then relaxed a little when I walked out of the room. I turned right though, away from the front door and went to look around the house. They scrambled to follow, but I had a head start and quickly found what I was looking for. On the side in the kitchen was a wallet.

The one with the broken glasses saw where I was going and lunged to beat me to it. It was a fruitless gesture though; I was closer and faster and a lot stronger. I swatted his hand away as he tried to snatch it from my grasp.

'Michael Shornecliffe?' I said, holding up his driving license. 'Care to give me your name?' I asked of the fellow standing next to him. They were hopping mad, but neither was brave enough to do anything about the intruder. I pocketed the wallet, which made them ever madder, then I started looking at paperwork strewn on the counter. I should have swept it all up when I went for the wallet, so now, when they saw me reading it, they lunged. I grabbed handfuls of it, but while I got some, I didn't get it all.

What could have turned into a scuffle ended as they darted away from me. 'Those are mine,' the man that was not Michael Shornecliffe said.

'Tough,' I growled as I stuffed them in my pocket. 'Like I said earlier. Call the police.'

He whispered something to his friend which I could not hear. The two of them grinned at me, which I didn't like. It suggested they knew something that I would want to know.

'Where are the drones?' I asked. I meant to scupper them, and they obviously understood that to be my intention because they suddenly found their balls. Michael opened the kitchen drawer nearest to him, removed a sharp looking kitchen knife and brandished it. His friend did likewise. I doubted they were brave enough to use them, but it seemed foolhardy to stick around to find out. I bolted for the front door, neither of them chased me and thankfully I slipped back out into the safety of the street. Stepping away from their house with a nonchalant air, I forced my heart rate to reduce after the brief burst of adrenalin. It was time to get back to the pub and find dad.

Let's Go Sailing

Holding my head in my hands, I said, 'Dad, I meant a boat with a motor on the back. A speedboat.'

'This is much better,' he said proudly as if the battered looking dingy was a treasure he had found. 'I haven't been in one of these things since I was a boy at the Naval Academy.' Examining the sorry looking Pacer dinghy, I wondered if it might be the one my father had last been in.

'How long will it take to get around the coast in this thing, dad?' I asked, fearing I already knew the answer.

'Oh, maybe a couple of hours.' He saw the disbelief on my face, 'They didn't have anything else.' He protested. 'The boat hire chaps all said there was no point looking for a boat in Cawsand or anywhere nearby because every one of them has been snapped up by treasure hunters.' There seemed to be little I could do about it, so it was this or I would not get to check out the coastline at all. Arguing about it would achieve nothing, so I hopped on board and hoped it wouldn't sink.

'I already rigged the sail,' he boasted. 'Amazing what you remember when you have to.'

Twenty minutes ago, I found mum at the pub by herself. She was in the room reading a magazine and debating what to do with her day. She had the dogs with her and was most likely going to drive to Bodmin to take them for a nice walk and get herself a cream tea she said. I told her it was a great idea. I didn't want her hanging around with Gretchen and Tilda while both dad and I were away.

Knowing the dogs would be taken care of, I walked back down to the jetty to look for dad as that was where mother assured me he had gone more than an hour ago while I was talking to Mr. Wainwright.

Now standing in the aft of the tiny vessel, I was calculating whether this was indeed a good idea. Dad was fired up for a day on the waves though, so I accepted that it was happening and looked about to familiarise myself with the sheets and tackle. There wasn't much to it. I was certain this model should come with a spinnaker, but the gear to raise it was missing. We had a mainsail and a jib though and dad was already casting off.

With the bowline released, we both watched the wind to make sure it pulled the front of the boat away from the mooring point. As it did so, I pushed the tiller to port to catch the meagre breeze just as dad released the stern line. We were away.

At a glacial pace.

'Oh yes,' dad exclaimed with glee in his voice. 'This is it. Bobbing about on the waves.' Bobbing about was exactly the right term for what we were doing. In my head, we were going to hire a boat the shape of a dart with a motor the size of a truck on the back that would have propelled us out of the cove and round the coast to either side in a matter of minutes. A little sulkily, I was silently telling myself that I was getting to spend a great day with my dad, and I should be thankful for it.

'I bought lunch for when we get hungry,' dad announced as he came to sit next to me in the small open area that served as a cockpit/cabin.

'What did you get?'

'Giant Cornish pasties with traditional filling. Would you believe they had a pasty with chicken curry in it?' he asked with utter disbelief and disgust. 'I ask you. Chicken curry. It just doesn't belong in a pasty. It's like making salt and vinegar ice cream,' he tutted.

A fat Cornish pasty sounded great but didn't exactly complement the healthy intentions I started the day with. I sighed mentally, then stared up at the mainsail and willed it to fill with wind. As if on command, a gust of wind rippled along the waves to starboard, the presence of the wind visible only as a fluttering of the wave tops. A quick adjustment to the tiller brought us across to starboard and into the airflow causing us to immediately pick up speed. This was much better.

Fifteen minutes later we were coming past the headland and could see the jagged coast stretching out either side of us. Flipping a mental coin, I took us East towards Plymouth first and handed the tiller to dad when I felt my phone vibrate with an incoming email.

I expected the signal offshore to be intermittent so that I might get messages and I might not. The email was from Jane. She had found the two drone pilots. Earlier, I tasked her with converting my new piece of information – the name Michael Shornecliffe, into something useable, like a link to find his colleague and then their mysterious employer. It didn't take her long. The other chap's name was Ralph Minchetti. They were two men that had briefly served in the Royal Airforce as drone pilots. This was a revelation. They were older than I thought as well, both twenty-three years old. To my knowledge, the drones used in the RAF were nothing like the squat models with a propeller on each corner that I had seen them with here. Instead, they looked more like small airplanes. They could be controlled from an entirely different part of the planet though; the pilot in England while his drone is in Syria for example, unless I had been suckered into believing exaggerated capabilities. It mattered not. They were professional drone pilots and the mysterious man they knew as Edington Hungerford had brought them to Cawsand to do something.

Jane ended the email by saying there was more to come, but she was still corroborating information and cross-referencing details with Lorna. I relayed the new information to Dad.

'Do you want to head back? This all feels like it's getting bigger than you and I should be handling by ourselves.'

I had to agree, 'You're not wrong, Dad. So far though all I have is intangible evidence. There is nothing I can show the police. Even if I cut Roberta out of it because of her family connections, what do you think Superintendent Charters will say? Or Sgt Andrews? I doubt they will listen until we can show them the murder weapon and the man that was holding it.'

'Keep looking for the ghost ship then?'

I nodded.

Forty minutes dragged past as we sailed slowly along the coastline towards Plymouth. Had I not felt a pressing need to get back to Cawsand and confront people, I would have been thoroughly enjoying myself. Maybe Dad and I would have to do this again another year, but without all the drama back on shore.

We were sailing very close to the jagged cliffs that form the coast in these parts. I could imagine ships wrecking against them in storms over the centuries. Driven against that unyielding black rock they would stand no chance at all. My thinking had been that a small craft could be hidden in a cove or inlet. Accessible by land or maybe even accessed by sea, the person creating the ghost ship illusion would sail it out at night and then back again. All under cover of darkness. That I could not perceive how they were creating the illusion didn't put me off, there were many things in life I had seen but could not explain: A magician sawing a woman in half for one. How many people had performed that trick? It was a trick, I knew that, but I had not worked out how they did it. This was the same thing to me. Maybe once I found the vessel they were using it would all be obvious.

Another fifteen minutes elapsed. 'Let's turn around, Dad. There's nothing here and the clock is ticking. It will take us an hour to get back to Cawsand anyway.'

'Coming to Port, son. Ready about?'

'Ready.' Dad pushed the tiller away and the boat swung around as we switched sides and I managed the jib sail. The boom swung over our heads and settled once more against its stops.

Thankfully, the tide was now flowing with us, pushing us along instead of slowing us down. Our return to Cawsand harbour would be far swifter than the outward leg.

My phone pinged another email. This one was from Lorna. I had specifically asked her to look at a singular piece of information. It was an absolute guess on my part, but I had been right. Her email had a photograph attached to it with a man's face. We had found Edington Hungerford and now I knew far more than just his name. I knew why he was here. What his connection to the place was and from that could fill in most of the rest of the blanks in this strange story.

Jane had been cc'd to the email, so I replied to both girls, asking them to find out if he owned property in Cawsand.

We were coming close to the turn into Cawsand harbour. Larger yachts were anchored there where the water was deep enough at low tide to not ground them. We had a few minutes yet before we would be sailing past them and Cawsand would be in sight. I was planning still to examine the coastline to the West of the village. It felt a little futile, but if I could just find the vessel being used the create the ghost ship, I believed I could blow the case wide open.

I abandoned that plan though as the next email arrived. Jane had taken all of five minutes to determine that Edington did indeed own a property in Cawsand, but that was not the bit that drew my eye. He owned a yacht. Jane even had its name, and we were sailing right past it.

'Dad.'

'Yeah.'

'Cut the engine.'

'We don't have an engine, son.'

'I know that, you daft old git. Hove to, for goodness sake.'

Dad shoved the tiller away as I killed the mainsail, effectively stopping the boat dead. Right between our current position and Cawsand was Chesapeake Dreams. It was a little old, but it was still impressive and must have been close to one-hundred and fifty feet in length. I gave Dad some quick instructions so that he would know what we were doing and grabbed the two oars from the bottom of the dinghy. A few strokes covered the remaining distance but as we approached the yachts hull, we collided with something, a dull thud echoing through our little boat.

Since we could not have hit the bottom, there had to be something under the water. Both Dad and I hung over the edge to peer into the water. Sure enough, there was something down there, anchored somehow right next to the man's yacht.

'What is it?' Dad asked.

'I'm going to guess and say that it's our ghost ship. But I'm not going to know until I go and look.'

'You're getting in the water?' Dad asked, horrified.

'Yup. Not thrilled about the idea, but I see no other way of getting a proper look at it. The water is clear enough that I will be able to swim around it. I won't be in the water long.'

'You better not be, son. It looks mighty cold, and we have no towel to dry you with.'

'I'm going on board that yacht first. Maybe I can find one on there.'

We steered the dinghy around the underwater object and alongside the yacht where, at the rear end, there was a step for access and egress. With Roberta's warning about piracy echoing in my head I slipped on board and went to look around.

The yacht was sitting low in the water, and I soon discovered why. We had noticed while bobbing up and down next to it, that the sea was resting a foot or more above the yacht's natural tide line. All vessels will sit in the water at a set depth according to the weight of the objects on board. A line forms over a period and this vessel was sitting far lower than the mark which was visible as the waves lapped against it. A new line was not forming yet though so the change of weight on board had to be something new.

It was. The new thing was a mountain of gold, and silver and jewels. I had stumbled across Aladdin's cave. Below deck, where the galley would house the people on the boat, provide them with a kitchen and both living and sleeping areas was nothing but treasure on every surface. I took pictures, a whole stack of them and then a quick video as I panned around.

I could fill my pockets and never think about money again. No! a voice in my head cried out. You could take the damned yacht and sail to the Caribbean! I ignored the voice, grabbed a handy tea towel and hurried back to my father waiting at the back of the boat.

'Find anything?' he asked.

'You should go take a look, Dad. You will never see anything like it again as long as you live. I need to get undressed and check out what is alongside the yacht so don't take too long. My core temperature will drop fast once I'm exposed.'

He scrambled across the side of the dinghy and onto the yacht. Reappearing less than a minute later with a look of stunned awe on his face. 'A King's ransom and then some more. How much did you take?'

'The exact amount my conscience could handle,' I replied, pulling off my trousers. I was down to my shorts and already getting cold. 'Be ready to help me dry off and get dressed. I doubt my fingertips will do buttons after a minute in the sea.'

I really didn't want to do it, but my desire to solve the case was greater than my fear of the cold, so with no further messing about I peeled off my pants and jumped over the side. The motion carried me under the waves where I had to fight the natural urge to draw a breath when the cold hit me. I stayed under instead, flipped myself around and swum over to the object we had bumped.

There was enough light to see it by, and I was able to find a handhold, so I could anchor myself to it and stay under. It was a submersible of some kind, a cylindrical shape with a propeller looking thing at one end but the dominant feature was the huge piece of what I believed to be Perspex jutting up from one side like a giant windscreen. I had almost swum into it and would have done so had I not seen the steel frame around the edge of the plastic at the last moment.

The top of the submersible's body was mostly flat, but a domed protrusion sat in the centre. It was glass, or Perspex also and looked to have some electronics in it. Maybe a camera lens; was what I was looking at? Then it hit me. I knew how they were making the ghost ship appear. At least I had a working concept that I would argue until proven wrong.

I surfaced. The dinghy was no more than a few yards away, but the cold had penetrated my muscles making my shoulders feel sluggish as I tried to swim towards salvation. Seeing my struggle, Dad held an oar out until I could reach it then pulled me to the boat and helped me clamber inside.

'Let's get to shore,' I managed through chattering teeth as I dried most of the water off and started throwing on my clothes. The small boat could be sailed by one man so that was what Dad did.

I made a phone call.

Where's Mum?

As we sailed around the yacht and pointed the hull at land, the village of Cawsand slowly came into view. It looked so tranquil, so picturesque laid out in front of us like that. The sun was peeking through the clouds creating sunbeams that lit up the village and made the sea sparkle as it moved. From our position out to sea, one would never know there was anything boiling beneath the surface of the welcoming streets. Behind us, the sun was setting, and a heavy cloud bank was moving in. It would be dark soon.

My phone pinged with an incoming text. Swiping the screen, I brought up the message. It was from mum.

'No. No. No. No. NO!'

'What's up kid?' asked Dad.

I didn't answer right away, I tried calling her instead. The phone rang but was not answered. I tried again with the same result. Dad was waiting patiently, a little concern on his face.

I showed him the message. Mum had decided to go undercover. She had been eavesdropping on Tilda and had overheard her talking about the need to do something with the Pirates tonight. Mother failed to tell us where she was going, but she was taking the dogs for a walk and was going to see if she could find out if my theories were true.

Dad's face was grim, as well it might be. Mum was rubbish at being inconspicuous. She was likely wearing dark glasses (on a cloudy day in November) and thinking she would not be noticed because of them. We needed to get back to shore and find her. I'll tell you this about boats though. If you have never sailed, you might not appreciate this: Boats move slow. When it feels like you are whipping along, feeling like you're barely sticking to the water because you're moving so fast, the little dingy thing you are in is maybe going eight knots. I can run faster.

I wanted to get back to land, ditch the boat and look for mum before she got herself into trouble, but land was a mile away and it was another twenty minutes before dad and I were impatiently tying onto the dock and abandoning it. The chap that had rented it to us was coming to inspect it and return the security deposit, but we were already running away as he yelled at us.

'Where do you think she is?' Dad asked.

I slowed to a walk. I had not the faintest idea. I wanted to say somewhere in Cawsand, and she almost certainly was, but even though it's a tiny village there are still a thousand houses she could be in, plus other buildings and there are boats going in and out all the time – it would be hard to find her if she were already on a boat. As we left the harbour to join the winding streets, there were still plenty of people about. Out of season tourists drawn by the buzz of excitement about the village, treasure hunters of all manner and of course the local populace.

I leaned close to Dad, so I could speak quietly to him,

'Let's get back to the room. Mum may have left a note for us there. If not then we need to change, call Roberta and start poking around.' Dad was looking worried as we hurried around the corner to the pub. 'Don't worry, Dad. We'll find her.'

'We could just go for a pint you know. If they have her it will not be long before they want to give her back.' He was making a joke to lighten our moods. Like me, he was an ex-serviceman, and this was typical behaviour when dealing with high-stress situations.

Mum wasn't in the room though and there was no note from her. The front door to the pub was locked for the first time since I had arrived, thankfully the key to my room had the second key for the front door on the same ring. I had been carrying it with me since I arrived. I opened up and let us both in.

Upstairs, at least the room was unmolested, but the dogs were gone along with their leads and mum was still not answering her phone. I gave up on calling her and rang Roberta.

She answered on the third ring. 'Hi, Tempest.' There was a slightly sexy purr to her voice like she was thinking private thoughts about naked romping, and I had just interrupted them. 'What are you up to right now?'

'Sorry, Roberta. I have a bit of an emergency, and I need your help.'

She switched to her serious voice. 'What do you need me to do?'

'My mother has gone missing. She left us a mysterious note saying that she was off to follow your aunt.' I needed to tell Roberta a little more now. 'Roberta, your aunt might be mixed up in the ghost thing.'

'Rubbish, Tempest.'

'Not just her, Roberta. I think others might be as well.' I held back from saying I thought her mum might be at the apex of the conspiracy.

'Tempest, do you have any evidence at all?' she demanded.

'Not yet. Not a damned thing.'

She was quiet for a moment as if thinking. I gave her a moment but then had to press her. 'Roberta, my mum is missing. Let's assume I'm wrong about everything, she has still followed your aunt somewhere. Where might she be?'

'Where might my aunt be at this time on a Thursday? I have no idea, Tempest. Somewhere in Cawsand.'

'Help me narrow it down, Roberta. Your Aunt owns a couple of businesses. I know their names but not their locations. I need to start looking in places where she might be, and I could do with your help before she gets herself into trouble.' I was pleading.

'Okay, Tempest. If we work together, I'm sure we can find your mum.' Roberta outlined three places we should start looking. One was down on the beach near The Cleve or just along from it, an old fisherman's shack that Tilda was planning to turn into a harbour tours business. It was closer to her, so she would check that out and meet us in front of the pub shortly. One of the others was at the far western end of the village, high up on the cliff overlooking the sea. Roberta had said it was possible but unlikely that they had gone there as it was abandoned and falling down. Dad and I were close to it though, so I was going to eliminate it anyway.

We disconnected. 'Ready?' I asked Dad. He had changed into dry gear but had on much the same rugged outdoor clothing as before. Wondering what we would be heading into, I wanted to put on my combat gear and armour. It was at home though where it belonged, so I settled for grey jeans and a pair of walking boots plus a dark sweater over the top. We were basically going to be sneaking around the village looking in windows for murdering conspirators. Bright clothing would not be appropriate for the task.

I left mum a note on the bed, just in case, and the pair of us rushed out, down the stairs and into the street. In the ten minutes we had been inside, the cloud bank had crept in and blackened out the little natural light that might remain at this time of day. It was getting foggy too. This close to the shore, the weather conditions could change suddenly. I knew that, but this had been threatening most of the day and had finally arrived.

The conditions were irrelevant. Moisture from the fog might penetrate our clothes if we are out in it for long enough but that would not matter and could not be allowed to delay or deter us. The first place Roberta had advised we look was a warehouse just out of town. It was less than a mile away, but even at a fast pace, it would take us a good ten minutes to get there as the winding streets prevented anything like a direct route. It was an old canning factory, if Roberta's information was correct, from back when they used to land huge amounts of sardines here. It had long since been closed but looking through the windows it was clear that some of the machinery was still there. It was tucked into the cliffside and well hidden behind overgrown foliage and trees. It would have made a great place for secret conspiracy meetings – the co-conspirators could slip away in the dark and find their way there using the moonlight. No one from the village below would be able to see them.

We approached slowly and with caution in case this was

where mum had followed Tilda to. It might be they could even have a guard outside looking out for intruders. There was no one though and it became quickly clear that no one had been here for days or perhaps weeks.

We turned around and headed back towards the village.

I checked my watch: 1815hrs. My stomach gave a rumble that was audible enough for my dad to hear. Neither one of us made any comment. It had been four hours since we left mum this afternoon to check out spots along the coastline. We had found what we needed to. I had enough to hand the whole thing over to the police now and I knew a few things that I was not doing anything about yet because doing so would not get my mum back. I could not be sure at what time she had set off as my phone had recorded when I received the message not when it was sent but I had to assume that she had been missing for the best part of four hours. It was not a welcome calculation.

My thoughts were interrupted by a light coming from ahead of us. We had just reached the edge of the village again. Stepping off the dirt path that led to the sardine factory and back onto the road where the two met, there were now houses before us.

Blocking our path were two skeletal pirates brandishing cutlasses and somehow pulling off a bored expression with their grinning skulls.

Really Dead Pirates

We both froze. My brain was having trouble deciphering the scene in front of me. I was looking at something that could not possibly exist, but here it was right in front of me. Two skeletons dressed in ragged clothing that appeared to have largely rotted away. There were scraps of flesh left here and there, and they somehow still had eyeballs, even though I felt certain the fishes would have eaten those first. They were wet as if they had just emerged from the sea, their clothing slick with water that was dripping from the cuffs and collars.

'What do we do?' whispered Dad from right next to me. The one on our right took a step forward and swished his cutlass.

Then his mouth opened, and he began to speak. He was able to orate in a most effective manner despite the lack of lips or tongue. 'Begone from this place. All who reside here are doomed to perish for their sins. Come back into the village and you will share their fate.' At his utterance, the other one brought his weapon to bear upon us.

I wanted my legs to move but my brain was still having trouble getting messages to them. I was scared. Genuinely, truly scared by the apparition in front of me and it was pissing me off. They could not be real, but they looked pretty damned real from where I was.

Then I noticed that the water that was visibly dripping from them was not appearing on the ground. I took a step forward, somehow finding the will to make my feet move. My Dad grabbed my arm lightly in a warning. I shook it off and stepped yet closer to them. We were only ten feet apart now. Having come closer I could see that their forms weren't entirely solid – I could sort of see through them.

If they weren't real, which I continued to tell myself they could not be, then what were they? Then a part of the puzzle clicked into place, and I looked to the sky.

'Dad?'

'Yes, son?'

'Help me find some rocks.' I bent down to the path next to me to pick up a loose chipping. I hurled it into the sky. I lost sight of it after a few feet as the dark and mist swallowed it up, so I tried again. This time with a handful of smaller stones. When I threw them, there was a faint pinging noise as a few of the stones hit something invisible in the air above me. One of the skeletons flickered.

Dad saw it too and started throwing chunks of flint into the night sky. The skeletons failed to advance on us, but they did swish their swords again and the one that had spoken repeated his message – verbatim.

It was Dad that scored the first proper hit. A distinctive clunk resounded as his most recent throw found a target. The pirate on the left suddenly vanished from sight. He just winked out like he had been turned off, which essentially, he had. A heartbeat later a drone crashed onto the path, skittering and sliding as friction with the tarmac slowed its motion.

The dead pirates were holographic projections from drones.

That we were still facing a skeleton meant that there was still a drone operational. They had been dispatched by the two pilots to scare us away. Were the pilots in their house? If the drones could be controlled from anywhere, I had to assume the only reason they were in Cawsand at all was because they had to recharge them periodically and maybe the transmission of the images had a short range.

Wherever they were being controlled from, I had to assume that they could see us and had some way of manipulating what the figures being projected were doing. Or had elaborate and complex motions stored as options that were then being queued and played by a computer. They must have realised they had lost one of the drones though as the remaining pirate also winked out of existence. The drones may have left or may have been tracking us, I could not tell, they were so silent. I wanted to find them and wring their necks and some more information out of them. I would only waste time going to their house though. Dad and I needed to meet up with Roberta. In my anger at the drone pilots, there was some jubilation. I now knew how it was that people had convincingly reported ghostly pirates wandering around the village.

'Nice shot, Dad,' I acknowledged as I bent to pick up the downed drone. It was evidence. Whether it could be traced back to the owner or not I didn't know. The drone was twitching, the rotors turning on one side, but not the other. Looking closer I could see that Dad's shot had broken one of the four propellers and the one adjacent was not moving.

'Someone is trying to scare us off. I guess they don't

want us to catch them doing whatever it is they are doing. I'm not interested in them at moment, or at least I am, but only so far as I need to be to get mum back. After that, we shall see who is guilty of what.'

'Let's get to the other address, kid.'

'Right you are, Dad.'

We started jogging down the road back into town. The fog was getting thick. It appeared to be eating the light coming from the lamps in the street. We could see dim glowing balls high above us but the illumination that would normally let us see our surroundings was lost in a murky blackness just a few feet ahead. I was navigating by memory, turning down paths only when we stumbled across them. We had crossed Earl's Drive between two houses and made our way down an alleyway to emerge on St Andrews Place. The second address that Roberta had given us was up towards St Andrews Street which was not that easy to get to unless one knew all the little cut through lanes.

On the road ahead of us two figures emerged from the gloom. Dad saw them at the same time as me, pointing ahead rather than speaking as we were both getting out of breath. At first, they were hard to see but as we drew near it was clear they were just another drone projected version of the dead pirates. These ones had a little more flesh to them, their clothes were a little fuller, but it was the same rubbish trick, and I wondered why they would bother trying to do the same thing again. They must have back up drones, or more drones than they had people to operate. How good were the cameras, if they didn't realise we already knew it was drones being used to make the pirates appear?

I planned to just run through them. If their plan was to stop me finding my mother, I had bigger challenges to worry about. Like where on earth she was for one.

As we came near them, they moved to intercept our path. Both raised their cutlasses threateningly as if they planned to cut us down when we passed them. Then a gap in the fog let a little more light through and moonlight glinted off the steel of the cutlass one was holding.

They were real!

We were right upon them. Their arms were swinging down. I roughly shoved Dad to one side as I reached up to grab the arm heading towards my head. The cutlass to my right swung harmlessly through thin air in the space where my dad ought to have been. I caught the very real and quite thickset arm above me and folded myself underneath it.

Blind luck more than skill on my part landed me exactly where I needed to be to break the man's grip on his weapon. I had kept hold of his arm as I came under it and slammed into him in a body check. My motion stopped by transferring my kinetic energy directly into his chest. The air rushed out of him as I turned my back and pulled the sword arm down over my shoulder. He was shorter than me, so the motion overstretched his shoulder joint and forced him to the release the cutlass.

With his right arm in mine, I span underneath it to come out behind him. His companion had recovered from his committed swing into nothing but was momentarily caught in indecision about whether to attack me or my dad. He didn't get to make a choice as my dad punched him in the side of his stupid face. As he toppled towards me, I kicked out the legs of the man I was holding by stamping my instep into the back of his knees. The pair were on the floor.

'Stay down,' I growled at them both. I examined the man I was holding. His face was slathered in make-up which someone had done a very good job of. His skin looked like it was falling off the bone in places. It wasn't though and when I looked closely, I could tell who it was. It was Thirty-Three. His muscular frame should have given it away sooner.

The sound of running footsteps brought our attention up again. From the gloom, another figure was running towards us. Thirty-Three was trying to get up, despite me having his arm in a lock that forced his elbow joint against itself if he tried to move. I reinforced my grip as it was guaranteed to keep him in place. My father was standing above the other chap, almost daring him to make a move. I wanted to get a better at look at him as I suspected I would be able to identify him as well. It would have to wait though as there was a potential third player joining the fray. I would need to make sure the chaps already down stayed there, which might mean some rather unfair violence, but then perhaps they shouldn't have taken my mother.

As I steeled myself to act, it was Roberta that emerged from the darkness. She seemed startled to find us with two pirates at our feet.

'What the hell?' she asked.

The man I was pinning started to talk.

'Shut up, Thirty-three,' she snapped at him.

'Roberta…' he started to speak again, but this time she kicked him in the face.

'I said shut up. I need to deal with these two,' she said. 'You should go and check out the place by the water.'

'Didn't you get to look at it?' That was what she was supposed to have been doing.

'I managed to check out the one by St Andrews Street, but then I spotted these two moving around and followed them. I lost them in the fog though and only just now when I heard them scuffling with you did I relocate them.'

'Was there any sign of anything at the place you checked?'

'No, nothing. There's a cut-through between the houses down there,' she said pointing off into the darkness. 'It's to the right of a yellow house with white shutters on the windows. Get going. I called for backup already but told them to approach stealthily. I will guide them in when they get here and bring them to your location. I just hope your mum is down there. Text or call me if you can.' She touched my arm tactilely as she moved in close to me and bent down.

Roberta was pulling cuffs from behind her back as she knelt to replace me in restraining Thirty-Three. I let her. Dad was pulling at my sleeve, wanting to get moving, but I needed no such encouragement.

I glanced back over my shoulder a second later, but the darkness and fog had already stolen her from view. We found the gap between the houses and slipped down it. The darkness we had been enduring was nothing compared to the cloak of nothing that now enveloped us in the narrow confines of the alleyway. I could touch both walls with my arms spread just a little to each side. I might as well have been blind, but we struggled forward. I could hear Dad stumbling and swearing behind me. It was only a few seconds, though it felt like much longer, then the alleyway ended, and we emerged from between the two houses to find ourselves on a road that led directly to the seafront. I could not remember the name of the road, but I recognised it even in the dark.

The final place that Roberta had suggested we look was a fisherman's shack close to the water's edge. I didn't know what it had originally been built for, probably storage of fishermen's gear, but now it was owned by Tilda and doubtless she planned to profit enormously from whatever development she had planned for it.

We covered the distance to it swiftly enough, jogging in our impatience. As we neared, it became clear the building was occupied, there was light flickering from a couple of high windows suggesting candlelight or a fire inside. I motioned to Dad that we should fan out a bit, come at it from both sides of the path leading down to it. In the fog, we might easily miss a sentry posted outside. It seemed an unlikely precaution on their part. However, I was not going to get caught out by rushing in blindly.

We stopped a few yards short and listened. The fog damped out sound more effectively than any other weather condition with the exception of rain. It would be my friend tonight if I wanted to sneak up on anyone, but it was also making it impossible to find anyone I might wish to sneak up on. All things considered, I would rather it was dry and clear instead. As we crept forward a little more, the sound of voices coming from the inside of the wooden building became audible. Was it them? We had no way of knowing.

'Do you see a window on this level?' asked Dad, his voice a quiet whisper. We were crouched by the edge of the wall that faced the village.

'No, not on the three sides we have been able to see. There's a large door just around this corner. I could see light framing its edges. We won't be able to tell if mum is in there or not until we go in and we have no way of knowing how many are inside or who they are.'

'We also don't know if they are doing anything wrong. It could be some fishermen in there cleaning their nets for all we can tell from here. My stupid wife could be back in the pub right now knocking back wine.' We both knew she wasn't of course. Dad was scared for his wife and his fear was manifesting in foolish words.

'Time to kick down the door, Dad?'

'Time to kick down the door,' he agreed. We would either make fools of ourselves because there were fishermen inside tending their nets or we would gain a brief upper hand over whoever was in there. I was starting to wish we had taken the cutlasses. They would make handy weapons right now.

I stood up, flexing my muscles to gee myself up for the task ahead. If there were hostiles inside, we would have only a couple of seconds to deal with them before those we had not reached would get over the shock of our sudden appearance and be upon us. The danger of finding ourselves outnumbered was very real and we were ignoring it.

I offered Dad my hand, he grasped it and let me haul him up from his crouched position. He was keeping quiet about any discomfort, but I knew he had bad knees, and we had run several miles now.

His jaw was set with a determined look. We turned to the door as one. It was a big thing, twice the size of a door one might find on a modern house and half as high again, but it also looked old and a little brittle. I held up my right hand with three fingers extended. 'On three,' I whispered.

I folded my fingers into my hand one at a time.

Three.

We heard movement inside the building.

Two.

Someone shouted something undiscernible

One.

We both lifted our right legs and kicked out hard just as Gretchen opened the door. On her tiny frame both our boots connected with her boobs. Dad kicked her in the right boob, I kicked her in the left. She flew backward into the building, tumbling onto her back then over on her head and shoulders to finally land on her front. She didn't move.

But neither did we. So dumbfounded by the door opening that we just stood still and watched the tiny woman spin end over end.

'Michael!' yelled my mother, snapping me back to reality. Dad was already moving. Mum was tied to a chair. Actually, tied to a chair with rope like this was some old detective movie. The dogs barked, bringing my attention to them. They were inside a lobster pot!

There were five people in the room not including myself and my parents. The two drone pilots were the only men, and they were both moving to intercept my dad. He was breaking into a run to barrel through them both to get to mum.

Of the two women, one was Gretchen, and she was down for the count and the other was Tilda. I was sure at least one of them was a murderer, so while they were small and fragile older ladies, I was not going to dismiss them as harmless.

Dad slammed into one of the skinny drone guys, attempting to push him off with a stiff arm to his face like one might in a rugby game. It might have worked if the other hadn't hit him at the same time. The second man collided with my dad. If I hadn't been snoozing by the door taking it all in, I might have been able to prevent it but now dad was falling to one side from the impact and the man was still shoving against him and throwing a few good punches to Dad's ribcage as he went.

You don't do that with me around though and get to enjoy it for long. Just as my dad was falling backward and both drone pilots were regaining their balance I arrived at their location. I had been no more than a couple of seconds behind dad, which had been enough for them to get to him first but now it was my turn, and I was going to show them what three decades of martial arts and fight training could do against two nerdy, skinny kids.

One swung a punch at where he hoped my head might be about to go, but I had already grabbed the other man as he was getting back to upright and swung myself around him. Using my body as a counterweight, I swung around him, holding onto his coat, planted my feet behind him and flung him into his friend. There was a crack of skulls as their foreheads collided. They fell away from me, neither one knocked out but both reeling from the blow to their heads. I turned to Dad and offered him my hand to get up.

'Let's get mum, shall we?'

'Oh, my boys!' she exclaimed, excitement and pride in her voice. 'My wonderful boys.'

We crossed the floor to mum, but we didn't get there. Just as we were a few feet away a shot rang out bringing us to an instant halt. The noise was deafening in the wooden building.

'Not so fast,' said Roberta. She was standing in the doorway behind us, flanked on either side by the two pirates we had left her dealing with.

Betrayal and Deceit

In her hands, she was holding a shotgun. The two goons in their pirate costumes had one each as well and they were all aimed squarely at me.

'It's about damned time, Roberta.' Tilda snapped as she crossed the room to see if her sister was alright. Gretchen still hadn't moved since dad and I kicked her.

'I told you not to trust her!' yelled my mother, raising her voice so that everyone would be able to hear that she had, of course, been right all along. 'I told you.'

Mum had a point. She has been trying to marry me to every woman that has walked too close to me for the last five years or more. Suddenly with Roberta, she changed her mind like there was some odd mother's version of Spidey-sense going on.

Dad and I were more or less in the centre of the room. The building was formed of a single space, there were no partitioning walls anywhere and there were no windows on the ground floor – or rather, what would be ground floor height. Near the roof, some three yards up the wooden

249

walls, there were a series of small openings on each of the two longs sides. There was no electricity in the building, so the light was being provided by a pair of hurricane lamps and several powerful battery-powered LED light strips. It was almost as light inside as one might find in a modern dwelling at night, but the building contained fishermen's equipment as I had guessed, so there were wooden beams crossing the expanse of the roof some two and a half yards up. They weren't loaded with anything currently, but there was other equipment stacked in piles around the room, the effect of which was that the light shining from different spots in the room where the lamps had been placed caused a map of shadows.

Ultimately, it meant that dad and I had nowhere to go, so when Roberta moved further inside the building followed by the two shotgun-wielding pirates we had no choice but to comply with her orders.

'On your knees,' Roberta ordered. Mum was squirming in her chair trying to get loose, but her bindings were too tight.

Tilda was getting Gretchen into a sitting position; she was conscious again.

'Are you okay, Mary?' Dad asked, ignoring all the madness around him. She nodded, perhaps not trusting her own voice. We were in trouble and they both knew it.

'Mike, Ralph.' Roberta took charge. 'We'll have to carry them to the boat. Stay there for now and don't let them move. We are going to need rope.' Ignoring us momentarily, Roberta strode across the room to check on her own mother.

'Any ideas?' Dad whispered.

He was rewarded with a whack to the back of the head with a shotgun butt. Mike and Ralph had taken up hostage management positions behind us. 'Keep quiet, old man,' Ralph hissed.

Satisfied that her mum was not seriously hurt, Roberta turned her attention back to us. 'You couldn't just leave, could you?'

'You gave me the address at the edge of the village, so you could get the drones in place.' I indicated behind me with my head at the two morons. I heard them stiffen but no blow to my skull arrived.

'Everyone else that has seen the drone-generated pirates has run away terrified. What makes you so special that you walk towards them?'

'I'm not stupid?' I replied. 'The drones have been operated by Mike and Ralph. They were both employed by Edington to help you keep people off the streets at night.' She had stiffened when I mentioned Edington. 'Did you really think no one would work it out?' I paused and looked around the room. 'What shocks me is that you managed to keep it all so secret that not even your mother knows.'

'What are you talking about, man?' chirped up Gretchen. 'I have been running this from the start. Tilda and I dreamed it all up.'

'Yeah, and who the hell is Edington?' asked Tilda.

'Yeah,' echoed John.

I looked around the room.

'Actually, I'm afraid you didn't dream it up. Any of it. You invested in property, businesses, real estate and land once Tilda learned that Julien Hogg was going to open a hotel on the cliffs above you and charter cruise ships into the harbour. Then, when he changed his mind you found that you had borrowed yourselves into enormous debt and the land and property was worthless. With no tourists to sell to all year round, this is just another sleepy Cornish fishing village that no one ever comes to. You needed to get your money back, so you set out to make the village more desirable. Tilda started pinning warning notes to houses and properties that were less than perfect and you waged a campaign against anyone who was not white because you are racists.' Neither woman protested. 'Where did the pirate idea come from though? Was it John? He worked on the set of The Pirates of Penzance in the West End as a make-up artist. He said he was good enough to turn himself and Edington into fake dead pirates, didn't he? Did you really think that no one would spot that? Where did he get the idea from though?'

I looked at John. Involuntarily he glanced at his sister. Everyone saw it.

'So, Gretchen you concocted the ghostly pirates and set out to enact your plan. Did you set out to just scare people away or did you think you could attract tourists with the rumour of ghosts haunting the village? You got ambitious because the ghosts worked so well and decided to use the pirates to scare off some of the less desirable residents. People whose property was in need of renovation, the Indian family with their restaurant, the smell from which failed to evoke the traditional smell of Cornwall. How you came to your plan doesn't matter actually Gretchen because the idea was never yours.' I had been staring at Roberta the whole time I was speaking.

I turned now to face to Gretchen and Tilda. 'Think about the timing of it, ladies. How soon after Gary Wainwright found gold coins on the beach did the idea of the ghosts come about?'

They looked at each other, their faces a mask of confusion.

'Enough stalling,' snapped Roberta. 'It's time to clean

up this mess. Get rid of these three and get back to business.'

I spun to face her now. 'Why did you kill your uncle?'

Dad nudged my arm. 'Look at Tilda, son.'

Tilda's face was a mask of pure rage. 'What does he mean, Roberta?'

I ignored the question. 'Did he see you coming out of the house? I understand he liked to visit other lady's houses at night. Isn't that right, Tilda? He could easily have spotted you exiting the house on Heavitree Road. Were you carrying gold down to the beach at the time? Or was it something else that tipped him off?'

'You killed my Philip?' Tilda growled.

'What was that about gold, Roberta?' Asked Gretchen.

Next with a question was John, 'What does he mean the property deal fell through, Mum? You said we were going to be rich.'

'You killed my Philip!' roared Tilda, this time abandoning Gretchen and running at Roberta, arms outstretched and ready to kill.

Roberta took a step back and swung the shotgun from me to her aunt. Tilda ignored it though, whether by calculation that her Niece would not shoot or through the blindness of her rage, she bowled into the smaller woman, knocking her over and grabbing for the shotgun.

Thirty-Three reversed the gun he was holding and whacked Tilda in the side of her head with the butt end. She dropped like a stone.

'That's quite enough of that,' he said, his voice no longer the slow slurring voice of a moron, but one that enunciated clearly in a clipped British tone. With one meaty hand, he reached down, grabbed Roberta by the hair and pulled her from the floor. He pressed the shotgun to her neck. 'Anyone moves, and I blow her head clean off.'

'Go for it,' I instructed.

'No!' shrieked Gretchen.

'What are you doing, Thirty-Three?' asked John, utter bewilderment on his face.

Briefly taking the shotgun away from Roberta's neck, he swung it backhanded into John's face. A spray of blood shot from his nose as he toppled backward. The shotgun John had been holding went skittering off into the shadows.

'Now?' whispered my dad.

I shook my head. 'Everyone, I would like you to meet the brains behind the crimes being committed.' I locked eyes with Thirty-Three.

'You must be kidding,' Laughed Gretchen. 'He couldn't outwit a piece of toast.'

'Actually, Gretchen, Edington has a Ph.D. in maritime history, and he was a commander in the Royal Navy. That's where he met Roberta. Isn't that right, Edington?'

He remained silent, the shotgun still pressed to Roberta's throat in the pretence that he might use it. I gave him a few seconds to speak, then pressed on with my own explanation.

'It was you who dropped the coins, wasn't it? An accident. A rip in a bag or something. Until then it was all going smoothly. Suddenly the secret you were keeping, that you had found the treasure, was out. You needed to throw people off the scent. So, your accomplice helped you create the ghosts and the ghost ship so that you could divert attention away from the village and have the treasure hunters all looking for it in the sea instead. The ghosts were to keep people off the streets so that you could continue to sneak the treasure out to your yacht at night. It's a nice yacht by the way. Caribbean Dream? Did you name it? Or was it on the yacht when you bought it. I'm sorry, I don't know how the yacht name registration thing works.' His face was becoming thunderous. I knew too much. I pressed on. 'How many houses did you search looking for where the pirates buried the treasure all those years ago? Did you anticipate that you would have to play the idiotic Thirty-Three for this long?'

Next to Edington, John began to rouse. The blow to his face had knocked him out briefly.

'Is any of this true?' Gretchen asked her daughter.

'Go on, Roberta. Tell her,' I goaded. Roberta was continuing the pretence that she was being held prisoner. I turned to look behind me. I was bored with being on my knees, but the two drone pilots still had their shotguns trained on my dad and me.

'Of course, Edington isn't your real name either, is it? He looked uncomfortable for the first time. 'It threw me for a while. Edington Hungerford. Edington is a village outside Hungerford. I had two very sharp ladies working on it today. Once I worked out that I could not find you anywhere because the name was made up, it was not difficult to track you down.' I turned to Gretchen again. 'Gretchen, I have the dubious pleasure of introducing you to Cameron Lake. Your son-in-law.'

'What?' Gretchen shrieked.

Now Cameron's face looked ready to murder.

'I told you not to trust her!' yelled my mother triumphantly.

'Now?' whispered my father.

'Almost.'

'What kind of man sends his wife to sleep with another man?' I asked loudly. 'Twice, Cameron. Just to keep me distracted. Wouldn't it have been easier to have killed me?'

'I tried,' replied Roberta. 'You have a surprisingly hard skull, Tempest.' She pushed the shotgun away from her neck, finally accepting that no one was buying the ruse anymore. 'I would have finished you off, but I was spotted, so I had to drag you into my house and tend to you instead.'

'Roberta, what are you saying? Did you kill Philip? Is Thirty-Three your husband?'

'Oh, shut up, you ridiculous woman. His name is Cameron. He's the most brilliant man I have ever met, and we are on the cusp of being ridiculously rich. Philip tried to blackmail me. That's why he's dead.'

'But your mother and your aunt and your brother have an important role to play in this, don't they, Roberta?'

'What does he mean?' Gretchen asked.

On the floor by Roberta's feet, Tilda's eyes had opened. She was listening. Behind me, the two drone pilots were whispering to one another, quiet insistent noises that I could not make out, but they were arguing about something and thus were distracted from the task of watching my dad and me.

It was almost time. First though, I needed to finish the distraction. 'How do they create the clean getaway, Gretchen?' I let the question hang in the air for a moment. 'By leaving the police with a neat solution to the case. I'm afraid Gretchen that your darling daughter and her husband plan to kill you and the others and make it look like you were fighting over the gold and turned on each other.'

'That's preposterous,' snapped Roberta with a derisory laugh.

'Then why did you plant gold at the pub?'

Roberta's mouth hung open. It had been a bluff on my part to turn Gretchen, John, and Tilda against her, but somehow, I had it right.

'I expect it has been found by now. I was worried that your call for back up might not have got through, so I called the police as well. Just in case, you know.'

'You bastard!' she screamed. Then she was running at me, but Gretchen moved to intercept her.

'Now?' asked my dad.

'Yup, now.' As I said the words I was already moving, coming around to grab the shotgun behind me and push its barrels away. As I grabbed the steel it went off, the noise deafening in the close confines. Despite the instant heat transferring to my hands, I ripped it from the lighter man's grip and swung it around in a backhand arc. My father had managed to get off the floor, but his knees were as old as the rest of him, his reactions slower than mine and he was locked in a death grip with Ralph who had been standing behind him.

The stock of the shotgun in my grip hit Ralph full in his mouth, knocking him backward and taking all the fight out of him. He dropped to the floor, leaving my father holding the shotgun. My dad and I locked eyes for a second but there was no time to talk.

One drone pilot was down, and the other had scarpered. That left Tilda, Gretchen, Roberta, John, and Cameron to deal with. I spun to face them. 'Get mum!' I yelled as I slapped dad on his shoulder. He needed no further motivation. I had hoped the damned police would have found us by now, but they hadn't, so my sole aim was to get my family safe. They could pick up Roberta, Cameron and all the others later. I would have given the police a location to find us at but when I had called them

I had no idea where we would be by the time they arrived.

Cameron was gone. Tilda and John were still down, and Roberta was fighting her mother. And she was losing. As I watched, glancing across to see my father get to my mother and start untying her, I saw Gretchen punch her daughter in the mouth. Roberta tumbled backward. I watched no more.

'I told you not to trust her,' said my mother yet again. She was free now and being led out of the shed by my father.

'Come on, boy!' he called to me with urgency, his right arm around his wife. In his left hand, he had the lobster pot with my dogs in. They were staring through the gaps at me. To hell with Roberta and the others. I was on holiday with my family and this case was solved.

I dropped the shotgun I was holding. It was empty anyway and I walked out the door after my parents. I had a fleeting fantasy about a cold pint at the pub then realised the improbability of that happening. There was another pub in the village that I had not yet been in, so I guess we were going there if there was going to be a drink tonight.

'Mr. Michaels,' a shrill voice called my name. It was the Superintendent. She was running down the path that led to the fishermen's shacks with half a dozen armed officers. The Officers trained their guns on all three of us. Dad was still holding the shotgun he had taken which was bound to make them nervous.

A quickly issued instruction from the Superintendent changed their aim.

'In there,' I indicated to the shack we had just vacated.

The armed police rushed past us. Pausing briefly as she followed them, the superintendent asked if we were hurt.

'Nothing of concern,' my father replied.

'Roberta and her family are in there along with one of the drone pilots I told you about. They were using some high-tech camera gear to project images of the pirates. I saw them for myself. They were very convincing. The chap behind it all escaped though, as did Michael Shornecliffe, the other drone pilot.'

'Where?' she asked, looking around.

'I didn't see which way either man went.'

'Nor I,' added my father.

'They will not be able to get far. The road out of the village is blocked.' There was noise coming from the shack now. Shouted instructions from the armed Officers as they secured the building. The Superintendent left us to join them, issuing orders to some other unseen force via her radio as she went.

I caught up with my father and took the lobster pot from him. 'Let's get the dogs out of there, shall we?' The catch was a little fiddly, mostly through unfamiliarity. Once I worked out how simple it was to open, my two dopey sausages plopped happily out of the confined space and into my arms, their kisses showering me in dog saliva.

'Isn't anyone going to ask me what happened?' demanded my mother. 'I got kidnapped.'

My father and I just looked at each other.

'How about a glass of wine, Mary?' Dad asked. 'Then you can tell us all about being kidnapped.'

Mother beamed a smile at her husband. 'Oh, Michael. You do know me well.'

Happily, and with my father and I either side of her, the three of us holding hands in a line and the two dogs trotting ahead of us, we left the beach behind and went in search of refreshment.

Are We Done Yet?

I didn't get far from the beach before I thought of something that turned me around. I sent my parents on without me, promising that I would be along shortly. The dogs followed me when I whistled for them. I had no idea what had happened to their leads. Fortunately, they were quite obedient and stayed close by.

I caught the flashing lights of more emergency services sweeping down the road into Cawsand. The strobe lights weren't accompanied by sirens, unnecessary to clear the way when there is no traffic to clear. I picked up the dogs and stepped to the edge of the road to allow the ambulance and two police cars to pass me. I was almost back at the shack, so the vehicles drew to a halt just in front of me, uniforms spilling from each vehicle in a rush.

I was looking for John, but it was Roberta I came across first. Sergeant Andrews was leading her out of the shack towards a waiting police van. Her hands were cuffed behind her back, any resistance well and truly gone now. Her pretty hair and face were a mess, blood visible on her lower lip and a chunk of hair sticking out perpendicular to her head where it had most likely been yanked.

I was quite content to dismiss her, but she called my name, 'Tempest.' I turned to face her. 'I'm sorry. I think you're a great guy.' She shrugged apologetically. 'For what it's worth, I don't regret sleeping with you. I wish I had met you sooner.' She was being very open and honest. For the first time.

I considered just walking away, but it irked me that she thought she could make things better with a heartfelt apology. 'Roberta you are a crazed, greedy, psychopathic murderer. I will regret meeting you for the rest of my life.' My own heartfelt reply delivered, I turned away from her desperately hurt face. I could hear her being bundled forcibly into the van as I went in search of John.

Inside the shack, Gretchen and Tilda were being treated by paramedics. By the look of things, Tilda had suffered a heart attack. Armed police were standing by but neither woman was restrained, the threat from either probably minimal.

I finally spotted John. He was in handcuffs being led away to the waiting police van outside. He would be taken to a cell, processed, charged and locked up. He was guilty of GBH or worse and he was a fairly despicable human. He also made the world's best granola, and I needed the recipe. I doubted he would give it up, but I had to ask.

He turned as I called his name. 'What?'

'John, I realise you probably have no desire to be a pal. However, I was hoping you would give me the recipe for your granola.'

'What?' his face was a mask of disbelief. 'You have got to be kidding.'

'John, you make the best granola on the planet. Let the

recipe survive this,' I implored. He was still being led away by the police, and we were nearing the van now. I only had a few seconds left.

'Okay, okay. But only because I think you're cute.' I steadied my mind to memorise the recipe and ingredients. 'First, I take whole blanched almonds and fire raisins and bake them in the oven. While they are baking, I take McVities original Hobnobs biscuits, not the chocolate chip ones, it has to be the originals, and I crush them by hand. This is important because if you use a machine, you will get dust and not the wonderful chunks that you want.'

'Hold on.' What he had said had just registered. 'The base for your granola is smashed up Hobnobs biscuits?'

'Yes. How else do you think I get it to taste so amazing? Next you...' I waved him into silence and walked away.

No wonder I was feeling bloated, and my trousers were tight. I had eaten a whole packet of cookies for breakfast every day this week. I patted my stomach and chuckled ruefully. 'Come on, boys,' I said to the dogs. They were by my feet, looking up at me hopefully. It occurred to me that I had not fed them this evening, they were undoubtedly wondering what was going on. 'Let's get some dinner, shall we?'

I would find my parents and deal with my own needs later. Quietly walking back up the street towards the darkened Sea Pilgrim the Superintendent's words echoed in my head. "He won't get far, the road out of the village is blocked." At the time when she had said it, I had felt reassured. There is only one road in or out, but he had been coming and going by sea all along. The gold would be too heavy or cumbersome to take through the village to a car, so he had been carrying it down to the coast and loading it into a boat to then row out to his yacht. I even knew where because it was where he had dropped the coins one morning.

What to do? Alert the Superintendent? Maybe he was already gone. I would take a walk and see. It seemed like a simple solution to my unanswered question. He had most likely headed straight there when he fled the shack.

He hadn't though. Displaying that greed can never be satisfied, he had gone back to the house for more gold. Coming along The Cleave I spotted him running back across the beach. In the darkness, it was just a darkened figure that could have been anyone, but the furtiveness of the figure's movements told me it was him.

He climbed back up to street level and crossed the road to head back up to the house. Was he really after more gold? I could soon put a stop to his greed. I pulled out my phone to call the police. They would route a message back to the uniforms here on the ground in seconds. My phone was dead though. It had been in my pocket all afternoon and not charged since last night.

I debated going back to find the police at the shack. I knew though that I was going to have to tackle him myself. If I went for help and he got away I would berate myself for months for my cowardice. If only I didn't have the damned dogs with me.

It was too late to do anything about it. 'Come on, chaps,' I called quietly to them as I set off at a jog towards the house on Heavitree Road.

The front door to the house was open when I got there. The lights were not on but there was a glow coming from somewhere deep inside. The dogs scrambled in ahead of me. They thought we were visiting someone, to a dachshund, going into a house that was not yours meant food and getting fussed. The noise of their claws skittering on the wooden floorboards sure to alert Cameron to my arrival.

I shut the front door behind me, trapping us all inside. I thought about waiting for him to emerge rather than go looking for him in the dark house and walk into whatever trap he might have hastily arranged. Waiting though would mean the dogs would be with me when Cameron and I fought. I went through to the next room and shut the door on the dogs, separating me from them. Bull immediately whined at the door. I ignored him.

The glow was coming from a hole in the floor. Lights had been jury-rigged on a cable that led from a socket in the wall down through the hole. A wooden ladder was poking out through the hole. I moved over and looked down through it. All I needed to do was pull up the ladder and he would be trapped.

I could get the police at my leisure.

I grabbed for the ladder, but I had missed my chance. Cameron was coming back up it. He looked up at me as I was looking down into the hole at him. His giant, meaty hands were gripping the ladder rungs. Staring up at me with a delighted grimace on his face, it was clear he fancied his chances. His thick-set neck and muscular shoulders were all I could see as he climbed. I remembered just how big he was. The question now was whether the muscle was for show, like a bodybuilder gets, or if it was truly functional in which case he would be as strong as an ox. I told myself the muscle would make him slow. I also told myself the sensible thing to do was grab the dogs and run for help.

He said, 'So glad you stopped by, Tempest,' as his head emerged above floor level. I wanted to kick it, but decency dictated I let him gain his feet before I attacked. 'Aren't you going to warn me the police are coming? Tell me I need to run?'

'No. My plan is to beat you to a pulp and hand you over to them.'

He chuckled. 'I have to admire your spirit, little man. I think your mirror might be broken though.' He was off the ladder now, squaring off against me. I was watching his eyes, waiting for the move. 'I'm twice your size and at least twice as strong.'

He twitched his eyes at my hands. The tell just before the move. We were six feet apart, no distance at all but the small room was barely more than twelve feet across so there was nowhere to go when he lunged. If he had expected me to dart away, he was sorely mistaken.

He came with both hands trying to grab hold of me. I made like I was going to try to take a step back then lunged forward to punch him squarely in the face. He reeled back from the blow as I grabbed his right arm and swung under it. His forearm was dirty and sweaty though from working down the hole and my grip failed.

Where I had intended to turn his arm against its elbow joint and force him down, I fell backward instead, landing on my butt and rolling quickly away. Not quick enough. A boot caught my ribs, right on the site of the injury I had sustained a couple of weeks ago and with a whoosh, the air left my lungs.

He kicked again, only this time I got my arms in the way, caught the leg as it hit me and pivoted my own legs around to sweep his remaining foot. He crashed down. I rolled away again, but right into the wall less than a foot behind me. I scrambled quickly to my feet to see that Cameron was across the room. There was distance between us once more so I could reset myself.

I brought my hands up and loosened my limbs, my knees flexed to react in whatever way I needed to convert his next attack and turn it against him. He chuckled though, reached down and produced a rusty looking cutlass from a pile of junk on the floor.

I was willing to bet that it was *the* murder weapon used to kill Philip Masonberg and very possibly to cleave open Matthew Todd's head. I wanted it for evidence. The more pressing task for me now though was avoiding getting cut to ribbons by it. I looked around for something I could use to defend myself. As he came for me, I grabbed the only thing I could see – the wooden ladder I had not been able to yank out of the hole earlier.

He swung the cutlass, aiming to take my head clean off. It thunked hard into the wooden ladder and stuck. Thankfully the weapon was blunt, but he was quick enough to kick me with a swinging boot that luck, not skill allowed me to catch on the meat of my right thigh.

The ladder was about eight feet long, giving me a ton of leverage. I cranked it hard through a perpendicular plane. I wanted to yank the cutlass from his grip. The result though was that he ripped the weapon free and hacked at me again. This time he put more force behind it and cut the top rung in two. His eyes flared triumphantly as he hacked again, this time lopping a piece off a ladder leg. My eight-foot weapon was shrinking.

I swung at him with it, boxing him with both ends. In turn, he stabbed at me point first meaning to skewer me. One, two, three times he thrust the blade forward. I parried the first one down, the second one up, but the third came right through the gap between the rungs.

Perfect.

I folded the ladder from perpendicular to the floor to

horizontal, trapping his arm as I do so. Inevitably it pulled his arm and thus his face downwards. Seizing my chance, I whipped the ladder back up before he could bring his greater strength to bear. The wood caught under his chin, the cutlass came free and he fell backward.

But he didn't fall over. He was still on his feet, his eyes locked on a point on my torso. Then he looked back up at me and grinned once more. I glanced down.

There was blood on the floor, and it was mine.

When his weapon had come through the rungs it had caught my side. Blood was coming through my clothing and seeing it I became aware of the damp sticky feeling and a stinging sensation low on the right side of my ribs.

We locked eyes. He was readying himself for the next attack. The Cutlass was halfway between us but off to the side where it was not convenient for either of us. If one of us dove for it, the other need only wait and then kick their opponent once he was stooping to pick it up. He was waiting for me to make my move. He was convinced he was going to win.

Well, stuff that.

I took the fight to him. He swung a punch. I parried it with my left forearm and hit him in the face with my right fist and kept going. He tried to kick me, a giant foot arcing up towards my face. My right arm went out and around to trap the leg under my armpit as it struck me. Then I took a fast step back to pull him off balance and kicked him in the nuts.

The blow hit home. I let his leg go as he folded into himself. Then I noticed our positions relative to the room, took two steps back and three to my left then ran, leapt and kicked him in the chest with everything I could muster. He flew backward, slammed into the wall behind him and fell down the hole. Triumphantly I picked the ladder up and walked towards the door as he howled his disbelief.

I tried to think of something cool to say.

Nothing came though, so I shrugged and went looking for my parents and a cold pint.

A Cold Pint

Before I could refresh my palate, I still needed to feed the dogs and alert the police to the location of the master criminal. I was getting a bit weary, finding the police again felt like a lot of effort but I did it anyway.

I found the Superintendent still down at the shack. There were crime scene type people there now, the armed Officers were packing up and of Gretchen, Roberta and the others, there was no sign.

'Ah, Mr. Michaels. I'm glad you are here. I need a statement from you. I will need to interview your parents as well.'

'I have Cameron Lake and the murder weapon, I think.'

'I'm sorry.'

'Cameron Lake. The guy behind it all. Your roadblock was never going to stop him because he was leaving by boat. I have him trapped in a basement. Oh yeah, when I called you to tip you off about Roberta, I forgot to mention that I found the treasure.'

'The treasure?'

Goodness, this was hard work. 'Yes, Superintendent. The treasure that twenty ships full of treasure hunters are at sea every day looking for. The half a billion pounds of gold, silver, and jewels that is supposed to have gone down on the Merchant Royal in 1641. Ringing any bells?' I waited to see if she had any questions.

'Oh. Oh, I see. Well, perhaps you should show me where he is then.' The Superintendent never seemed to get excited. She did react though, calling Sgt Andrews over and having her round up three more uniformed Officers so they could all follow me back to Heavitree Road.

I turned to start the walk back to Heavitree Road yet again. I talked as we walked. 'The ships are looking in the wrong place. The treasure, at least quite a lot of it, was buried in the basement of a house on Heavitree Road. Quite how it had stayed hidden there all these centuries I cannot imagine, but Cameron tracked it down, probably by reading several of the same letters, logs and accounts that I have plus an awful lot more besides.'

'I would guess that he has been excavating in that house for months, taking it out to his yacht at night under cover of darkness. He dropped some coins one night and their discovery was the catalyst for everything else. You probably ought to get on the radio and get a police launch out to look on board a yacht called Caribbean Dream. It's moored out near the harbour entrance.'

'Tempest?' The call came from behind me. I didn't need to turn around though to know that it was Rebecca Franks. Undoubtedly drawn by the flashing red and blues that had swept through town and were still flashing their strobe lights even now. I turned anyway, resignation in my movements.

Rebecca was jogging along the road towards me, the two men that formed her crew trying to keep up. Bull and

Dozer assumed their natural defensive posture, appearing from nowhere to run headlong at the woman, barking for all they are worth. Fortunately, being attacked by a miniature dachshund is not that terrifying. A little startling maybe, but there really isn't much danger of injury unless they manage to trip a person.

'Goodness!' She exclaimed as they ran at her feet.

'Dogs,' I called to them so that it sounded like I was at least trying to bring them back to heel. They had arrived at her feet and seemed confused about what to do next. She had stopped running in her surprise, so they were giving her a sniff.

'Tempest, might I ask you what is happening please?' she had learned some manners since our last meeting.

'Good evening, Rebecca. Perhaps you would like to accompany the Superintendent and me. The master criminal is trapped not far from here in the basement of a house where pirates buried treasure many hundreds of years ago. If you want a fantastic exclusive for the ten o'clock news, then this is it.' As I said it, I wondered if her face might not make it right around the world. The treasure story was quite something.

'You will give me all of that?' her voice full of barely suppressed awe and excitement.

'And more. I have a lady that was kidnapped for stumbling across the conspiracy earlier today. I believe she will be only too pleased to give you her story. There are layers here Rebecca. A week's worth of stories.'

'I may want to have your babies,' she squealed.

We were nearing the house on Heavitree Road once more. The dogs were being very good about me failing to feed them. Perhaps I would give them something special for their dinner tonight. Rebecca had positioned herself in front of me, walking in reverse, the camera trained on me, the Superintendent, Sgt Andrews and the other Officers behind us.

'Hold on,' said the Superintendent, a thought occurring to her. 'I have a question. I saw the ghost ship for myself. How was this man managing to make that appear at will? It looked so convincing.'

'Tethered alongside his yacht is a submersible. On it is fitted a huge sheet of Perspex, behind which is a projector of some kind. I believe the submersible to be remotely controlled. The projector sends an image of the ghost ship to the Perspex screen, and he can make the ship rise from the waves and vanish again at will. Doubtless, it's more complex than that or works slightly differently to how I have described, but I looked at it today and that is my best guess. Your tech chaps can work it out for themselves once they impound it.'

Inside the House on Heavitree Lane

Cameron had recovered from his kick in the spuds but was still stuck down his hole. He had some choice threats to make about my future when they dragged him out and handcuffed him. I paid him no mind.

The ladder that I had used to defend myself was used to gain access to the hole again so that the Superintendent could inspect the basement for herself. I followed her down. Inside was lit by mains powered lamps that branched off from the cable I had seen coming into the hole. Had this originally been a smuggler's hold carved into the floor of the house to keep goods away from excise men? A memory of reading Daphne Du Maurier's Jamaica Inn as a schoolboy told me that sort of thing went on continually a few centuries ago. Regardless of its original purpose, the pirates had brought the treasure to shore, probably killed the people that lived in the house and had hidden everything they could carry in this hole in the ground. Had they then backfilled it to bury it? Had they had time? Had someone else done it? Someone like the Captain of HMS

273

Cruelty. Bury the treasure, pay off a few local officials and the men you employed to do the work and come back for it later. Then something happened, an untimely death perhaps and the treasure remained where it was. Forgotten for generations until one man, one determined man tracked it down. Had Cameron Lake made his discovery public he would have been famous, and his reward would have made him quite rich enough. But then the greedy are never rich enough, are they?

The space he had dug out was large enough to be called a room. I called back up to Rebecca that she should grab a camera and come down. There was room for one more. The work of excavating the space must have been back-breaking. He had erected timbers to shore up where he was digging out. There might have been some original timbers in here that had long since rotted away and it was clear that whatever the treasure had been brought ashore in had also rotted away as there were gold coins just spilling onto the floor from the dirt of the walls.

'My God,' Rebecca whispered breathlessly. She reigned in her composure then and turned the camera to herself. As I moved away, I could hear her begin reporting what she was seeing. As she began jabbering away, I heard one of my dogs whine from the room above me. I was done here.

I climbed up the ladder, telling the Superintendent that I needed to eat and needed to feed my dogs and where she would be able to find me this evening. She said I was free to go, but honestly, I would have liked to have seen anyone try to stop me.

I picked the two dopey dachshunds up and carried them out to the street, kissing them both on top of their heads as we went.

Around the corner, I knew there was a fish and chip

shop. I had not gone far when I caught the first smell coming from it. My stomach gave a groan.

'You can't come in here looking like that,' The lady behind the counter snapped.

I looked down at myself. I looked like a homeless person. Dirt, blood, and goodness knows what else had stained and marked my clothing. I turned to check myself in the reflection of the glass door. My hair was a mess, and I had dirt on my face as well.

'I just want a fish and chips,' I implored. 'I have money.' I added just in case she did think I was homeless.

'I don't care. This is a clean establishment. People expect hygiene where they buy their food.'

A hand clapped me on the shoulder. I turned to find the three men left over from Gina's crew. I really didn't have the energy for another fight right now but doubted I would get a choice in the matter.

'Thanks for what you did for Matt,' the nearest man said. I raised an eyebrow. I thought his name was Ivan. I couldn't remember.

'Sorry about giving you grief this week,' Danny piped up. 'Can we get you something from the shop?' he offered.

This was better than finding treasure. I thanked them and asked for a large fish and chips, open with lots of salt and vinegar. I offered them money to pay for it, but they insisted it was on them.

I fell onto the hot food hungrily when they brought it out of the shop, the woman inside scowling at me through the glass. Just to be contrary I sat on the floor to share it with the dogs right outside her shop door. I thanked the guys as they walked away and almost lost a finger because I was watching them and not what the dachshunds were doing.

The large portion was plenty to fill all three of us. Satisfied, I clawed myself back to a standing position. I still wanted a cold drink, and it had been an hour since I sent my parents to the pub without me. I hoped they weren't worried about me.

They were not as it turned out because Rebecca Franks had already found them. It was my first time inside The Star Inn, I got a few looks as I came through the door, but no one tried to stop me from joining my family.

Dad was keeping quiet while Rebecca Franks, the professional journalist, was trying to get a word in edgeways with my mother. He spotted me, jumped up and came to shake my hand.

'Okay, kid?' he asked, taking in the obvious wound to my side.

'It's fine. No big deal.'

'Cold one?'

'Damned right.'

Postscript

I plugged in my phone to charge and lay my head down to sleep. I was bone tired. The phone did nothing for a second or so, but just as I was closing my eyes it sprung to life with incoming messages all coming at once now that I had given it some energy.

I reached across to look at the screen, just to check.

Seven missed calls from Big Ben. Four missed calls from Amanda and finally a text message from Jane.

The text message read:

Boss, I think Amanda and Patience have been taken by the Voodoo priest. Big Ben went to investigate, and I have not heard from him since. That was hours ago. Call me when you get this.

I called Jane's number. No answer.

I sat up in bed suddenly sober and awake. I called Big Ben. It went straight to voicemail:

'Hey there, you have reached the voicemail of Big Ben. If you're a girl just leave your number after the tone along with your address, then get naked, and wait for me. I won't be long. If this is a dude calling, then take it easy and try to not feel too bad when your girlfriend sleeps with me.'

I didn't bother to leave a message. I tried Amanda and got no answer from her either. I had no number for Patience and I was getting angry, my ire rising due to frustration. Still sitting on the edge of the fold-out bed, I tried to quickly review my options.

I didn't appear to have any. My friends were in trouble somewhere. It didn't matter that I was tired, or that I was sore from fighting this evening. It didn't matter that it would take me hours to get back to Kent and that I had no idea where they were. I had to go.

I started packing my bags, shoving my things in as quickly as I could. I was leaving right now. I would call my parents from the car. They were still at the pub, so unless I bumped into them as I was going, they would return to the room and wonder where I was. They were enjoying their break, and they could not help with my latest problem. I would not even tell them about it.

'Come on, dogs,' I called as I opened the door and stepped outside.

They both hopped off the bed. We were off for another adventure, and they were my willing wingmen. With the two small dogs scampering along behind me, I headed once more into the dark and an uncertain future.

Afterword

Hi there,

Firstly, thank your purchasing this book. I hope that you enjoy reading it anywhere near as much as I enjoyed writing it. If you did, then I have a growing library of other books to make you laugh and keep you turning pages when you really ought to be going to sleep.

The next book in the series overlaps the timeline of this one as Amanda Harper, Big Ben, and Jane get into hot water back in Kent while Tempest is in Cornwall. Originally, I wrote and published the two series separately but then had to combine them when I found myself inundated with requests for the correct reading order. It came as a demonstration of how much I had to learn. Crafting a fun story that draws the reader in is just one small part of the business. As a self-published novelist, choosing that route because I don't then have to share the money with editors, publicists, bookshops, agents, and goodness knows who else, meant I could make a healthy living from my hobby. It also meant I had to do everything myself and the only bit I knew how to do in advance was write. I wasn't even that good at that as people possessing an early copy of my first book will testify.

A little more than a year after writing this book, I got to transition into writing full time, shedding the shackle of my day job to do something that inspired me.

There will be many more books to come. I'm about to start on my thirty-eighth and wonder just how many I will write before the sands in my timer run out. One thing I feel certain of, is that I will not run out of ideas.

Take care

Steve Higgs

June 2020

vinci-books.com/doodoo-voodoo

Amanda Harper has been left in charge and this case will leave bodies.

What was she thinking quitting her job in the police for an uncertain future at Blue Moon Investigations? And now her new boss has taken a week off leaving her to run the business. There's no time to dwell on it though as she has a new client, cursed by a voodoo priest. When Amanda's friends start vanishing and the police won't help her, she heads into a climactic ending that threatens to leave a trail of bodies that might include hers.

Turn the page for a free preview…

In the Doodoo with Voodoo:
Chapter One

LAST SHIFT

Sunday, October 30th 1156hrs

I hate running. I was sure I shouldn't have to run this much as a police officer. Surely, when I shout for a criminal to stop running, they should stop. This guy hadn't read the rules though, so he was tearing down Week Street in Maidstone with no intention of slowing down.

He was just a petty pickpocket, one of a gang that had been targeting Maidstone town centre recently, snatching purses and pilfering wallets. Or lifting people's shopping bags when they weren't looking. There was always a crime being committed in Maidstone town centre, it was just that kind of town where people with money mixed with those who did not, and certain parties tried to even the balance.

I was posted in plain clothes to observe and ultimately find the gang. Basically, I' been sent window shopping for the day with a side order of try to pay attention to what's going on around you. It was my very last shift with the police.

I quit several weeks ago when I finally admitted that my career wasn't going anywhere. It coincided with meeting Tempest Michaels, a local, self-employed paranormal investigator. I asked him for a job, and he signed me up right then and there. Now I work for him, but I still have a week of notice left in my old job, so I was kinda working both simultaneously.

Sipping a salted caramel hot chocolate and telling myself that ordering it skinny meant it was really low in calories, I was paying almost no attention to anything, when right in front of me the dopey looking kid with the spots and the dreadlocks walked up to a pram, opened a lady's handbag, and pulled out her purse. He even looked up at me as he slid it into the pocket of his dirty hoody and had the audacity to wink.

I thought he was going to try me with a chat up line until I yanked out my warrant card and shouted for him to stop.

He didn't of course. Which was how I came to now be chasing the ugly, skinny little turd down Week Street towards the river. He was faster than me, but he also wore his jeans hood style, so they were flapping around his backside and threatening to fall down and trip him the whole time. He probably thought they looked cool.

I yelled into my microphone that I was chasing a suspect and needed back up in position. There were three of us working undercover today in different parts of the town centre, but it's so big that we couldn't easily coordinate between us. Uniformed police are also never far away in Maidstone though and today two were positioned at the top of Fremlin Walk where the confluence of roads creates a hub of sorts.

The youth ran by them almost before I could react,

certainly before I could raise a warning to anyone, so my backup was essentially backing me up now by running along behind me.

Not much help.

A cyclist came out of the cut through by Earl's pub, almost knocking the kid with the dreadlocks over. He leaped over his front wheel though as the cyclist saw him at the last moment and hit his brakes. The move put the cyclist directly in my path and I ploughed right into him, the pair of us going down to slam into the ground. Me on top of him with his surprised face jammed between my boobs.

The guys in uniform leapt over the tangle of bike, cyclist, and me to continue the pursuit, but the pickpocket had gained valuable yards. Despite that, the likelihood of him escaping remained slim. Maidstone is too open. There are no clever alleyways to duck down to aid his evasion. His only hope was to pick up a bike or get into a car.

No sooner had the thought left my brain, than a brand-new white Mercedes C220i AMG flew out of the gap by the Hazlitt Theatre. Someone inside threw the passenger's door open, and it skidded to a halt. The youth was going to make it. He had too great a lead to be caught now.

Until Patience clotheslined him.

I didn't even see where she came from. I was still picking myself up and making sure my boobs weren't hanging out of my top. One second, he was home free, the next his body was spinning through the air while his head rotated about Patience's right forearm.

Score one for the girls!

Patience is one of the other officers placed in town to look for the pickpocket gang. We had been sent to different areas of the town to cover the most amount of territory, but she'd been messaging me since we arrived to meet up and work together because she was bored and wanted to quiz me about my boyfriend.

I apologised to the poor cyclist and got moving again.

Seeing his accomplice get taken down, the driver of the Mercedes hit the gas and belted down Week Street towards the A229 where he could filter into the freely moving Sunday traffic and escape. He wasn't having a good day, though.

Ahead of him, the lights changed, and an Argos truck swept out of Pudding Lane. With nowhere to go, I watched the brake lights flash accompanied by the screeching of tyres before he slammed nose first into the side of the truck, ruining the beautiful new German car. To be fair, it was probably stolen.

Patience stood over the thief. I was out of breath, but there was no longer any cause to hurry, so I ambled towards her at a fast walk. Downhill from me, Duncan and Sylvester, the two chaps in uniform, caught up to the ailing car just as the driver tried to bail out. In moments, was cuffed and forced into a sitting position by the car's rear wheel.

'Hey, butt monkey!' Patience was making her arrest. The youth was lying on the pavement groaning a little and slowly writhing around in pain. 'Hey! I'm arresting you for the crime of having a ridiculous haircut, terrible clothes and for being a dirty little purse snatcher.' Patience didn't worry too much about doing her job properly so long as she enjoyed herself.

I arrived at her position where a small crowd was beginning to gather. Human nature dictates shoppers or passersby are always ready for a little street theatre.

'Hey, girl.' She offered me a high five. 'Did you see the sale on at House of Fraser? I nearly spent next month's wages. They have too much fine clothing.'

Thinking what we needed to do was our jobs, I said, 'We should get this one to the station.'

'The uniforms can pick him up in a minute. Patience needs some lunch.' She was staring at my chest. 'You know your boobs are lopsided right?'

I looked down. Dressing this morning for undercover work in town, it hadn't occurred to me to put on a sports bra. I wasn't expecting to chase anyone. I turned away from her to rearrange myself, then realised I had a three-hundred and sixty-degree crowd. My boobs were going to have to wait.

A squad car made its way past the wreckage at the bottom of the road, being waved on by Sylvester. A second car was behind it and behind that a third car which would probably contain Chief Inspector Quinn. The second car peeled off to stay with the crashed Mercedes, so I groaned internally as CI Quinn's car kept on coming.

Both cars ground to a halt right next to us, the crowd parting only when Patience yelled at them to do so.

Three uniformed constables exited the cars, the driver of CI Quinn's car opening the rear door to let him out. He's pompous and pretentious and doesn't realise that having people to open doors for him demonstrates that more clearly than anything else could.

Regardless, he was heading to the top of the ladder and acting as if he ought to be there already worked for him. He and I had an unsteady relationship that went back about six years to when he was my sergeant, and I spurned his advances.

In a few days, it would no longer be of any concern. I didn't hand my ID card back officially until November 8th, but due to overtime coupled with vacation days I never got around to taking, I was finishing today. My uniform and all the paraphernalia that went with it was in the boot of my car ready to be handed back. I had hoped I could wrap the undercover thing up quickly enough to get back to the station and hand it all in, but alas it was already too late for that, so I would have to return tomorrow or the day after.

'Woods, report,' Quinn demanded.

'Got us an ugly idiot with a head full of dreadlocks, Chief. Woman's purse still in his possession. I think he looks like he might try to run again. You want me to kick him in the bollocks?'

The guys in uniform snorted laughter they tried hard to control.

'Woods, you know how I enjoy your reports. Please stick to the facts and try not to embarrass yourself perpetually?' CI Quinn replied deadpan. He's not known for his sense of humour.

'Was that a yes or a no on the bollocks?' she enquired, seeming genuinely unsure. 'A no, then.' She decided, seeing his expression.

I was getting peckish. I had managed one small swig of my hot chocolate before I had to abandon it to chase Mr Dreadlocks, so now I was both hungry and thirsty and it was getting close to lunchtime.

'Do you need anything further from us here, sir?' I asked CI Quinn directly. 'Perhaps Patience and I should return to observing the crowd in case there are more of his gang operating here?'

Ben Swanscombe cuffed the youth and got him to his feet.

'She hit me,' the boy protested. 'She's not allowed to hit me.'

'I stopped you is what I did. You ran into me. I was stationary, and you were moving. You can't claim I hit you if

STEVE HIGGS

I didn't move.' Patience was well used to defending her slightly violent streak.

The youth continued to complain as he was led away and bundled into the back of the squad car.

CI Quinn turned to leave, but over his shoulder, he said, 'I want you both back at the station. You have paperwork to fill out.' He ducked into his car, either to ensure we couldn't reply or probably because he's so disinterested in anything we might have to say that he'd already forgotten us.

'Well, Patience is going for lunch, Chief Inspector. What do you think about that?' she said to the departing car. 'Damn that white boy sure has a stick in his butt. What do you want for lunch girl? Patience is buying?'

'You're buying? You win the lottery or something?' I'm not saying Patience is tight with her money, I just don't remember her ever having any.

'Girl, it's your last day. Or at least it's your last shift. Patience is going to buy you lunch.' Patience was displaying one of her rare moments of seriousness. She's a good friend. The kind I suspected I could rely on if I ever needed to. We had already promised to stay in touch even though we would no longer be working together every week.

'Lunch sounds good,' I replied. It really did.

'And a large glass of pinot,' she added.

'We're still on duty. We're not allowed to drink.'

'Girl, it's your last day. When are you ever going to break the rules if not now? What are they going to do if they catch you?'

She had a point. 'Okay, Patience. A glass of pinot.'

'Large glass.'

'Large glass,' I conceded.

'And shots.'

288

In the Doodoo with Voodoo: Chapter Two

A NEW CASE

Sunday, October 30th 1643hrs

Lunch with Patience had not been a good idea. It seemed like one at the time, especially when the first half glass of cool, crisp, perfect white wine wound its sensuous tendrils of relaxation into me and removed the stress I was feeling. After that took hold, I remember deciding that another glass was a great idea and my planned lunchtime skinny salad had been abandoned in favour of a pizza. Then a third glass had happened and the two of us had slunk back to the Station three hours later, armed with a quickly concocted lie about having seen some probable pickpockets and feeling the need to tail them.

No one asked us where we had been though, as if they hadn't even noticed we were absent. I finished my paper-work, writing up a report about the event in town, the chase, and arrest, while next to me Patience worked her way through several doughnuts she'd picked up on the way back to the station because all the wine had made her hungry.

Whether I was stressed because it was my last day with a steady sensible job and the pay check for it was about to run out, or if I was worried about my new career as a paranormal investigator, I hadn't been introspective enough to work out. When I talked to Patience about it, somewhere between glass two and glass three, she said it was neither thing. In her opinion, I was getting stressed because I knew I was going to have to sleep with my perfect boyfriend soon and now I was worried that she had it right.

I had met Brett Barker about a day after I took the job at the Blue Moon Investigation Agency. He was a prime suspect in the murder of his grandfather, not least because he'd inherited the Barker Steel Mill in Dartford and a sizeable fortune upon the man's death. Tempest Michaels, that's the owner of the Blue Moon business and my boss, thought Brett was guilty, and all the evidence suggested he was. I had arrested him, as I was still a serving police officer, but released him the next day when we determined he was innocent, and he asked me on a date.

That was two weeks ago, and we had been on several dates since. I'm counting him as my boyfriend already, but we haven't yet managed to get to the intimate part of our relationship. Honestly, I don't know why we haven't. There has not been a conversation where we have decided to take it slow. I'm certain he's not gay, and we are both old enough to not be tiptoeing around, yet nothing beyond some passionate kissing has occurred thus far.

Patience assures me that if I don't take him to bed soon, I will lose him. Actually, that wasn't what Patience said. She said … never mind. Let's just say it was a more graphic version of hurry up and take him to bed.

And it was what I was planning to do. He was gorgeous. He was lean and athletic with a handsome face that smiled easily. He's an absolute gentleman and he is seriously rich. Like, buy me an island for my birthday kind of rich. We were taking it in turns to entertain each other. One date he would call the shots and take me out. Sometimes it had been swanky and expensive, like the first date when he put me on a commercial jet flying first class to Paris for an overnight stay at the Penthouse of the Ritz, but he'd also taken me out for dinner in a perfectly ordinary restaurant.

That we earned vastly different amounts was of no concern to him it seemed, it would only be a concern in our relationship at all if I decided it was, so I had to get over it. When it had been my turn to entertain him, I had brought him to my house for pizza, or out to the local cinema because there was a film I wanted to see. Five dates had elapsed now though. Was that too many without some intimacy creeping in?

I had answered the question for myself days ago but had done nothing about it yet. Now it was time to fix the problem before it became one. I would call him tonight, invite him to my flat tomorrow night and shag his beautiful brains out.

The clock on the wall assured me it was nearly finishing time for me. I would have to return in a couple of days to hand back my uniform and again on November 8th to hand over my ID card. I felt no pang of separation at the thought of being without that vital piece of equipment. It was just something I had carried around with me for the last few years.

Just as I was getting out of my chair to leave, my phone rang. The caller ID on the screen told me it was Jane/James calling. Jane/James is Tempest's cross-dressing, gender fluid office assistant. A young man who with a wig, some makeup and a dress, looks more convincing as a woman than I do.

'Amanda Harper,' I answered the phone.

'Hi, Amanda. It's James,' he said. 'Are you coming to work tomorrow? We have a couple of promising cases.'

'I will be there. Just one question: Where is there now?' Two days ago, the Blue Moon office had been subjected to a firebomb and had burned to the ground. It would be rebuilt, but for now, it was very much unusable.

'Tempest has set me up in the office in his house. It feels a bit odd wandering around his house without him here, but at least we are still in business.'

'Tempest isn't there? Where is he?' I asked.

'I'll tell you about it in the morning. Or Tempest will call you I guess,' he replied.

That was cryptic. I dismissed it though. Tempest would come and go in pursuit of cases as he saw fit. He wasn't there to hold my hand and had hired me because of my ability to work independently. The pair of us might work together on cases at times but would just as often attend to separate clients.

'What are the cases?' I asked him.

'There are a few actually. The Tonbridge ghost tours are once again claiming to have a ghost that they want us to investigate, there are some farmers out towards Cliffe that have reported mysterious crop circles coupled with odd behaviour from their cattle. However, the most pressing seems to be from a young lady that has become the target of a voodoo priest.'

'Voodoo?'

'Yes.'

'In Kent?'

'Apparently so. She met some guy on a dating website. He got a little scary and when she broke it off, he cursed her, and her hair has fallen out.'

I had picked my phone up, air-kissed Patience and headed out the door. I had to leave my car in the space behind the station as I wasn't at all certain I was sober enough to drive home. Fortunately, it was only a little more than a mile to my flat by the train station. I was still talking when I got outside and discovered it had started to drizzle.

Nuts.

'Are you still there, Amanda?' James asked.

'Yes, still here. Just fighting with my umbrella.' I needed both hands. 'James, I will see you at Tempest's house at nine o'clock tomorrow. Okay?'

'Sure thing.'

'I expect the cases can wait until then.' I said goodbye and disconnected. The damned umbrella catch was sticking and refusing to open. I was hovering in the doorway at the back of the station grunting and swearing. Finally, it popped, and the handbag-handy brolly flung itself from closed to inside out and then mockingly refused to go back to a useable state. It learned to rue the day as I shoved its useless arse into the first trash bin I came to.

I trudged home through the increasing downpour, my hair a sodden mess on my shoulders by the time I got there. Mrs Stone was just wheeling her bin outside when I came hurrying up the path towards our building. I lived in a four-story block of flats not far from Maidstone East train station. The location was favoured by city commuters heading to London as the price of living here was far more affordable than the cost of living inside a London postcode. I was fortunate enough to have secured a flat on the top floor when they were first built five years ago. It was a small place but was still easily big enough for me and had been fitted out with good quality cupboards and appliances in the kitchen and was also well-appointed in the bathroom. The rent was affordable – more so now that I was going to earn more with the switch in jobs and I saw no reason to move. A small, but insistent voice at the back of my head, that sounded suspiciously like my mother, told me I should marry Brett and move into his twenty-five-bedroom palace.

I ignored it.

I hadn't actually been to Brett's house yet as a girlfriend. The last time I was there I was tossing the place looking for evidence. I would get there soon enough but I was in no hurry to be a wife, or a mother or anything other than what I was. Mostly I struggled to look after myself, all too often discovered that I had no clean knickers to put on and regularly opened the fridge to find there was no food in it. Each time I did so I promised to organise myself better. But I never did.

'Hi, Mrs Stone,' I called out in passing. She was wearing a pink warm-up suit and pink sparkly fake Ugg boots. Her silver hair was also dyed a shade of pink and to contrast it all, she had on a terry dressing gown in a lemon hue.

She waved a hand in reply as she manoeuvred her bin into place by the kerb ready for the morning. I made a note that I needed to do the same as they only came every other week and I had missed the last two collections.

Pushing open my door, I stepped over the mail I found on the floor inside, then scooped it up and quickly sifted it on my way through to the kitchen area. Mostly rubbish I concluded but there was one envelope that looked suspiciously like my credit card bill, I left that one for later, and a postcard from my Mum. I dumped everything but the postcard on the kitchen counter along with my handbag as I continued through to the bathroom where I set the bath taps to run hot water. My hair was already wet, so a bath seemed perfectly timed. I swiped my phone to connect to the speaker and pressed play. A heavy base started thumping through my apartment as I sashayed into the bedroom to peel off my damp clothes.

I put the postcard face down on my dressing table, so I could read it as I fumbled with my clothes. My mother and her boyfriend, Max were on a round-the-world cruise. Mum had retired earlier this year when Max had convinced her she should. Dad had died six years ago when his battle with cancer was finally done, and I thought mum would never smile again. Then last year, about eighteen months ago now, she met Max at a friend's sixtieth birthday party. He was a few years younger than her but pointed out that at their age it didn't make all that much difference.

I was happy for her, but her relationship with Max came with one unfortunate side effect – her renewed sex life. I had learned, not that I wanted to, that my mother had married the first man she slept with. A fact she only came to regret after he'd died, and she found out what she'd been missing. Now she was, so far as I could tell, only sleeping with the second man ever, but he was more experienced or more adventurous or more something and she wanted to tell me about it every time we sat down to chat.

Thankfully, there was no mention of sex in the note she sent me. They were now on the final leg and having passed through the Panama Canal were in Miami. It would be another couple of weeks before they were home although, of course, the postcard took a while to get to me even in the 21st century and mum liked to send them rather than emails that would be instantly delivered. She was having the time of her life, and I was happy for her.

Now naked and getting cool, I hurried to the bathroom and slipped into the tub. I had expected to feel buoyant this evening. I need never put my uniform on again. I ought to be celebrating. Oddly though, I felt a little uncomfortable, as if I had done something wrong and was about to be exposed for it.

My phone rang. It wasn't a number I recognised so I Ignored it, let it ring off and I flicked the button to silent as I slipped into the bath. Ordinarily, I would have taken a glass of wine with me, but after the overindulgence this afternoon I was sipping water instead.

Forty-five minutes of soaking, scrubbing, exfoliating and moisturising later I was getting hungry. The pizza, eaten in a wine induced haze of false hunger was now forgotten, demanding I forage for sustenance again very soon.

First though, I would call Brett. It was a call I had been planning in my head for a couple of days. I wanted to get him naked, and I wanted him to know that this was my plan, but in a subtle, sexy way that would leave him hopeful, but not certain of my intentions.

I really ought not to feel nervous. I found it both exhilarating and worrying that I did. Brett Barker was very much unlike any other man I had ever met. Ignoring the bank account that equalled a small European Country's GDP, he was a man that was at the same time utterly confident and yet still somehow unsure of himself. That he could nurture in me a desire to look after him while also willingly giving myself up as his sex-slave gave me a rush. He was exquisitely handsome, and I could only imagine what he would look like naked. On the few occasions when my hands had touched his arms, or torso or anything else, it was clear he was lean and muscular beneath his clothing. Not like a bodybuilder, but like a well-toned athlete.

Grab your copy...
vinci-books.com/doodoo-voodoo

About the Author

When Steve Higgs wrote his debut novel, *Paranormal Nonsense*, he was a captain in the British Army. He would like to pretend that he had one of those careers that must be blacked out and generally denied by the government, and that he has to change his name and move constantly because he is still on the watch list in several countries. In truth, though, he started out as a mechanic - not like Jason Statham in the film by that name, sneaking around as a hitman, but more like one of those sleazy guys who charges a fortune and keeps your car for a week even though the only thing you went in for was a squeaky door hinge.

At school, he was largely disinterested in all subjects except creative writing, for which he won his first prize at the age of ten. However, calling it the first prize he won suggests that there were other prizes, which is not the case. Awards may yet come, but in the meantime, he enjoys writing mystery and thriller novels and claims to have more than a hundred books forming a restless queue in his mind because they are desperate to be written.

Now retired from the military, he lives in southeast England with a duo of lazy sausage dogs. Surrounded by rolling hills, brooding castles, and vineyards, he doubts he'll ever leave, the beer is just too good.